HE TRAVELED HALFWAY AROUND THE WORLD
TO FIND THE ANSWER . . .
TO UNTANGLE THE BAFFLING MYSTERY
SURROUNDING THE SHROUD OF TURIN . . .

**IS THIS THE LINEN CLOTH
JESUS WAS BURIED IN?**

Before you accept or reject Robert K. Wilcox's
shroud theories—read this book. Meet the
people he interviewed. Weigh the written evidence. Examine the photographs. Contemplate
modern reconstructions of the pain-wracked
body that imprinted a 2,000-year-old linen
shroud. Then decide for yourself . . .

**SHROUD**

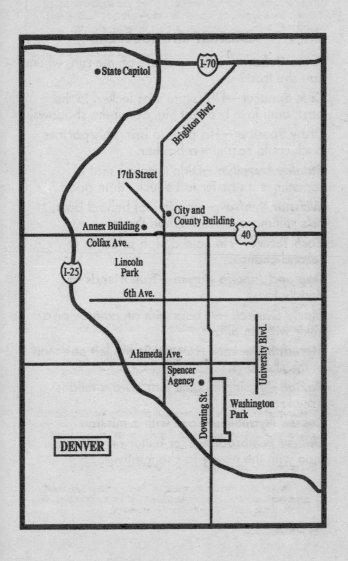

# CAST OF CHARACTERS

**Anne Osborne**—As a witness on the run, whom can she trust?

**Cole Spencer**—His future was locked in the past, until love brought him out of the shadows.

**Drew Spencer**—His plan to bring his partner back could cost him a brother.

**Stanley Lewellyn**—Didn't realize that sometimes it's better to be lucky than good.

**Webster Renfrow**—A criminal behind bars, he's still more powerful than the law.

**Zach Turner**—He paid a high price for a second chance.

**Dan and Janetta Hagen**—True friends or deadly foes?

**Marty Gartrell**—A boss with an attitude or a killer with an alibi?

**Meredith Hackett**—Her tragic life left one man in the shadows.

**Paxton**—A single name that always means trouble.

**Russell Nyguen**—A cop with a mission.

**Gilbert Pembrooke**—For better or worse, a man with the power to change lives.

# Prologue

From where she stood in the hallway, looking across the darkened outer office, Anne couldn't tell if Stan was dead or alive. The dime-size wound at his temple held her momentarily transfixed, trapping the scream that exploded inside her brain. A thick stream of crimson seeped through his soft blond hair to form an eerie liquid halo of deep red on the rug beneath his head.

His pale blue eyes, open but unseeing, reflected bewilderment in a wrenchingly childlike stare.

Numbed, she took a few entranced steps into the shadowy outer office. But halfway across the room, she stopped at the sound of a man's voice registering through the haze of her shocked senses. At first her reaction was one of almost hysterical relief.

Thank God she wasn't alone in this horror!

But even as she digested the fact that someone was in Stan's office, some inner warning, as distinct as an electric shock, went off inside her brain. Whoever was in there with Stan was not tending to him, was not administering first aid or calling for help. Something was wrong. Dreadfully wrong!

From her position in the middle of the room, Anne caught a glimpse of her reflection in the window behind Stan's desk. With the night behind it, the glass had become a mirror, and in that mirror she saw her worst fear confirmed—the glint of a gun and the shadowy figure holding it.

A surge of terror paralyzed her thoughts for what seemed like endless moments before raw instinct kicked in, assuring her that the gunman hadn't yet seen her, that she still had a chance to escape. *Not enough time to get out,* an inner voice screamed. *Quick! Hide!* Noiselessly she obeyed, sliding into the narrow space between two tall filing cabinets in the corner.

Miraculously, the gunman still hadn't seen her. If he had, she knew somehow that she wouldn't have lived long enough to scream.

But her hiding place was, at best, only a temporary haven. At any moment she could be discovered, and then what? There was no one on the fourth floor to hear her cries of help. No one to come to her rescue, to deliver her from this waking nightmare. The security officer at ground level—what *was* his name?—would never hear her screams.

The voice came again, this time louder. She held her breath, straining to hear what was being said.

"Damn it!" The sharp curse flew out of Stan's office before it slid back to a low, almost unintelligible murmur. Even though her senses had suddenly become painfully fine-tuned, Anne only caught a few words. "Didn't I tell you...outside...security...quick...."

Another voice, so low she couldn't distinguish if it belonged to a man or a woman, replied with words that sounded like "explosion" and "kid."

"Come on!" the first voice ordered. "Get us out...." They were moving toward the door. "...the hell out of here before someone...and we have to kill them, too."

*Kill!* The word echoed in her mind, and even though her heart cried no, the truth of what she'd seen could not be denied, even if the snippets of overheard conversation hadn't confirmed it. Assistant District Attorney Stanley Lewellyn was dead. Murdered!

If the faceless gunman or his mysterious companion said anything else, their words were lost in the scuffling sound, which Anne interpreted as their exit.

In the silence that ensued, she dared not move a muscle or take more than a shallow breath. Even after several minutes of torturous silence, she still hovered in her shadowy niche, terrified that Stan's attackers might come back—or worse, that they'd never left and were waiting in deadly stealth for her to show herself.

Her muscles ached from remaining motionless for so long. Only her thoughts raced.

Remembering the words "Before someone...and we have to kill them, too," she shuddered. The words might have seemed jumbled, but the meaning was clear. If the intruders knew that anyone had witnessed their crime, they wouldn't hesitate to kill again.

She told herself to remain hidden, at least for a few more minutes, to make sure they'd gone. She hadn't heard the elevator arriving or departing, and that meant they'd either taken the stairs or they were still on the fourth floor.

Suddenly, another horrible thought flashed through her mind. Her office door was still open. The lights were still on. She'd planned to go back to her office and lock up after she'd said good-night to Stan. The way she'd left her desk, it would be obvious that someone besides Stanley Lewellyn had been working late in the deserted County Annex building on this Friday night before the long weekend.

In what seemed now like a lifetime ago, Stan had confided to her that the Labor Day holiday would be just like any other work day for him. The project he'd been working on would keep him busy all day Monday and at least another week.

"Two years of circumstantial evidence," he'd said, finishing the last of the pizza they'd shared. "And now, I'm this close—" he'd held up his thumb and forefinger to indicate a scant inch "—to finally getting the hard evidence I need to crack this case wide open." He hadn't given her any details, but he'd hinted that his November election hopes were riding on this one case.

The eager spark in his eyes and the ambitious energy he'd radiated said he'd expected an easy victory.

"Good luck," she'd wished him.

"When you're good, luck has nothing to do with it," he'd quipped as he walked out the door.

*Better to have been lucky, my friend,* she thought with a grim shudder.

And then, after he'd gone, Anne had become so absorbed in compiling notes for a probationer's hearing scheduled for Tuesday morning, she'd worked for a solid hour before she looked at her crystal desk clock again. It had been just after ten when she'd walked down the hall to tell Stan she was calling it a night.

When she'd stopped in the doorway, she'd seen him—dear God, just what *had* she seen?

Suddenly, she had to know. If by some miracle Stan was still alive, every moment he went without medical attention narrowed his chances for survival.

Focusing on helping Stan gave Anne the courage to chance a peek into the dark receptionist's area. The room was empty. All she could do was hope and pray that Stan's attackers wouldn't come back before she could summon help.

On rubbery legs, she crossed the outer office, moving cautiously around the desk of the assistant district attorney's personal assistant.

She stood a moment in the doorway of Stan's office and cast a wary eye over her shoulder. The hallway was empty. The awful possibility that Stan's attackers might return at any moment sent shivers up her arms even as she bent down beside his lifeless form.

With trembling fingers she searched his throat for a pulse. "Oh, Stan," she cried. "Oh, God, what have they done? Why would they do this to you?"

Forcing herself to breathe, to ignore a light-headed sensation that threatened her equilibrium, she shoved her shoulder-length hair back and placed an ear to his chest. Her spirits rose when she thought she detected a faint fluttering. But all hope was dashed when she realized the sound was nothing more than the whir of the oscillating fan beside the desk . . . and the thudding dread of her own heartbeat.

Rising, she reached for the phone. Her hands shook so hard she realized that if the number had been more complicated than nine-one-one, she probably couldn't have dialed it. As it was, her fingers jabbed the keypad automatically.

The sound of the operator's voice startled her, but somehow she managed to put into words the horror that, even as she cried for help, still didn't seem quite real.

"Help! Please! A man's been shot!" Afraid to raise her voice above a hoarse whisper, Anne replied to the operator's question with an urgent, "What.... Yes, shot!" Without taking a breath she rattled off her name and the address. "Please send someone," she cried. "And for God's sake, hurry!"

# Chapter One

The city lay steeped in shadows, and the traffic was light by the time Cole Spencer pulled his dusty pickup into the private lot. Before he could angle his four-by-four into the empty space near the sidewalk, a woman in a small red sports car zipped around him and claimed it, forcing him to take the space with the name Spencer stenciled in white. For three years it had been his space, situated next to the one reserved for Drew, his brother, his former partner and his best friend for as long as he could remember.

Cutting the engine and reaching for the chocolate brown Stetson laying on the seat beside him, Cole fought the eerie feeling of déjà vu. Like the shadows cast by the glass and steel behemoth across the wide boulevard, the shadow of his past seemed inescapable.

The memories intensified as he walked around the front of his truck toward the entrance of the building that had once been the center of his professional world. He hadn't set foot inside the offices of the Spencer Agency since the day he'd renounced his half of the partnership. Two years, but today it seemed like yesterday.

After Meredith's funeral, all he could think about was getting the hell out of Denver as fast as he could. The turn-of-the-century three-story house he'd spent nearly a year restoring, the agency he and Drew had spent even more time building, his friends, his colleagues—everything and everyone—he'd left all of it behind without a word of explanation. There had been no need for explanations. Everyone who mattered knew, and the rest of the world had ceased to count.

At the corner, a metal newspaper stand caught his eye. He'd been standing in this exact spot, staring at that same stand, the morning he'd read the headline that had announced his personal nightmare to the world. Young Heiress Commits Suicide.

A city bus groaned to a stop in front of him, interrupting his retrospection, which had been so intense that for a moment he'd half expected to see that same headline glaring at him.

He blinked and read the headline of the day: No Arrests in D.A.'s Murder. Almost without realizing what he was doing, he shoved a couple of coins into the slot.

But before he could lay claim to his purchase, a scream jerked his attention to the nearby alley. His response was automatic, his boots pounded the pavement as he raced toward the sound.

When he rounded the corner, what he saw taking place dispelled his morbid musings and sent a wave of anger rushing through him. An old woman, standing with her back to an overflowing Dumpster, was still screaming, stopping only long enough to rattle off a string of four-letter words at the three teenage boys on bicycles who swooped around in circles in front of her.

The louder she shrieked, the more they taunted her, bringing their two-wheelers closer with each pass.

She screamed again and stabbed the air with a twisted walking stick just as one of the boys zoomed past, snatching the bright blue-and-orange windbreaker from her cart.

The boy who'd snagged the jacket waved it over his head in triumph, while his buddies cheered. Their jubilation stopped, however, when they spotted Cole. With one glance, they received his warning loud and clear and sped off, deserting their friend, who was still so busy gloating over his ill-gotten gain that he didn't see Cole coming up behind him.

When Cole grabbed him and dragged him off his bike, he yelped like a scalded pup. "Hey, man! What the—"

"Stop it!" a voice yelled, startling Cole and the kid. "Let him go!"

Cole nearly obeyed but quickly reconsidered, and when he spun around to see who had delivered that shouted order, the kid was still his squirming captive.

"What do you think you're doing?" a tall, blond beauty demanded.

Tightening his grip on the wiggling kid, Cole eyed the young woman standing in front of him. Her hands-on-hips stance almost amused him, but her all-business demeanor, including the tailored blue suit and crisp white blouse, said she was a woman who was accustomed to being taken seriously. She was also the woman who'd stolen his parking space.

"Let him go!" she said again, and even though a pair of funky-looking wire-rimmed sunglasses hid her eyes, Cole knew she was glaring at him.

"Not yet," he said.

A flash of color rippled across her smooth, high-boned cheeks, and her full lips drew themselves into an unnaturally stern line.

"Hey, what's up with you, man?" The kid tugged and pulled, trying without success to free himself from Cole's unrelenting grip.

"Give it back to her," Cole ordered. When the teenager hesitated, he added, "Now!" in a voice that reverberated with authority, echoing off the brick walls that enclosed the alley on two sides.

Grudgingly, the kid held the jacket out to the old woman.

With a quick movement, the blonde interceded, grabbing the coat before the bag lady could take it. "Wait a minute," she said. "This isn't your jacket, is it, Polly?"

If her initial interference had surprised him, she'd shocked Cole again when he realized that, as unbelievable as it seemed, this impeccably dressed woman seemed to know something about this back-alley situation that had so far escaped him.

"No, it ain't her jacket!" the kid said. "It's mine!"

The old woman glared at all three of them.

Although Cole wasn't ready to relinquish his hold on the boy yet, he loosened his grip.

"Did you take Zach's jacket, Polly?" the blonde asked.

All eyes shifted again to the old woman, but she ignored the question as if it had never been asked. In fact, she seemed suddenly oblivious to all of them. The hidden treasures buried in the overflowing Dumpster seemed infinitely more interesting than the jacket, Cole, the kid and the blonde.

"That's what I thought." The young woman sighed and turned to Cole. "It's his jacket. Let him go."

Though still unconvinced that the kid was the real victim in this strange scenario, Cole released the squirming teenager. "Pick up the cart," he ordered.

The boy complied, his eyes sparking defiantly. "Crazy old bag lady," he grumbled as he took back the jacket the blonde held out to him. "She steals my stuff and I'm the one who gets busted." Tying the jacket around his waist, he complained, "I wasn't going to do anything to her. I just wanted my jacket back."

"I understand. And by the way, nobody's *busted* you, Zach," the blonde corrected. "At least not yet," she added, a hint of dry humor curling the sides of her pretty mouth. "Were you in school today?"

"Sure," the kid announced proudly. "Been to every class, all day, all week, just like I told you I would. But I gotta go now, I'm working the night shift at Burger Shack."

The blonde smiled. "Good for you. Now go home and stay out of trouble. And don't forget we've got a court date on the fifteenth."

Zach nodded, suddenly sobered. Swinging his leg over the bike, he jammed the pedals into motion and raced off to join his friends, who had reappeared at the end of the alley.

The blonde watched him go before reaching down to gather the old woman's scattered belongings. Cole bent to help her when out of the corner of his eye he saw the old woman spin around with surprising speed to defend the possessions she mistakenly believed were being stolen.

Without thinking, Cole grabbed the blonde around the waist and spun her out of harm's way seconds before the walking stick sliced the air where her pretty head had been.

With his free hand, he jerked the stick out of Polly's hand. She gasped and ducked, and Cole realized she thought he was about to strike her. A wave of disgust swept through him. The city hadn't changed, a cynical inner voice told him. The law of hurt or be hurt still prevailed.

"You can let go of me now," the blonde informed him icily. He released her immediately. "And you didn't have to manhandle Zach, either," she informed him, tugging at her jacket and straightening her skirt, which barely covered her pretty knees.

"Are you related to that punk?"

Ignoring his question, she spoke to the woman who had resumed probing the Dumpster. "It'll be cold tonight, Polly. You should plan to get down to the mission early."

Polly gave no indication that she'd heard, but set to work rearranging the menagerie of her belongings in the rickety cart. Cole placed the walking stick in the cart once the blonde had turned to leave the alley. In two strides he'd caught up to her.

"I don't think she'll take your advice," he said.

She slowed down so they were walking side by side. "No. I don't think she will, either." He detected weariness in her voice. No wonder city dwellers clung to a cloak of anonymity. Some people just couldn't or wouldn't accept help, no matter how desperately they needed it. For others, help came too late. He thought of Meredith again, of how she'd needed help, of how he hadn't been there to give it.

"I'll call Father Michael. He'll come pick up Polly and drive her to a shelter. He's about the only one she listens to."

"How do you know her name? Do you work at the mission?"

She laughed. "Only on holidays." Her voice intrigued him. The slightly husky quality resonated with an honesty he found extraordinarily appealing. "Everyone who works or lives in this area knows Polly," she explained as they rounded the corner. "She hangs around the arcade when the kids congregate after school, and she walks away with anything that isn't nailed down."

"She just about nailed you with that stick. You really shouldn't have stepped in like that."

"Oh, yeah?" She stopped and looked at him, one golden brow arched above the dark glasses. "Then why did you?"

"I guess I didn't like the odds."

"And they say chivalry is dead."

"They're right," Cole replied.

"Hmm. I wonder..." She studied him out of the corner of her eye as they resumed walking. Even though he couldn't see her eyes behind the dark glasses, he knew she was staring at his hat. "Hey, wait a minute. Aren't the good guys supposed to wear *white* hats?"

He couldn't resist exchanging a smile with her. "I wouldn't know about that. I guess I haven't run into all that many good guys lately, have you?"

"Come to think of it," she admitted wistfully, "I guess I haven't, either. But that doesn't mean they don't exist, now, does it?"

He shook his head. "No, I guess it doesn't. But if I were you, I wouldn't make a habit of charging into alleys on the chance that one will come riding to the rescue." Even as he said it, he wondered if that was what Meredith envisioned, that he'd be her white knight.

At the building's entrance, he prepared to say goodbye to the lovely lady with the unsavory friends when she surprised him again by walking into the lobby ahead of him. "Well, so long, cowboy," she said. She smiled again and pushed the dark glasses up into her hair. Her blue eyes danced. "Thanks for riding in, as you put it. Even if your hat is the wrong color and your rescue was a bit mis-guided.''

He acknowledged her with a touch to the brim of his hat. ''My mistake.'' With the memory of another misguided rescue still haunting him, he had no problem conceding the point. The past proved his lack of judgment when it came to damsels in distress.

They parted when she stopped to study the building's directory, and Cole stepped into the elevator. But before the doors slid closed, he found himself unable to resist one last look at the beautiful blonde who still believed in heroes in white hats.

''COLE SPENCER, you good-lookin' thing! What a sight you are for these sore eyes!'' Despite being old enough to be his mother, the receptionist seated outside Drew's office loved to flirt.

''It's good to see you, too, Francine,'' he said, removing his hat and holding it with both hands in front of him. ''How've you been?''

''Can't complain,'' she declared, plucking the bifocals off her nose to let them dangle by the hot pink cord around her neck. ''Your brother says I'm as bossy as ever, but you and I both know he couldn't run this place without me.'' She laughed and folded her hands in front of her on the desk. ''So, what brings you down from the mountains, Cole? Finally had enough of all that fresh air and sunshine?''

''Never,'' he declared, finding it curious that Francine hadn't known he was expected. When he'd been an active partner in the agency, she'd known more about the day-to-day comings and goings of the Spencer Agency than either he or Drew. ''To tell the truth, I don't exactly know why I'm here,'' he admitted. ''I guess you could say I've been summoned. And when big brother calls...''

She feigned a frown. ''Believe me, I know how he is. Well, go on in. He's with someone, but if I remember correctly, you two never had any secrets.''

*Only one,* Cole thought. The one that had brought him back to Denver today, despite his better judgment.

Unfortunately, when Drew had called last night, Cole had been outside, assisting the vet tending to a mare with colic. Bess had taken the call. "All he said was that he needed your help, and that he'd appreciate it if you could come to Denver tomorrow," his aunt explained. "He said it had something to do with a case, that he wouldn't take no for an answer, and that he'd fill you in on the details when you got there."

Telling himself he wasn't about to embark on the nearly seven-hour drive without more information, Cole had tried to reach Drew several times last night, to no avail. With each unanswered call he'd grown more frustrated by the sound of his brother's recorded voice on the answering machine. *If it had been anyone but Drew,* he reminded himself again.

When he opened the office door, he saw his brother sitting behind his desk talking on the phone. Drew looked up and smiled, and despite his best resolve, Cole felt his irritation toward his sibling evaporate. He'd never met anyone who could stay angry with Drew for any length of time—even as a child his brother had possessed an irresistible charm.

Cole's focus shifted to the dark-haired man pacing the floor in front of Drew's desk, and he acknowledged Russell Nyguen with a nod.

"It's been a long time, Cole," Russell said as he moved forward with his hand outstretched.

"It has," Cole replied, taking in Russell's spit-polished appearance and expensive blue suit. Either Nyguen had just come from a funeral or he'd finally made detective.

Drew hung up the phone. "Come in, Cole. Glad you could make it." His smile was bright, but he didn't stand up, even when Cole reached across the desk to shake his hand.

"I tried to reach you last night. The message you gave Bess was pretty vague."

"And now you want answers." Drew's electric smile dimmed a little. "Okay, shoot."

Cole opened his mouth to fire off the first of a dozen questions when the office door opened and, to his complete surprise, the blonde from the alley walked in.

Their gazes met and held for a questioning moment before shifting to Drew.

Nyguen moved quickly across the room and closed the door. "I'm glad you're here, Ms. Osborne."

"I'm sorry I'm late," she said a bit breathlessly. "I didn't have any trouble finding the building, but the Spencer Agency isn't listed on the directory in the lobby, so I had to do a bit of investigating of my own to find the office."

What a terrific smile, Cole thought. A smile like that could single-handedly brighten the darkest day.

"The officer who drove you here should have known the suite number," Nyguen said. "He should have escorted you through the building." His expression reflected irritation. "Where is he, anyway?"

"I don't know," she replied. "When he called and told me there had been some kind of mix-up, I decided to drive over myself."

"What kind of mix-up?" Nyguen asked.

She sat down in one of the wing chairs opposite Drew's desk and crossed her long legs. "He just said that he was running late—some kind of scheduling glitch or something. Anyway, I didn't see the point in keeping everyone waiting."

"Who called you?" Nyguen reached into his jacket to withdraw a small, folded cell phone.

"Johnson, I think he said—no, wait a minute, I think it was Johnston."

Nyguen gave her a measured look as he walked out of the office, punching in numbers as he went.

"Ms. Osborne," Drew said after the detective had left, "this is my brother, Cole."

She offered him her hand. "Mr. Spencer and I ran into each other outside."

"It's just Cole."

"And please, call me Anne." Her intelligent eyes demanded his attention. "Your brother and Detective Nyguen insisted on this meeting when they met with me at my home last night. But to tell the truth, I'm still not convinced I need a bodyguard."

He released her hand abruptly. "Bodyguard?" he shouted at his brother. "I think you'd better start explaining."

Drew attempted to diffuse the supercharged air with words. "She needs our help, buddy. What was I supposed to do?"

*Damn it!* Cole seethed. Why had he allowed himself to be put in this position? And, furthermore, what had possessed Drew to set him up this way? His brother knew better than anyone how he felt about coming back to the agency in any capacity, but especially as a bodyguard.

"I'm afraid there's been a mistake," Cole told Drew's pretty client. "Now, if you'll excuse me . . ." He settled his hat on his head and started for the door. "I've got a long drive ahead of me back to Telluride."

Cole's hand was on the door when Drew said, "She's a witness—the only witness to Stanley Lewellyn's murder. Assistant District Attorney Stanley Lewellyn," he added pointedly. "The killer didn't know she was there, and she's talked to no one but me and the police since it happened."

Cole matched his brother's intense stare. "Then why does she need a bodyguard?"

"That's been my question from the beginning," she murmured, leaning back in her chair and folding her hands in her lap.

"So far she's received three phone threats, beginning the day after the murder," Drew said.

She bolted to the edge of her seat. "I thought we agreed those calls could have been pranks." She turned her appeal to Cole. "I'm a probation officer for juveniles. I work with a lot of angry, stressed-out kids and parents. Any one of a dozen people could have made those calls."

She'd said something about a hearing to the kid in the alley, Cole remembered.

Drew went on. "The day after the murder, an anonymous caller told her he knew who she was, where she lived and what she'd seen."

Cole winced. As a partner in the agency, he'd heard variations of the story countless times—a message, in the form of a note or a phone call, delivered by desperate or even obsessed individuals. Some of them turned out to be nothing more than jilted lovers, unable to except rejection. But, too often, the kind of messages that sent clients to private investigators were the kind of messages left by people who were nothing short of walking time bombs, desperate people under tremendous pressure. Too often the thin, tight line they walked was a temporary path that led to ultimate violence.

"It sounds like Denver PD has a major security problem," he ventured. He caught her look of open surprise, and he immediately assumed she'd heard this same conclusion from Nyguen and Drew.

"It could be even worse," Drew said.

"You think someone in the department might be involved with the murder?" Cole asked.

"It's a possibility we have to consider."

Anne Osborne crossed her arms and released an exasperated sigh. "That's the only possibility they'll even consider. I've tried to tell them that this whole bodyguard idea is absurd. Like I said, I deal with angry people day in and day out. It's part of my job, and I know how to take care of myself."

What Cole had witnessed a few minutes ago in the alley raised serious questions about that claim, but for now he had a much bigger question that only his brother could answer.

"So why call me?" he asked Drew, leaving unspoken what they both already knew, that he'd made it clear when he'd resigned his partnership in the agency that he wouldn't be coming back. That he'd lost whatever he'd once had that made him believe he was capable of protecting anyone from anything.

Hadn't the disastrous results of his last case convinced everyone that he no longer possessed the kind of sixth sense and special judgment required to be an investigator, much less anyone's personal bodyguard?

"I wouldn't have called if I hadn't needed your help," Drew said simply.

*But why me?* The question hung unspoken between them until an ugly realization began to form in Cole's mind. "I think I'm beginning to understand," he said finally. "You called me exactly *because* of what happened before." Because he'd been a former cop, a large segment of the force had known about his relationship with Meredith Hackett. The media, in its coverage of the highly sensational story, had unearthed every juicy detail of their ill-fated relationship. A shadow of doubt loomed even larger when his investigator's license had been temporarily suspended while the department investigated Meredith's death. After her death, he hadn't cared whether they ever reinstated it. Why would he? In his mind, his career was over the day Meredith took her life.

In a stinging flash of insight, Cole realized exactly what his brother had been thinking. It was precisely because of that publicity and that smudge on his record that no one would suspect he was working again—which, in fact, he wouldn't be. Not as a private investigator, anyway. And there was no license required to act as someone's protector, someone's personal bodyguard. Even if someone did discover that Nyguen had turned Anne Osborne's protection over to the Spencer Agency, no one would suspect that Drew's brother—a washed-up investigator who'd fled the city under the cloud of scandal—would be brought in to protect the state's only witness in this high-profile case.

For the first time in his life Cole felt betrayed by his brother, and for a long, angry moment, all he could do was stare at Drew, into the eyes that, despite the subtle differences, were so similar to his own.

"Was calling me in on this case Nyguen's idea or yours?" Cole asked, doing nothing to sweeten the bitterness in his voice. "Or did you decide together that your renegade brother would be the perfect choice?"

He felt Anne's scrutiny, and his insides tightened. He could almost feel her heartbeat accelerate. When their gazes met, he despised the flicker of recognition he thought he saw in her wide blue eyes.

*Yes, I am the one you read about in the newspapers, the one involved with the poor little rich girl who killed herself.*

"It was my decision to ask for your help," Drew admitted. "And yes, if you must know, I did have your past in mind when I decided to call you. But not for the reasons you assume. I needed someone I could count on, someone who would have no inadvertent contact with the police department that might tip our hand or compromise my client's safety."

Despite Drew's logical explanation, Cole felt the past still lodged between them. The silence between them crackled with a dozen different unspoken accusations.

At last, Cole turned and headed for the door again.

"I wouldn't have called you if I'd been able to handle this myself," Drew said in a low voice, tinged with what Cole recognized as barely contained anger. "There *is* no one else. Not for this case. Surely you can see that, in this instance, security is everything?"

Cole opened the door, but before he walked out, he glanced over his shoulder to see Drew finally rising out of the chair, which until now he'd seemed glued to. For the first time, he saw the heavy plaster cast that encased his brother's left leg from hip to ankle.

"What the hell happened to you?" he gasped.

"Close the door," Drew said, leaning against the desk for balance.

Before Cole could comply with his brother's order, Russell Nyguen brushed past him.

"The officer I sent to pick her up was involved in an accident," Nyguen announced. "His car was broadsided at an intersection a block from your office. Witnesses said the van that hit him didn't even slow down."

"Was the officer hurt?" She was on her feet and, for the first time, her voice and her confidence seemed to falter.

Cole moved to her side almost without realizing what he was doing.

"The hospital lists him as serious. Now, Ms. Osborne, are you sure the officer who called you said his name was Johnston?"

"Reasonably sure. Why?"

"My guess is no one by the name of Johnston has been assigned to your case," Cole said, more to himself than to her.

She blinked and turned the question on Nyguen.

With a nod, the detective affirmed Cole's supposition. "Since the phone threat, I've restricted the investigating team to half a dozen handpicked men. No one named Johnson or Johnston is part of that team."

"Can you remember anything else the caller—this Johnston—told you?" Cole asked, slipping into the role of investigator far too easily for his liking.

She thought for a moment before she shook her head. "All he said was that the plan had changed, and that he'd meet me at my home instead of my office. He even confirmed my address and then said I should leave work and drive straight home. He said he'd be waiting for me in a police cruiser in front of my building—" She stopped short, and Cole watched her expression change as the deadly implications of what might have happened began to dawn on her.

"Did he say why the plans had changed?"

She shook her head. "No. I was too frustrated by the delay to ask." The look on her face said this whole ordeal had been one long frustration for her. "I'm really behind at work, and I'd already canceled one appointment to make

this meeting. Any further delay meant rescheduling my entire week, so I decided to drive myself."

Nyguen's frown deepened. "In the future, if anything—
and I mean anything—out of the ordinary happens, you
must call me immediately."

"I tried to reach you," she told him. "But you weren't
in, and I figured you and Drew were here, waiting for me.
So I left a message at the precinct for Officer Johnston,
saying I no longer needed a ride, and I drove here myself."

Nyguen and Drew exchanged a meaningful glance.

"What's wrong?" she asked.

"It means that their first guess was right. That there's a
leak in the police department big enough to float a battle-
ship through." It wasn't that Cole missed the disapproving
glare from Nyguen. He'd just decided to ignore it. He
glanced again at the massive cast on his brother's leg.
"When this is all over, you owe me one hell of an explanation, big brother."

Drew smiled, driving the matching dimples into cheeks
darkened by a serious five-o'clock shadow. "When this is
all over, you'll get one," he promised.

Cole nodded. "Tell Francine to call the towing company and report a red sports car illegally parked in your
lot." With his simple declaration, Cole had anted up. He
was in the game, despite the fact that the rules were being
made as they went along.

"Towed?" Anne gasped. "Hey, you can't do that! And
how did you know I drove a red car?"

Drew almost laughed, but masked it wisely with a cough.

"I don't think it would hurt to file a missing-person report," Cole suggested to Nyguen.

"I agree," Drew put in. "If it's an insider we're chas-
ing, that bit of news should give our murderer something
to chew on."

"Wait a minute," Anne protested, rising. "What's going on here? Nobody's doing anything with my car without my permission. And who's missing?"

Cole crossed the room and pushed a beautifully framed watercolor aside to reveal a small black wall safe. After a few deft turns of the dial, the safe swung open. Before he closed it again, he withdrew a small handgun, a battered Colorado license plate and an envelope he knew contained enough cash to keep him operating for at least two weeks.

"Cole's right," Nyguen said. "And when the car winds up at the police impound, it will add credibility to the missing-person story. Don't worry, Ms. Osborne. Your car will be perfectly safe."

Cole slipped the envelope into his back pocket and the gun inside his belt.

"My car will be perfectly safe with *me,*" she corrected.

Next, Cole opened the closet beside the filing cabinet and withdrew a gym bag, a denim shirt, a pair of jeans and a black ball cap. "The bathroom's in there." He pointed to the door across the room as he handed her the clothes. "Put these on, and be sure to push all your hair up under the cap. You can put your clothes in this bag if you want to bring them with you." He had some real doubts as to how well a couple of yards of denim and a ball cap would work in making anyone believe this stunning young woman was a man, but he was working with limited resources. All he had to do was get her out of the building and out of town. With night encroaching, they just might have a fair chance at pulling it off. "Meet me in the alley in five minutes."

"Now wait just a damn minute," she demanded, dropping the clothes on Drew's desk. "I'm not doing anything, meeting you anywhere or letting anyone tow my car until one of you tells me what's going on." Her glare was hot and accusing as it ricocheted between the three of them.

"What's going on," Drew began in that patently smooth style that Cole had seen soothe more than one female feather, "is that my brother has just agreed to become your bodyguard." He paused and looked to Cole for confirmation, which he gave with a curt nod. "As for where you're going, I guess somewhere well out of the city limits would be the logical destination."

She spun to face Nyguen. "What if I refuse to go?"

The detective shifted uneasily from one foot to the other. "In that case, I'm afraid my only other choice would be to place you under house arrest. For your own good, of course." He shook his head. "But under the circumstances, I'm not sure even that would work."

"There's always the city jail," Cole suggested. He didn't have to wait long for the explosion he knew he'd ignited.

"Jail!" she shouted. "Have you all gone crazy?"

"It *would* be an extreme remedy," Nyguen admitted, with complete seriousness. "But I'm afraid I'd have no other choice if you refuse to accept the protection I've arranged. From now until we can apprehend Stanley Lewellyn's killers, I'm responsible for your safety, Ms. Osborne. And the best way I know to fulfill that responsibility is to either put you in jail, where you can be guarded twenty-four hours a day, or place you in the protective custody of Mr. Spencer."

"Custody! Jail!" she exploded. "I'm the *witness*, remember? Not the criminal."

"I think she's beginning to get the idea," Cole remarked dryly. "You know, you can make this all real easy by just doing what you're told, Ms. Osborne."

The look she shot him was scalding. "Easy? You want easy? I'll give you easy." She snatched her purse and stalked to the door. "I'm leaving now. And you, Cole Spencer, can ride back to whatever Saturday matinee you rode out of and forget you ever met me. Is that *easy* enough for you, cowboy?"

Cole stepped in front of her at the door. She glared at him but didn't try to push past. Everything about her told Cole she was unaccustomed to taking orders from anyone or allowing anyone to do her thinking for her. Independence was a quality he admired, generally, but couldn't tolerate in excess, if the objective was keeping her alive.

Nyguen came up behind her, and she whirled around to see him holding the bundle of clothing Cole had laid out for her. "Ms. Osborne, I think you should know that when I made that call a few minutes ago, I also got a report from the plainclothes detective I stationed outside the building. He saw someone tinkering with your car. A young man.''

"My car is a red sports convertible," she explained. "Kids always want to check it out."

"Do they always try to disable it?"

"What do you mean, disable it?"

"I mean, loosening the lug nuts on your tires—"

The color drained from her face. "But why would..." She swallowed. "Maybe he was just trying to steal the hubcaps."

Nyguen shook his head. "If he'd wanted to steal your rims or your hubcaps, he wouldn't have left the bolts partially on, would he? By the time the officer spotted him, the kid had loosened all but one bolt."

Cole started to explain what would happen when a wheel flies off a car going sixty miles per hour, but the look on her face told him that dangerous scenario, or one equally grim, was already spinning with graphic detail through her mind.

"Is the kid in custody?" Drew asked.

Nyguen frowned and shook his head. "He took off before the officer could get to him."

Immediately Cole's thoughts jumped to the teenager Anne had defended in the alley. "How well do you know this Zach kid?"

The blood rushed back to her cheeks in a flood of red. "It wasn't Zach," she said confidently. "He would never do anything like that."

Cole could hardly remember the time when he had that kind of trust in people.

"Give me the boy's name, just to be sure," Nyguen ordered, pulling a slim notebook from his pocket. "I'll check him out. If it turns out to be someone other than Zach, my man will work up a sketch with a police artist and we'll get it to you. Maybe it was a kid you've worked with in the past. If we could get that lucky, we'd have our first lead."

After Anne reluctantly gave Nyguen Zach's last name and address, Cole said, "We need to get going." The incident with her car told Cole what he'd already suspected, that she'd been spotted by whomever was tracking her. "Get changed," he said. "And remember what I said about the cap."

She nodded, but her tilted chin told him she wouldn't always give in so easily, that she'd never allow herself to be led blindly by anyone, regardless of the risk. He did notice, however, that her hands were shaking when she finally accepted the clothes Nyguen held out to her.

"Just one more thing," she said. "I have a very important hearing scheduled for next week, and I can't postpone or cancel it. I have to be there."

"We'll do everything we can to help you honor your commitments," Drew said.

"That isn't good enough," she said stubbornly. "A young man's future is riding on that hearing, and I want your word that I'll be allowed to attend."

Cole opened his mouth to respond, but before he could, Drew said, "You have my word."

"And I need to stay in town, in my own apartment," she said stubbornly.

Cole shook his head. "No way."

"Now wait a minute, Cole," Nyguen interrupted. "That might not be such a bad idea. You'd stay with her, of course."

"It won't work," Cole said, resenting the direction he knew Nyguen's thoughts were heading. "It's not worth the risk." He wouldn't allow his client to be used as bait to draw the killer out in the open. Sure, he'd be there to protect her, but mistakes happened, and Cole wasn't about to gamble his client's safety just to make Nyguen's job easier.

"But I have to go back to my apartment, at least for a few minutes, tonight," Anne insisted. "It's important."

"Whatever it is, it isn't important enough to take that kind of risk," Cole said flatly.

"To me, it is," she shot back.

She met his gaze without flinching, and for a long, uneasy moment no one spoke.

Finally, Drew said, "I have to agree with Cole, Ms. Osborne. You shouldn't go back to your apartment tonight." He turned to Cole. "But if you could stay in the city at least long enough for her to take a look at that sketch . . . Well, who knows, maybe this whole thing can be resolved much sooner than we think."

Nothing they'd said had convinced Cole, but he did have to concede that his brother had a valid point about the sketch. Why make the trip all the way to Telluride only to drive back tomorrow so Anne could get a look at the police artist's rendering?

"My apartment has a security system," she said with a hopeful tone.

"And my den has a fax machine," he countered. "If need be, you can send a copy of that sketch to the ranch," he told Nyguen.

"Can't we at least stay in the city tonight?" she pleaded.

Cole felt all eyes shift to him, but hers were the ones that most demanded an answer. "All right, but just long enough to see that sketch, to see if you can identify the kid."

"Great. And since we're not leaving town, there's no need to tow my car. Right?"

"Wrong!" It was bad enough that he'd agreed to this dangerous compromise, he might as well paint a bull's-eye on her back—a bright red bull's-eye in the form of one very conspicuous red sports car, a target Lewellyn's killer had already spotted. "We'll swing by your apartment just long enough for you to do whatever it is that's so all-fired important. But be advised, all of you, that at the first hint of trouble, we're leaving town. With no arguments."

"Of course," Anne said, but the glint of victory in her eyes belied her quick agreement.

He turned to Nyguen. "Once we're moving, I won't stop to check my decisions out with anyone, understand?"

"I wouldn't want it any other way."

"Russell knows how we operate," Drew assured him.

It wasn't Russell Nyguen or Drew who worried him, Cole thought, and when she said, "Is this charade absolutely necessary?'' he knew he'd have his hands full trying to protect this headstrong and defiant lady.

"Absolutely," he said.

She hesitated at the bathroom door, and he knew she was deciding if she could go through with what was being asked of her. In her eyes, he saw her pose the question to Drew first, and then to Nyguen, and finally to him. But he had no answers to give her about what to expect in their near future together, not when his own heart and mind were filled with so much doubt.

"Nyguen will escort you down the back stairs to the exit," was all he said. "I'll drive around and meet you in the alley." It would take only a moment to change the plates on the truck.

As he walked out of the office, he heard his brother say, "He's not so bad when you get to know him, but I wouldn't keep him waiting, if I were you. Patience has never been his strong suit."

# Chapter Two

With the physique of Hulk Hogan and the predictability of a rattlesnake, the man everyone in the neighborhood knew as Paxton was not one to be argued with. Zach didn't know if Paxton was the dealer's first name or his last. All he knew for sure was that trouble was just another name for any kind of contact with the big man.

Zach also knew when trouble was stalking him and, even from a block away, he could feel the shadow of Paxton's particular brand of evil heading straight for him in a long black limo. The car slid to the curb noiselessly before Zach could drag his bike up the stairs of the run-down apartment building, where he and his mom and Karli were working on a record—eight months and two days at the same address.

He cringed when the car door opened.

"Hey, Zach. What's up?" The expression, a staple of conversation in Zach's neighborhood, sounded stupid coming from the middle-aged white man with diamond-encrusted rings on each finger, including his thumbs.

"Hey, man. I'm talking to you! Get over here. I don't like to yell."

Moving cautiously closer to where Paxton waited, Zach was careful to position his bike between them. "What do you want, Paxton?" he asked, doing his best to paste a don't-give-a-damn expression on his face.

"What do I *want?*" Paxton's face turned red. His starched white collar barely contained his corded neck. The muscles in his back and shoulders bulged beneath the expensive black fabric of his three-piece suit. "Hey, man, you should show a little more respect for your old friend."

*Friend!* Zach thought bitterly. Paxton didn't know the meaning of the word. "I gotta go," he said, and turned to leave.

One hand landed on his shoulder, the other shoved the bike away as if it were made of paper. If only he were big enough, or tough enough, or even drunk enough, he'd plant a fist in the center of Paxton's face. Unfortunately, Zach was none of those things, and he wasn't stupid enough to think he had a chance against this bull of a man, either.

"Hey, I saw your sister today," Paxton said. His smile was more a sneer.

Zach winced at the thought of Paxton anywhere within a million miles of twelve-year-old Karli. "Leave me alone, Paxton. And leave my sister alone, too." He stumbled backward as he jerked out of Paxton's grip and headed for the stairs again.

"Did I mention that I saw your mom, too?"

Zach stopped in his tracks.

"She didn't look so good, you know? Kinda sickly and pale...all strung out."

His mom was a drunk. She drank up the rent, the groceries, the winter coats and gloves and the lunch money. She drank up every holiday. She usually drank until she was sick.

But she'd never done drugs. Not so far, anyway. But what if she got desperate, what if Paxton or one of his friends pushed her?

"Come on, kid," Paxton said. "Let's take a ride."

Zach allowed himself to be ushered into the back seat of the limo where a sheet of Plexiglas separated Paxton and him from the young driver, who sat stoically behind the wheel.

"Nobody tells me what to do," Paxton said, his hot breath on Zach's face. "Nobody!" He drew a gun from his jacket pocket and pressed the barrel to Zach's temple. "You got that?"

Zach nodded. Fear and rage took turns pummeling his stomach, and he felt like he had when, as a kid, he'd stuck his mom's house key in a light socket. He knew Paxton wouldn't think twice about killing him. He might worry about messing up the interior of his sixty-thousand-dollar car, but it wouldn't keep him from pulling the trigger. A dealer could always get a new car.

"Now listen up, kid. I got another job for you." That he'd put the gun down gave Zach little relief. A man like Paxton had a dozen ways to destroy someone.

"What kind of job?" Zach's voice was all high-pitched and trembly.

"Nothing big. Just a simple little delivery."

*Simple.* That's what he'd said last time, when a simple little delivery had resulted in Zach being sent to Mountainview Juvenile Detention Center for a year. While he'd been there, his mom had gone on a real bender and ended up in detox at City Hospital. What bothered Zach the most was that Karli had been forced to go through all of it alone.

Since his release from Mountainview, his family was doing better. His mom was on the wagon more often than she was off, Karli was going to school, and Anne Osborne had signed his work permit, allowing him to land a job at Burger Shack.

A lot of guys complained about their probation officers, but Zach knew he'd been lucky to be assigned to Anne Osborne. Not that she couldn't be tough, because she could. He knew she meant it when she said she'd take him back to Mountainview herself if she heard that he was even thinking about messing up again.

"I can't make any more deliveries for you," he said. "I've got a probation hearing next week, and I might get an early release. I'm saving up for a car." Or a pickup. How he'd love to sit behind the wheel of one of those really cool four-wheelers!

Why he'd bothered telling Paxton any of his plans for the future, Zach didn't know. Maybe because, for the first time, thanks to Anne Osborne, he felt as though he actually *had* a future. She'd promised to talk to someone about getting him a job at Discount City when he got off probation. It was a good job, and a good job meant money for a vehicle, and when Zach turned sixteen, he meant to have both. With a decent job and a vehicle, he could get his mom and Karli out of this stinking neighborhood . . . and away from the likes of Paxton.

The big man glared at him for a long, dangerous moment before he said, "You're smart, Zach. That's what I like about you. And you're right. You're no good to me behind bars. But this is a special job. I promise it won't be anything like the last time." His voice dipped low. "After all, we can't afford anything like that to happen again, now, can we, Zach? Hey, wait a minute . . . I guess with you getting hauled off to jail, you probably never heard how that whole thing ended."

Zach held his breath. "What are you talking about? What else *is* there?"

"The end of the story, that's what," he said. "The part where the junkie dies." Paxton smiled and tapped the glass, and the limo pulled away from the curb, taking Zach and all his hopes for the future with it.

FROM THE MOMENT they merged onto the westbound interstate, Anne began to wonder if Cole was planning to ignore the deal they'd struck in his brother's office. "We *are* going by my apartment, right?"

"We are." His stoic demeanor unnerved her, especially with her own emotional state so uncharacteristically frazzled.

"Well, then, would you mind telling me why you're driving seventy miles per hour in the wrong direction?" She made no effort to tone down her annoyance.

"I have a dozen good reasons, but only one that counts. I'm your bodyguard. I've agreed to protect you."

Good lord, the man was insufferable! He'd been more pleasant in the alley dealing with Polly. "Is it just me, or are you this charming to all your clients?"

One dark brow lifted and he almost smiled. "I'm taking a roundabout route as a precaution, in case we're followed."

Automatically, she jerked around in the seat to peer out the back window.

His laugh was a humorless snort. "And your reaction just now is exactly why I didn't explain earlier."

She turned around again, feeling a bit sheepish. "Right."

"It's okay. There's no one back there." When he glanced at her, some of the black ice in his dark eyes seemed to have melted. "I just wanted to be sure. Trust me, when I think you're in real danger, I'll let you know." It was twice the number of words he'd spoken since they'd left Drew Spencer's office twenty minutes ago.

"Gee, that's so reassuring."

Seemingly oblivious to her sarcasm, he said, "When we get to your building, I'll drive by without stopping. If you see anything out of the ordinary—cars, people or even a trash can out of place—let me know."

"Out of the ordinary seems to be the operative phrase for this entire situation."

He glanced in the rearview mirror. "If it makes you feel better, I doubt you'll be in this situation very long. If you or that cop can identify the kid who tampered with your car, this whole case could open up fast."

"And if not?"

He shrugged.

"You think it was Zach, don't you?"

He glanced in the rearview mirror again, this time for what seemed to be a longer, harder stare, and it took every ounce of Anne's willpower not to turn around again.

"Let's just say he seems a likely candidate. He knows you, knows your car—"

"You're wrong."

He shrugged again. "It wouldn't be the first time."

The silence that ensued seemed suffocating, and Anne rolled her window down a few inches to inhale a breath of cool evening air. They were west of the city limits, almost to Golden. "Hmm. The air out here smells like pine."

"You like the mountains?" His attempt at casual conversation caught her completely by surprise.

"Yes, but unfortunately, I don't get the chance to enjoy them as often as I'd like."

"You may be getting the chance sooner than you think."

"Is that where we'll go if we have to leave Denver?" In her mind, she envisioned him taking her to Evergreen or Conifer, two of several small towns nestled west of the city in the foothills but still within commuting distance of the city. Perhaps this enforced hiatus wasn't going to be so dreadful, after all.

"If we leave Denver, I'll be taking you home with me to Telluride," he said without taking his eyes off the road.

*Telluride!* "But that's hundreds of miles from Denver, isn't it?" She didn't give him a chance to respond. "I can't possibly go that far. We'll have to think of something else."

"If things go wrong, it's our next stop, so you'd better get used to the idea," he said flatly.

"You can't be serious! You'd take me against my will?"

"I'm hoping it doesn't come to that." The determined thrust of his square jaw said he'd never been more serious about anything.

"But I've got a job, commitments...a life to keep living." And besides all that, what would she do with Tabitha? She sighed, imagining Cole Spencer's reaction when she told him the reason they were swinging by her apartment was to make arrangements for someone to care for her cat. "I might as well be stuck on the moon as in Telluride. There's no way I can even consider it."

When he didn't respond, she said, "I can't believe you're doing this to me!"

"Three hundred miles is hardly the moon," he pointed out, his voice maddeningly calm. "And just for the record, I haven't done anything to you."

"Listen—" she unsnapped her seat belt so she could turn in the seat to face him "—there's just no way I can be that far away from Denver. I work with kids whose worlds are unsettled enough. For some of them, the weekly visits to my office represent the only constant in their lives. Surely you can see why I can't just up and leave them."

"Put your seat belt back on."

"What?"

"Put it on. I'm responsible for your life, remember?"

With a disgusted sound, she jerked the belt around her again and buckled it. His stony expression told her that her appeal had landed on unsympathetic ears. Desperation, however, forced her to try again. "Look, try to put yourself in my shoes, will you? What would your reaction be if someone forced you to just walk away from your job— from your life—for an indeterminate amount of time?"

She watched him mull over the question for a minute before he said, "When you think about it, we're in exactly the same situation."

"But not because anyone forced you," she reminded him. "And since we're setting the record straight, please try to remember that *I* didn't ask for a bodyguard."

"I'll keep it in mind," he said absently.

When they finally meandered into her neighborhood, Anne felt a surge of relief. At her street, he signaled and she said, "It's that two-story red brick building midway down the block, on the right."

"Nice neighborhood." He surprised her by reaching over and adjusting the brim of her cap a bit lower. "Now, when I drive by your building I want you to take a good hard look." His voice was so low and serious it raised goose bumps on her skin. "If you see anything—anything at all—"

"Out of the ordinary," she finished for him. The note of sarcasm she'd tried to reach fell flat as she peered up and down both sides of the street.

By the light from street lamps at each corner, the ordinary seemed suddenly ominous. Had she noticed that old blue van before tonight? Were those two guys talking at the corner her neighbors? Had she ever seen the woman jogging past her building before? And who was that young man in the hooded sweatshirt just getting out of the black Camaro in front of her building? Did he have a reason for being there, or was he waiting to do her harm?

"Well?" he asked when they reached the end of the block.

"It—it's hard to say. Everything looks all right, I guess..." She despised the wimpy sound of her uncertainty.

Stopped at the intersection, his dark eyes narrowed. "But you're not sure. So what is it? What did you see? Something or someone who shouldn't be here?"

She turned and peered out the back window. "I just don't know." And that's what frustrated her. "I guess I'm always so caught up in my own routine that I haven't taken the time to notice much of what goes on around here after dark."

Cole turned at the next corner to make another sweep of her block.

Anne hated the anxious feelings that gnawed at her stomach. After her bitter breakup with Gregg, this cozy city neighborhood had seemed so safe, so welcoming. She'd been lucky to find an apartment in this popular area of town, which was bordered on the east by Washington Park—or Wash Park as the natives called it—where giant elms lined both sides of the quiet street to form a lacy canopy of green. Each lawn, though small, was well-tended, adding to the subdued and homey feeling of the neighborhood.

Cole guided the pickup onto her street again. "Is there a back entrance to your building?"

"Yes. You can drive down the alley."

"I want to check it out. Get down in your seat."

"What?"

"Get down, Anne," he said as he rounded the corner and turned into the alley.

She slumped down in her seat, feeling foolish, depressed and peeved. "I can't see a thing."

"And with luck, no one will see you." After a moment he said, "All right. You can come up for air now."

"Thanks," she muttered and looked out to see that they were turning down her street again. Did he really have a legitimate reason for all these theatrics, she wondered, or did he just enjoy scaring her?

When he edged the pickup to the curb in front of her building, she reached for the door, but before she could open it, he leaned across the seat and covered her hand with his. His face was mere inches from hers, and his breath was warm on her cheek. "Rule number one, I always get out first. If everything's all right, I'll come around for you."

"Rule number one?"

"Yeah." He almost smiled. "Spencer's rules. We'll discuss the others as they come up."

She rolled her eyes. "I can't wait."

When he lifted his hand from hers, his warmth lingered, a not altogether unpleasant sensation. "I'll always come round and open your door," he said. "But if for any reason I don't make it, get behind the wheel and drive away as fast as you can. Don't slow down for anything, and don't look back." Pulling open the ashtray in the center of the dash, he withdrew a set of keys and handed them to her. "Hang on to these. I hope you'll never need them, but just to be safe..."

Anne nodded, fighting a shiver. If the man was trying to scare her, he was doing a great job of it, she thought, as she tucked the set of spare keys deep into the pocket of the baggy jeans he'd forced her to wear. At least the denim getup was warm, which was a comfort, since the cloak-and-dagger events of the last couple of hours seemed to have driven a deep chill into her bones.

She saw him sweep the area with a seemingly casual gaze as he walked around to open her door. With his hand at her back, they moved up the sidewalk to her building.

Inside, she followed his gaze down the length of the deserted hallway to the back door.

"My apartment is on this floor, at the end of the hall."

At her door, when he asked her for her keys, she hesitated.

"Just give me your keys, Anne."

"Spencer's next rule? A lady can't open her own door?"

He didn't smile when he took the keys from her and unlocked the door. He raised his hand, signaling for her to wait in the doorway while he edged inside and looked around.

In a few seconds, he seemed satisfied and, without speaking a word, motioned her inside.

"Gee, thanks," she muttered.

Reaching past her, he closed the door noiselessly and slid the dead bolt closed, again without sound. Anne dropped her purse on the table beside the door and watched Cole move quickly and quietly from room to room. With an economy of movement and unexpected speed, he checked each room before walking to the living room, where he headed for the phone and the answering machine on the end table beside the couch.

Before she could stop him, he hit the button to play the message indicated by the blinking red light. Suddenly his commando-style actions felt like a most flagrant intrusion.

"This *is* my home, you know—"

With a finger to his lips, he motioned for her to be quiet.

The message played, but the woman's voice was unfamiliar, and Anne could make no sense of the message. "This is Mrs. Reilly from U.S. West. The problem you reported with your line has been turned over to our service department."

She opened her mouth to speak, but again he gestured for silence. For the first time, she noticed that he held a small metal gadget in his hand, which he pointed at the brass table lamp beside the phone.

He stared at the gadget for a few seconds, and then motioned for her to follow him into the hallway. When she hesitated, he took her hand and hauled her with him into the bathroom and closed the door.

"What the . . ."

He pulled her down to sit beside him on the edge of the tub and turned the faucet on full blast. He leaned close and said in a low voice, "Your apartment's bugged."

She stared at him. "I don't believe it!"

"Believe it. There's a device in the lampshade in the living room. And I'd wager there's another one in your bedroom. Come on. I'll show you. But you mustn't say a word."

Despite her wariness of him—of the entire situation, which was growing more uncomfortable by the moment— she followed him to the living room. Aiming the small metal gadget at the lamp again, he pointed to the flickering red needle at the center of the device. Perplexed by what she'd seen, she followed him into the bathroom.

"Your phone line has been tapped, as well," he said. "Drew checked it out from his end. That message on your machine was from our—that is, from Drew's secretary, calling to let me know."

Anne could only stare at him in disbelief. "But what does this mean? What can we do?"

"It means we're getting out of here."

"But I can't just . . . I'll need to pack a few things . . ."

Reaching past her, he snatched her toothbrush from the plastic holder on the wall and handed it to her. "You're packed and we're leaving."

"But—"

"Now." His hand was on her arm as he guided her down the hall to the front door.

"Wait a minute!" she whispered, jerking out of his grasp. "At least let me grab a change of clothes."

This just couldn't be happening! This was her home, the place where, for the past two years, she'd retreated from the cold realities of the world—a world where husbands hurt their wives, and parents hurt their kids, and nothing was fair or safe. And now, not even her own apartment was safe. *Damn it!* This was all just so unbelievable.

His hand was on her arm again.

"Will you wait just a minute!" Unintended, her voice rose. "At least let me get my—"

He grabbed her purse off the table beside the door with one hand and opened the door with the other.

She was halfway out the door when she said, "My cat. I have to get my cat."

He frowned.

"Her name is Tabitha," she explained, mouthing the words. "I can't leave her." Before he could pull the door closed, she darted back inside.

He caught up to her in the bedroom. "There's no time." He wasn't bothering to whisper. "They've heard us by now. It isn't safe. We're going. Now." He reached for her hand, but she spun away before he could grab her.

Tabitha didn't like strangers. When she'd heard them come in, she'd probably made a dash for her favorite hiding place, Anne thought, dropping to her hands and knees to peer under the bed. Her heart sank when she saw that Tabitha's flannel-lined basket was empty.

"Darn it," she muttered. "Where the heck are you?"

Before she knew what had happened, he slipped his arm round her waist and hauled her to her feet. She jerked away from him and spun around to see a look on his face that should have scared her to death.

"I can't just leave her," she said. Who knew when she'd be back?

The fire in his eyes scorched her. "We've got to leave now!" His voice barely contained his anger.

"Not without my cat. Now help me find her!"

He hesitated only a second before he turned and jerked open the closet doors behind him. Anne shoved the blankets that were stacked on the floor to one side, but Tabitha wasn't there.

"Tabitha," Anne called in an urgent whisper. "Tabitha, come here." But still the skittish little animal wouldn't show herself.

"Well? Are you satisfied? She's not here. Now, let's go."

"But she has to be here." A possible answer to the mystery of Tabitha's whereabouts began to form in her mind. "Unless she darted out when—"

Cole seized the opening. "When whoever wired the apartment broke in, she could have dashed out. She's not here. Now, let's *go!*"

Grudgingly, she allowed him to herd her to the door.

"She'll turn up," he promised when they were in the hallway.

Another possibility struck her, and she headed toward the stairs that led to the basement. "She loves to go with me when I do my laundry," she said over her shoulder.

He caught up to her in two strides. "There's no time!"

"This will only take a min—" The sound of glass shattering preceded a giant roar that drove her to her knees and erased every thought but escape from her head.

# Chapter Three

Stunned, Anne almost didn't recognize the whimper as her own.

"Anne!" He was beside her on the floor, his arm draped over her back.

"I'm okay," she said, not really knowing if she was.

"Stay down."

"Wh-what happened?"

"I don't know. Let's get out of here." Taking her hand, he pulled her with him when he rose. "Follow me and stay low."

Thick smoke tainted the air above their heads. "I'm right behind you," she assured him.

With his hand tightly wrapped around hers, they ran to the end of the hallway and the back door. Cole stopped long enough to trip the alarm mounted on the wall beside the door, then shoved the door open. Before it closed, Anne glanced back long enough to see fingers of smoke writhing out of a black hole where her apartment door had once been.

She coughed, choking on the acrid air that seared her throat and brought tears stingingly to her eyes.

"This way," he said, his arm around her shoulders again. Moving quickly, almost running, they rushed to the end of the alley. Just before they reached the cross street, he pulled her into the shadows, where a flowering hedge had taken command of someone's back fence.

They were both breathing hard, and Anne felt her pulse pounding in her ears.

"Are you okay?" Even in the dim light, she read the concern in his eyes.

She nodded to assure him. Her throat felt raw and so tightly constricted, she didn't want to speak for fear she'd start coughing again. For the first time, she realized she was shaking from the inside out.

He put his arms around her and, instinctively, she nestled against him. "It's okay," he promised, stroking a large, comforting circle over and over again on her back. In a moment she felt the trembling subside.

"I'm all right," she said and pulled far enough out of his arms to allow a deep, cleansing breath. The shadows played across his face, enhancing the well-defined features. When she realized she'd been staring, she took another step back and wondered what was wrong with her to choose this particularly strange moment to notice his deeply appealing looks. "Get me out of here, cowboy," she said. "I think the smoke is affecting my brain."

At the moment, she would have felt better if he had relented to give her even the most fleeting smile, but there wasn't time, as he was quick to point out.

"When we reach the sidewalk, keep your head down. That alarm will bring out the whole neighborhood, so with any luck, you'll be just another face in the crowd."

His expression grew even more serious when he adjusted the bill of her cap—the ball cap she'd all but forgotten she was still wearing. When he tucked a lose tendril under the cap, his fingers strayed to her cheek and rested there for only a moment before he inhaled sharply. "We'll figure out what to do about your cat after we get you out of here."

Immediately, a lump swelled in her throat and she spun around to stare at her building. "Oh, Cole, what if she was in there?"

"She wasn't." He sounded so completely sure she almost believed him. "We looked, remember? Don't worry, we'll find her."

Again, she could only nod.

A few minutes later, they were walking quickly and deliberately down the street toward his truck. As they moved closer to the front of her building, Anne felt her heartbeat accelerate. The fire alarm was still screaming, but the wail of another siren, a fire truck rumbling down the street, drowned out the lesser sound.

Cole had been right. The street was a jumble of activity, and a crowd had gathered on the lawn in front of the building. Smoke poured from the direction of her living-room window. On the street, passing cars slowed, drivers and passengers absorbed in trying to snatch a glance of the spectacle. Her neighbors, the building's residents, stood on the lawn, staring in stunned disbelief.

It took all of Anne's strength not to join them, to count every head to be sure everyone was out of the building, to help where she could, to let her neighbors know she was all right and to beg their forgiveness for bringing this hell into their lives.

As she and Cole quickly closed the distance between them and his truck, Anne felt her legs go weak, and for a moment she thought she might faint. Although she'd walked away without a scratch, the terrifying thought that someone had just tried to kill her hit with sudden and full impact. Even now, whoever had ignited the blast could be standing right next to one of her neighbors, watching and waiting to see if the explosion had served its deadly purpose. The mere idea filled her with fear. What if he saw her now? What if he stepped out of the crowd and gunned her down the way he'd gunned down poor Stan? Would there be enough time for Cole—for anyone—to intervene?

As if he'd sensed her panic, Cole squeezed her hand and whispered, "Just a few more minutes and we'll be out of here. You're doing fine. Don't worry, we're almost in the clear."

Despite the fact that he was still a virtual stranger, Anne clung to his promises. Right now he was her compass, her guide in the midst of directionless fear.

When Cole opened the door, he said. "Keep your head down and don't look back."

To Anne, the moments seemed endless before he jumped in behind the wheel and started the engine. In truth, it was only a matter of seconds before they were pulling away from the curb.

Across the street, a familiar-looking car pulled away at exactly the same time, but in the opposite direction. Anne turned around in her seat and stared out the back window, straining to get a better look.

If she didn't know better... but no, it couldn't be...

"What is it, Anne? What did you see?" He eased off the accelerator as she continued to stare.

"I'm not really sure." The car's red signal light indicated a left turn at the corner, but instead the driver pulled the car into a sharp U-turn in the intersection and slowly cruised past the building again. Anne watched the car pull up to the curb in front of the building. Then, suddenly, the car accelerated, made another wide turn in the middle of the street and sped off in the opposite direction.

"Anne?"

"It's nothing. Just someone trying to get a closer look."

One dark brow lifted almost imperceptibly. "Are you sure that's all it was?"

"I think so." The actions of the driver of the blue car had seemed strange, but strange was not necessarily sinister, she told herself. Although why anyone would get a kick out of following emergency vehicles to the sight of someone else's misery, she'd never understand. Besides, she wouldn't have even noticed the car had it not looked so much like Jenetta's. Forcing herself to think logically, she told herself that in a city the size of Denver there were probably thousands of cars just like her assistant's blue compact. Besides, if for some reason Jenetta had been in her neighborhood, she sure as heck wouldn't have left the site of a disaster taking place in the building where her friend resided.

Cole slowed for a four-way stop, then turned to face her. "I think you need to understand something, Anne. From now on, you need to alert me to anything you see or hear that doesn't seem quite right. That Molotov cocktail wasn't tossed at random through your window. The threatening calls, the tampering with your car, they're all related. Someone very dangerous and very desperate is sending you a very clear message. Tonight he upped the ante.''

"If you're trying to frighten me, you're too late," she informed him. "I'm not underestimating the situation. But I can't allow my imagination to run wild, either." Nor could she allow some kind of groundless suspicion to take root in Cole Spencer's mind. "I was mistaken, that's all. I thought I recognized someone—a car, that is—because it looked similar to a car a friend of mine drives. But it wasn't her, okay?"

Cole signaled to pull onto the highway. "Whose car did you think it was?"

"A good friend. The secretary for our department."

"Would she have reason to be in your neighborhood this time of night?"

"It wasn't her, all right?" she informed him tersely. "Now let it go, will you?" Closing her eyes, she leaned her head back and massaged her lids, trying to ease the tension headache that was taking on a life of its own. *You're the one who needs to let it go,* an inner voice warned. Her emotions were definitely getting the better of her. Gregg had always accused her of being too emotional—an ironic charge coming from someone whose own moods could shift between joy and anger with little warning.

Her thoughts of Gregg surprised her, but then again, perhaps it was only natural that in this fearful, out-of-control situation, he'd come to mind. "I'm sorry. I shouldn't have snapped at you like that," she said.

"It's all right." His quiet, almost gentle tone disarmed her. "I just want you to keep in mind that sometimes the solutions to a very big puzzle can hinge on the smallest pieces, the seemingly unimportant details."

"I'll keep that in mind."

As they rode through the night in silence, Anne tried to envision the faces of the crowd that had gathered in front of her building. With any luck, the bomb that had been meant for her hadn't harmed any of her neighbors. The newlyweds who'd just moved into the building last week, the retired couple who lived next door and Mrs. McKee, the seventy-year-old widow who jogged around the park every morning with her fluffy little Pomeranian, Pansy, at her side. Anne thought about them all and prayed that they were safe.

From thoughts of her neighbors, her mind drifted to her own predicament. By the look and feel of the explosion, everything in her apartment must have been destroyed. It wasn't that she had anything of great material value—most of her possessions could be replaced, if not easily, at least eventually. The material items she treasured were few and, when taken as a whole, probably wouldn't have even raised next month's rent at a garage sale. Those things she'd miss would have been of no value to anyone but her—the books and photographs, the special notes and cards, her diary, the secondhand piano she'd lovingly salvaged and refurbished. And, of course, Tabitha, the scruffy little three-legged cast-off she'd rescued from the pound.

Without warning, tears, spurred as much by anger as grief, pooled in her eyes. She inhaled sharply and put her hands over her face. Cole's arm slid down from the back of the seat onto her shoulders.

"I'm sorry," he said simply, and steered the pickup across three lanes of traffic and onto an exit ramp, which seemed to have appeared out of nowhere. In the dark, with emotion gripping her and tears clouding her vision, Anne couldn't identify the neighborhood. All she knew for sure was that they were on the west side of town, near the foothills.

At the first side street, Cole pulled to the curb, shut off the engine and killed the lights.

"I know what you're going through. How frightened you must be."

She tried to answer, but chose to nod instead. He held her with his eyes for the space of a couple of heartbeats before he took her into his arms, into the shelter of an embrace where she found herself wishing she could stay forever.

After a few minutes, Anne forced herself to draw slowly out of his arms. Embarrassed by her sudden and uncharacteristic display of emotion, she stammered out an uncomfortable and awkward apology. "I'm sorry. I can't believe I did that."

"No apologies," he said softly. "You didn't do anything wrong. If you weren't having some reaction to what's happened, I'd be worried about you."

Two hours ago she wouldn't have thought Cole Spencer capable of this kind of gentle understanding.

"It just all seems so...unreal. First Stan and now this...." She sighed and dragged the ball cap off her head and ran a hand through her hair, causing it to tumble in a mass to her shoulders. "I hate feeling like my life is out of my control...like I'm not handling anything very well."

"I think you're doing just fine. You know, it isn't every day someone tosses a bomb into the middle of your life."

She shuddered. "You said something about a Molotov cocktail. How did you know?"

"It was just a guess. It's hard to say exactly what they used without talking to the fire inspectors and the police lab. But if I had to guess, I'd say some sort of homemade gasoline and gunpowder concoction. Lots of smoke, lots of bang. But, if we're lucky, not much fire."

She longed to share his optimism. "I hope you're right."

"I'll be in touch with Drew. He'll make arrangements to salvage and store whatever wasn't destroyed. And I'll see what can be done about finding your cat."

"Going back for her could have gotten us killed. I'm sorry, Cole."

"It's all right," he said. "I know just how you feel. I have animals I'd risk my neck for, too."

It was a simple declaration, and yet exactly the kind of reassurance she needed to hear.

"So what happens now? When do we call the police?"

His smile was patient. "If I know Russell, he's probably already on the scene. And until we know more than we do tonight, he's our only contact with the police. Remember that if he thought the police could protect you, Drew would never have called me, and the city wouldn't be paying me to protect you. I know it's hard to accept, Anne, but for now we can't trust the police."

Something about the way he'd said her name suggested an intimacy that warmed her and caused an unexpected awareness of him, which she found extremely unsettling.

"For now, let's just concentrate on getting you out of Denver." He started the engine, flipped on the headlights and headed to the highway. Neither of them spoke for several miles.

Finally, Anne said, "I'm not even a real witness, you know. Not an eyewitness, anyway. As I tried to explain to Detective Nyguen that night, I didn't actually *see* anything. I heard voices, and I hid until they were gone. When I was sure they'd left, I called for help. In reality, I'm not a witness to anything, and yet no one seems to understand that."

"It doesn't matter what Nyguen understands. What's important is what Stanley Lewellyn's murderer believes. And right now, he seems to believe you can identify him. Even if he isn't sure what you saw or heard, he still considers you a threat—a very big threat—if you could recognize his voice."

A series of shivers prickled up her arms to the back of her neck and across her scalp. She thought about Stanley, about his family. She thought about her apartment, how it had been and what it had probably been reduced to tonight. A cold, dark, nameless fear settled inside her.

"You said you heard two men talking in Lewellyn's office that night."

She shook her head. "No, I only really heard one voice. The other voice was so muffled and low, I couldn't even say for sure if it was a man or a woman's voice."

"And you didn't see anyone in the building before the murder?"

She swallowed before answering. "Only Stan. We were working late, though not together. I work in juvenile probation, and Stan works...worked at the other end of the hall in the prosecutor's office."

"Were you the only one in your department working late?"

She nodded. "Normally, my boss, Martin Gartrell—Marty—might have been there catching up, like I tried to do, but he'd been on vacation all that week. As a matter of fact, that's why I stayed late, to catch up on paperwork I hadn't had time to deal with because I'd been filling in for him all week." What a difference it might have made, Anne thought, if Marty had been there that night. Perhaps they could have apprehended Stan's murderers, or even prevented the killing altogether.

"You said something about an assistant?"

She nodded. "Yes. Jenetta Hagan. But she left early that day. It was the Friday before the long weekend. Everyone skipped out a bit early. Jen and Dan, her husband, have a cabin near Dillon where they spend a lot of their free time, especially the three-day weekends. Dan picked her up around two so that they could beat the traffic out of town."

Anne noticed a green highway sign that said Idaho Springs and was surprised that they'd already traveled fifty miles while she'd been engaged in answering his questions.

"What about Lewellyn's office? Was anyone working late, working with him, maybe?"

She shook her head. "No one."

Whether Cole had made any assumptions from her answers, she couldn't tell. His face seemed immobile, impassive. But her job put her in contact with enough investigators and cops to recognize when someone was absorbed in the mental sorting and examining of the information they'd been given. How many times had Jenetta complained about Dan's lapses into himself? Although Anne had sympathized with her friend, she couldn't help admiring the way Dan and others like him on the force did their jobs. Even after retirement, Dan kept up his work with juveniles through the police department's benevolent society.

How unnatural it felt to suddenly distrust the very individuals with whom she had worked so closely and come to respect so deeply over the years. Not only mistrust, she reminded herself, but run from . . . all the way to Telluride.

She frowned at the thought of the distance. "I don't suppose I can talk you out of taking me all the way to Telluride?"

He shook his head. "For now, it's the best, safest solution."

She sighed, resigned but still not pleased. "Will we drive straight through tonight?"

He glanced at her and then at the road. "You know, people travel from all over the world to vacation in the San Juans."

"Hey, I love the mountains as much as the next person. I just don't think you understand how I feel about being forced out of my home and away from my commitments."

His expression said she was wrong.

"Look, I didn't ask—"

He held up a hand, interrupting her. "I know, I know, you didn't ask for my help." Had he almost chuckled? "And I'm not asking *you* for anything, either, except to allow me to do my job."

"A job you didn't want."

"Right."

"A job you hate."

"Right again."

"Then why *did* you agree to protect me, Cole?"

All traces of humor, wry or otherwise, evaporated. "Because my brother is one of those good guys you believe in. He needed my help, and I owe him."

Why did he owe his brother? she wondered, though she couldn't bring herself to ask.

He rubbed the back of his neck, for the first time betraying any trace of weariness. "Face it, Ms. Osborne, we're stuck with each other, at least for awhile. We can fight it or make the best of it. It's up to you."

TWO HOURS LATER, Anne still felt chilled—deeply chilled—and shaken by the unbelievable events of the day. Wrapping her arms around herself, she huddled against the seat and tried to quell another bout of trembling.

"There's a jacket behind the seat," he said.

Reaching into the slim space behind the seat, she pulled out a man's flannel-lined jean jacket—his jacket, she knew instinctively, recognizing the soapy, leathery smell. The soft, worn flannel felt good, almost as good as his arms. With that thought, she stole another glance at him. Even in the dimly lit cab, the well-defined planes of his silhouette spoke of an inner strength. And looks weren't deceiving in this case, she told herself.

When put to the test tonight, Cole Spencer had exhibited confidence and expertise in abundance. In all likelihood, his ability to act and react had saved both their lives.

Almost without realizing it, she found herself wanting to trust him. She felt safe with Cole Spencer. At least physically. And although she'd be loath to admit it aloud, it was the first time since the night of Stan's murder.

Tonight, she'd found immeasurable comfort in Cole Spencer's arms. What impact that would have on the rest of their very unlikely relationship, she had no way of knowing. *Relationship?* Was that the word to describe an arrangement with a man who was forced to protect her and was being paid to care?

"We need to stop for gas soon," he said, preventing her from exploring further that odd train of thought.

Anne's watch had stopped, but she guessed they'd been traveling for at least another half hour when Cole signaled and guided the truck off the interstate and onto the exit marked Georgetown. Anne had visited Georgetown a few times, and she always admired the small mountain community nestled in the hills halfway between Denver and Loveland Pass. Like so many of the communities that dotted the Colorado Rockies, Georgetown reflected the state's affection for its nineteenth-century history. Carefully restoring and treasuring its past, the quaint community had become a popular tourist stop.

As they drove into town, Anne allowed her gaze to wander among the town's lights, which extended in a scattered handful up into the hills. An unexpected nostalgic feeling stirred within her. Growing up alone in the city, the only child of an irreparably broken home, Anne had often fantasized about living in a town like this one. She'd dreamed about what it would be like to be part of a real family who lived in a Christmas-card kind of community such as this. Tonight, with the lights from all those anonymous houses twinkling like ornaments on the hillside, she remembered her childhood dreams, and how, with Gregg, she'd thought she'd found a man to share them.

How could she have believed he'd wanted to build that kind of life with her, to create the kind of family she'd longed for as a child?

Sadly, by the time she'd recognized Gregg for who he really was, he'd not only shattered their marriage vows but destroyed most of her personal dreams in the process.

For the past two years, she'd been so consumed with rebuilding her self-confidence she'd had little time to dwell on the romanticized dreams of her childhood or start building new ones. Tonight, despite everything that had taken place earlier, she felt those dreams coming to life again. Like an old friend, whose face she'd almost forgotten, they came back to her, and she not only recognized them but felt the familiar tug on her heart.

Cole pulled into the gas station, filled the tank and paid the attendant. As he turned the key in the ignition, he said, "That place over there serves a pretty good burger. And I could use a cup of coffee. How about you?"

"Never touch the stuff, but I wouldn't turn down a cup of herbal tea."

They pulled up in front of the small, A-frame establishment, and Anne smiled at the sign that boasted, We Never Close!

"Put your cap on before we go inside," he instructed as he parked and killed the engine.

"Oh, please. You can't really believe I could be in any danger up here?"

"We have no way of knowing. Just put it on, Anne. I don't want to take any chances. One close call per night is enough."

Grudgingly accepting his logic, she gathered her long hair up in a twist on top of her head and settled the cap over it. "So, tell me, is this how it's going to be from now on, you giving orders and me obeying?"

He opened his door and stepped out without answering.

"I hate this," she muttered to the empty cab, "I *really* hate this."

When he opened her door, she was ready for him. "I think I should warn you, I don't take orders well."

"So I've noticed." He smiled and leaned into the truck, one arm on the back of the seat and the other on the roof of the cab. "I think you should leave the jacket on, too."

"Right." She buttoned the jacket and tugged on the cap to keep it from slipping. "Now I have a request. Please keep in mind that I'm not a child—" even as a child she'd had only herself to depend on, she remembered, but she didn't bother to tell him that "—and you don't have to tell me when to inhale and exhale."

Even as she let him have it, she knew she wasn't being fair, that it was the fatigue, the strain and a lot of false pride talking.

She was not so blind nor too stupid to recognize how badly she needed his help—the attempt on her life tonight had made her a true believer. He was in no way responsible for her predicament. He *was* responsible, however, for the sardonic spark in his eyes that hinted that he might actually be enjoying the challenge she represented, and that galled her.

Grabbing her purse, she climbed out of the truck and slammed the door unnecessarily hard.

"I'm not the enemy, Anne," he said, coming up behind her. "I'm just doing what I promised my brother I'd do. From now until this thing is over, we'll get along a lot better if you try to remember that. I am your bodyguard. I'm being paid to protect you."

He couldn't make their non-relationship any clearer than that, she told herself, so forget about his arms and forget about his tenderness. For him, offering comfort was just part of the job.

"However else you think of me," he added, "just remember that your safety is my sole concern."

*As if you'd let me forget,* she almost said.

# Chapter Four

The small, surprisingly cheery café wasn't crowded. The red vinyl booths and Formica-topped tables echoed back to the fifties, and the smell of burgers and fries that mingled in the air, along with the sound of clanking silver, almost succeeded in piquing Anne's appetite. A popular country song played on the jukebox, assuring late-night diners that despite cheating, lying lovers, life went on.

"This way," Cole said, directing her to an empty booth in the corner. Before she could sit down, he said, "I need to be able to see the door."

She traded places with him, but not without muttering, "Is this really necessary?"

"Yes," he said simply and handed her one of the laminated menus that stood wedged between the salt and pepper shakers and a ceramic sugar bowl in the center of the table.

With a smile Anne had never seen before, Cole thanked the jeans-clad waitress for the coffee she brought to the table. The young woman's naturally pretty face glowed under his unspoken approval. Absorbed with batting her heavily mascaraed lashes at him, she seemed oblivious to Anne's presence.

"And a cup of herbal tea, if you have it, and some honey," Cole added. The young woman was in full meltdown mode now, like an ice cube tossed onto a hot griddle.

"I could have ordered my own tea," she informed him when the waitress moved away, all smiles and eager to do his bidding. "I've even been known to order an entire meal."

His wry smile said her sarcasm had been duly noted. "I'll keep that in mind at our next stop."

"Thanks," she said, feigning intense interest in the menu to avoid looking at him.

"And *you* should keep in mind that the last thing we want is for you to draw attention to yourself."

As if ordering tea was the act of an exhibitionist. "I think we're safe," she said, laying her menu aside. "Since you walked in the door, our waitress hasn't seen anything but you."

Before he could respond, the subject of Anne's comment returned, grinning and carrying a tray that held a small metal pitcher of hot water, two tea bags and a pot of coffee. She refilled Cole's cup and he thanked her—before she walked away still carrying Anne's tea. It only took a few steps for it to dawn on her what she'd done, and she rushed back to their table, flustered and blushing.

Because Anne could remember herself at sixteen, and because her first impression of Cole Spencer was still vivid, she offered the girl an understanding smile. The guy really was incredibly attractive. Although when she stopped to study his face, she realized that handsome wouldn't be the right word to describe him—at least not in that golden-boy, Hollywood way, which is how she'd once regarded Gregg. Cole's appeal was far more intense than that—a disturbing reality that Anne had been fighting from the moment their lives had inadvertently collided in the alley behind his brother's agency.

Something about his face, with its rugged lines, high cheekbones and solid square jaw, fascinated her. His bronzed skin identified him as a man who spent most of his hours outdoors. Gregg had started working on his tan each year just after Christmas, visiting the tanning bed at the mall until he attained just the right glow for the first day on the links. By contrast, she couldn't imagine Cole engaged in anything as civilized as a game of golf, or as contrived as a tanning bed. In fact, he seemed as oblivious to his good looks as he was to the young waitress still ogling him.

But how could Anne blame her? His hair was fine and thick, that stunning blue-black color that no hair-care company had yet been successful in duplicating. His eyes, so brown they appeared at times almost black, snapped with innate intelligence and ready wit. They simmered with sensuality. If it was true what they said, about the eyes being the windows to the soul, then Anne had to conclude that Cole had been touched by great pain and loss—and touched deeply, judging by the few unguarded glimpses he'd allowed.

"Are you sure you wouldn't like to order something to eat?" he asked.

"Just the tea," she said, praying he hadn't guessed it had been thoughts of him that had been distracting her.

Each time the young woman returned to the table to refill his cup, Anne found herself experiencing an odd mix of emotions. The feelings of irritation she could accept—the waitress was flirting shamelessly, after all. But those other feelings, the ones that felt too much like jealousy, had to be examined when she felt stronger and the distance between them was more than a three-foot slab of Formica and a cup of tea.

"I hope you're not feeling as grim as you look," he said, surprising her. "It won't be that bad. Some people would jump at the chance for an unexpected vacation." He leaned forward, resting his forearms on the table. "You know, if you give it half a chance, you might actually enjoy it."

She felt a bit sheepish. After all, it wasn't his fault the police department had a security problem. "You're right, of course. And in a way, I'm looking forward to spending time in Telluride. Has the ski area opened yet?"

"Not yet. It's still a little early." He went on to explain how autumn could turn to winter overnight in the high country. As he launched into a description of the area,

Anne began to realize that maybe this was the best way to inoculate herself against his potentially lethal charm. By getting to know him, by getting him to reveal more of the mundane reality of his life, perhaps he'd become less of a mystery. And in dispelling the mystery, perhaps he'd lose some of his appeal. It was worth a shot. After all, as un-believable as it seemed to her now, she remembered a time when she'd found Gregg charming—before she'd discov-ered who and what he really was.

"I think there may be enough snow in the high country to cross-country ski," he was saying, and although Anne couldn't care less about downhill or cross-country skiing, she forced herself to concentrate on every word he said. The intense physical attraction she felt wasn't easy to ignore, but she told herself she'd better find a way if she hoped to emerge with her pride intact from whatever length of time they'd be forced to spend together.

"I hear the town is booming," she said. "Some are call-ing Telluride the next Aspen."

He shook his head. "I guess I wouldn't know about that. I don't spend much time in town. The ranch is eight miles south and another five miles off the main highway."

The concept of true isolation took immediate shape in her mind. "Sounds pretty lonely."

"It might seem that way to some."

"But not to you?"

He picked up his cup and studied the contents before he answered. "I guess I'm used to the solitude."

Solitude or loneliness. A surge of compassion filled her. "I remember as a kid longing for a room of my own," she confided. "Thinking back, I always remember feeling crowded. What I wouldn't have given for just a little pri-vacy."

He smiled. "My brother and I shared a room, but with a thousand acres to roam, I don't think either of us ever felt crowded. Our folks gave us free rein."

"Hmm. Sounds idyllic." In and out of foster homes most of her formative years, Anne had often shared a home with as many as six or seven kids at one time.

"In a way, we were lucky," he continued. "My father was the quintessential self-made man. My mom was ahead of her time, I guess. I always remember her as fiercely independent. I know they were determined to make us as independent and self-sufficient as possible. They gave us space, but also responsibility. My dad was a great one for letting us learn the hard way about consequences. I always thought the way he raised us gave Drew and me a certain edge, a kind of..."

"Confidence?" she offered.

He nodded. "Yes. I guess you could call it that."

"Your father sounds like a very wise man," she said, remembering that when she was a young, newly married woman, Gregg had begun immediately to squash her every effort to achieve any kind of self-confidence or independence. In the beginning, she'd blamed his erratic bursts of temper and obsessive nature on the demands of his career.

Later, when all that anger and control became more sharply and singularly focused on her, Anne had been ready to take the blame for their failing marriage. *If only I could be more dependable,* she'd told herself, *more frugal, more efficient, prettier, smarter, sexier.* The list seemed to grow even as his power over her became more complete and her feelings of self-worth eroded. Gradually, she'd found herself totally dependent on him to make even the smallest decisions. In short, Gregg had turned her into an emotional cripple, and what was worse, Anne had allowed it to happen. Now, she almost couldn't remember the woman she used to be. It felt sometimes as though that life had happened to someone else.

What part of Cole Spencer's life had he left behind? she wondered. The way he'd corrected himself after referring to Drew's secretary as *their* secretary led Anne to believe he'd once been an active member of the Spencer Agency. That, coupled with the resentment she'd sensed when he'd questioned his brother's motives for asking him to take her case, made her wonder what had caused the split.

Was the man she saw now, this rugged cowboy body-guard, as uncomplicated and straightforward as he appeared? Or was there another side, a side he was trying to forget? Was that solitude he claimed to enjoy his emotional haven—or a hideout?

The waitress picked up their check and the cash Cole had laid on top of it. "Are you sure you don't want anything else?" he asked. "We still have a long way to go. It will be close to morning before we're . . . home."

When she didn't answer immediately, he ordered tea in an insulated cup. "Herbal," he specified, and handed the waitress another dollar. "Maybe you can get some sleep on the way," he said as they waited for the young woman to bring the tea.

"Since Stan's death, sleep has become a rather vague concept," she admitted. "I just keep going back to that night . . . remembering how he looked." If she'd ever felt more helpless or more frightened, she couldn't remember when. Since that night, no matter how exhausted she'd felt, the moment her head hit the pillow the questions began again. Who killed Stanley Lewellyn and why? Could anything she'd seen or heard that night help solve the deadly riddle?

It would take a clear head to sort it all out. Ironically, the sleep she needed to unfog her mind seemed to evade her just when she needed it most, and tonight would be no exception. At least tomorrow she wouldn't have to drag herself to the office.

"The office," she blurted.

"What?"

"I just realized what a mess my assistant will be facing in the morning when I don't show up for work."

The waitress arrived with her tea, and Cole stood. "Ready?" he asked.

"Wait a minute." Remembering her cell phone in her purse, she formed a quick plan. If Jenetta found a message waiting for her, perhaps she could get a jump on re-scheduling appointments before her first client arrived.

She pulled the phone from her bag, flipped it open and started punching numbers.

"Put it away," Cole said.

"What?" She gaped at him, startled as much by his tone as his command, so different from the easy, conversational tone he'd used only moments earlier.

"The phone. Put it away."

"But I need to leave a message for my assistant." Ignoring his scowl, she brought the phone to her ear and heard the first ring. But before she got Jenetta's voice mail, Cole reached across the table and grabbed the phone out of her hand.

"What the...what do you think you're doing?"

He leveled an angry gaze on her. "You really don't get this, do you?" He jabbed the disconnect button while his dark eyes continued to simmer.

"Who the hell do you think you are?" she demanded.

Their glares locked for a full ten seconds before he responded. "I'm the idiot who agreed to be your bodyguard, remember?"

"Well, at least we agree on something!"

After a dangerous flicker of rage, his face softened and, to her utter surprise, he smiled. "Touché, Ms. Osborne." And as quickly as it had appeared, his smile died and his expression turned stone cold. "But the fact remains, you're in hiding. And in order for me to protect you from the kind of people who toss explosives into other people's living rooms, the world has to believe you've disappeared."

*Was there anything more maddening than a patronizing man?*

"I trust Jenetta." Her anger caused her voice to shake.

"Don't." He rose and shoved the small cordless phone into the pocket of his leather jacket. "At least not until this thing is over."

What had she ever done to deserve this arrogant man?

"Jenetta Hagan has been my friend for almost four years," she explained through clenched teeth. Dan and Jenetta had been almost like family, especially since her divorce. Anne couldn't count the number of times they'd call her with extra tickets to a ball game or a concert, or just to invite her to share one of Dan's special Sunday barbecues in their suburban backyard. "Jen would never betray me," Anne insisted, matching his stride as they walked out of the café and into the cold, clear, star-studded night.

Upon reaching the pickup, he opened her door. "You could be right. Maybe she wouldn't do anything to hurt you, not intentionally, anyway. But listen to me, Anne. You don't know what kind of individuals you're dealing with. Someone who would walk into a government building and gun down a D.A. is either crazy or supremely confident. Maybe both. But, in any case, extremely dangerous. Beyond any danger you could comprehend. You can't know to what extremes that kind of person will go to track you."

The sparks of angry black diamonds were gone, but his eyes still burned, underscoring his message with breathtaking intensity.

"So, unless you have some kind of death wish, I'd advise you to follow my rules. I'll do my damnedest to protect you, but if you've got some kind of point to prove here...well, just give it up, damn it!"

She felt stunned by the things he'd said—stunned and speechless. She didn't know how to respond—or even if she could—and before she could decide, he muttered, "Oh, hell!" slammed the door, stalked around the front of the cab, jerked open the door and slid in behind the wheel, where he sat for a moment staring straight ahead without talking.

She could feel the anger coming off him in waves, and her own anger swelling like an overinflated balloon in her chest.

Finally he started the engine. "I tend to take it real personal when I lose a client or when anyone I care about gets hurt."

Anne could only stare at him, wondering. Could all this anger really be traced to her? To her defiance of him over the stupid cell phone? It seemed unlikely.

Despite her attempt to rationalize his behavior, she still felt more than a little bewildered by his outburst, especially by the extreme emotion behind it.

*Anyone he cared about? Well, he certainly doesn't mean me,* she told herself.

From the beginning he'd been as reluctant as she to engage in this bodyguard-client relationship. However, the fact remained that they'd both agreed to go through with it. So for now, at least, they were stuck with each other. Until things were resolved and Stan's murderers were caught, she and Cole would have to find a middle ground. In the meantime, she refused to be bullied by him. Even giving him the benefit of good intentions, she could not allow herself to be intimated.

*Damn you, Nyguen! You and your protective custody!* If she had called the detective's bluff, would he really have resorted to some kind of house arrest?

After fifteen crackling minutes of silence, she took a deep breath and said, "I think we need to get a couple of things straight. First, I will need to contact my office from time to time. And since you are the expert on such things as tapping phones and tracing calls, I'll defer to your judgment on where and when to make those calls. But I *will* make them."

She braced herself for his response. When none came, she told herself, *Don't stop now, Anne, you're on a roll.*

"I have responsibilities and people depending on me, and I intend to honor those responsibilities as best I can, under the circumstances."

A pulse point on Cole's temple was working overtime.

"I also intend to make sure you honor your brother's promise and get me back to Denver for my client's hearing on the fifteenth." If she still had a client on the fifteenth, she thought morosely.

He didn't look at her but kept his eyes trained on the road. His jaw was still set in a hard line, but his grip on the steering wheel seemed to relax some.

"I can't make good on any promises but my own." She opened her mouth to protest, but he cut her off, adding, "I will promise you this much. The minute the police have a suspect in jail, I won't waste time getting you back to Denver, where you can get on with your life and forget we ever met."

She stared at him, wondering again at the source of his anger. Although she had to believe he'd made his promise in good faith, Anne knew better than to expect a quick arrest of Stanley Lewellyn's murderer. And as for her forgetting him, well, she had no unrealistic expectations about that, either.

AFTER WHAT SEEMED like an endless stretch of rough gravel road, Cole finally stopped the pickup in front of a large, two-story log home. Without waiting for him to come around to her side, Anne shoved the door open and stepped out into the velvety, pine-scented darkness. She stretched, her weary muscles aching from stress and the hours spent on the road.

Despite her fatigue, the cool, fresh mountain air seemed to revitalize her. When she exhaled, her breath misted in front of her, and she immediately realized the difference between Indian summer in Denver and autumn in the high country.

Surrounding the house, giant pines were silhouetted in black by the light of a half moon. A porch light illuminated a deep front porch above a small yard surrounded by a white split-rail fence. She had no idea if the Spencer ranch would look this welcoming in the morning, but tonight, with her mind and body begging for a break from unrelenting stress, she couldn't imagine any place looking or feeling more like a real home.

"This way," Cole said and directed her across the unpaved driveway and through a wooden gate and into the yard. The dizzying events of the past several hours seemed suddenly to blur, taking on an almost surrealistic feel as Anne walked beside him across the porch toward the double-door entrance to his home.

*His home,* her mind repeated, trying to find perspective in her present reality—a reality that included a killer without a face and a bodyguard who'd made no secret that he'd been coerced into protecting her.

The entire situation had her reeling inside, feeling lonely and cut adrift, unsteady and uncertain. Ever since she'd been placed in his custody, her feelings for Cole hadn't stopped shifting. His overly confident, swaggering machismo annoyed her, his orders irritated and chaffed, and his outbursts triggered memories of some really awful confrontations with Gregg.

But even with all that, she didn't really feel threatened by Cole. Not in the way she'd felt threatened by Gregg—that wrenching way that had not only made her fear for her life, but had shredded her confidence and stripped her identity. Perhaps tomorrow she'd feel differently about this tall, brooding cowboy bodyguard. But for tonight, she felt safe.

When he opened the door and ushered her inside, he offered her a tired smile, and Anne realized with a flash of insight why she didn't feel threatened by this man. It all had to do with the circumstances of their first meeting—not in Drew's office, but when she'd seen him in those first unguarded moments, when he'd rushed to rescue poor Polly.

That impulsive act had been the reaction of a man with a heart, a noble, decent man capable of deep compassion, with a sense of old-fashioned justice. Although she might not have approved of his methods, she respected his motives.

"My aunt lives with me," he said, jerking her out of her introspection. "She's a heavy sleeper, so there's no need to tiptoe."

Although she wasn't afraid of him, just knowing there was someone else—another woman—in this remote, high-country hideaway made Anne feel immeasurably better.

After all, lack of fear and blind trust were hardly synonymous.

"The guest room is upstairs, second door to the right," he said, switching on a brass lamp that sat atop a sturdy oak table. The massive leather sectional beside it seemed perfectly scaled to the room, which epitomized the "great" in great room. "Nights can get pretty cold up here," he said. "You'll find extra quilts in the chest at the foot of your bed. The bathroom's at the end of the hall." He pulled his hat off and hung it on a coatrack beside the door, then accepted the cap and jacket she handed to him. "Bess will drive you into town tomorrow, and you can pick up whatever you need."

Without her asking, he explained that Bess was his aunt on his late father's side. She realized then that, other than her minimal observance of his interaction with his brother, it was her first real glimpse into Cole's personal life.

"You'll like Bess," he said. "Everyone does. She'll be tickled to have someone to go shopping with." As he spoke, he reached into his jacket and withdrew the envelope she'd seen him take out of his brother's office safe. He counted out a few bills and handed them to her. His simple gesture reminded her of how Gregg used to judiciously dole out the despised monthly allowance.

"I have money," she said tersely.

"Cash?"

*Not much,* she remembered. "Enough," she lied.

"Don't use your credit cards and don't write any checks. A paper trail is the easiest to track." The dark beard stubble that had risen on his cheeks, along with the faint smudges of purple beneath his eyes, triggered an awareness in Anne that this was a man who'd spent too many of the past twenty-four hours on the road.

"When you're in town, try not to strike up conversations with strangers," he went on. "Telluride isn't the small town it once was, but there are still quite a few old-timers who know my family, and seeing you with Bess will naturally raise questions."

"I'll be discreet," she promised. Although it had been a long time since she'd needed to exercise the skill, she'd once known exactly how to assume the lowest of profiles. It had been an especially useful trick she'd employed as a child in uncertain and unstable circumstances. In some situations, like a new foster home or a stint in a group home, she'd found it easier to blend in than to fight. Later, as a young wife faced with the frightening and volatile behavior of an obsessive and abusive mate, she'd become a master at the technique, which by then had become a survival skill.

"I'll never be noticed," she assured him.

Cole looked at her a long moment, his expression openly dubious. "Hmm...well, I have my doubts about that. But do what you can. Wearing that cap might help." He handed the ball cap to her, and it dawned on Anne that he'd just paid her a compliment.

"I guess that's all for tonight." He seemed more than ready to dismiss her, and Anne felt suddenly awkward.

"How long do you think I'll be—"

He was shaking his head, and before she could finish, he said, "Stuck out here? There's no way of knowing—not tonight, anyway. Why don't you go on up and try to get some sleep. There's a hot tub on the deck, if you think it would help relax you. If you need a suit, Bess keeps some extras in a cupboard in the guest bath." He inclined his head toward the back of the house.

"Thanks, but I don't think I could keep my eyes open that long." She started for the stairs, then stopped. "Will you call Drew tomorrow?"

"I will. With luck, they've identified the kid who tried to rig your car. We might get some quick answers."

*At least to that piece of the puzzle,* Anne added silently. What bothered her most was that tomorrow, even if they found the kid, even if they arrested a murderer, there would still be some questions that could never be answered. Like why a decent man like Stanley Lewellyn had to die. Without warning, her facade of control slipped.

"Damn it," she muttered under her breath. "This is just *so* unfair. Stan was one of the most honorable people I'd ever known. Kind, funny..." Her voice broke.

"You're tired, Anne. Don't put yourself through this tonight." He was studying her face as though looking at her for the first time. "You need to get some sleep." His expression had softened so obviously that she was taken aback by the change.

"You're right," she agreed and then, afraid she might give in to the emotional reaction welling inside her, she turned and headed for the stairs. When she felt his gaze on her back, it took all the discipline she possessed not to spin around and rush into the reassuring embrace she remembered experiencing all too well just a few hours ago in Denver. Why his unexpected kindness affected her the way it did Anne didn't know. But when he said, "Everything will be all right, I promise," in such a tender tone, she nearly came undone.

"Thank you," she managed to say, but didn't turn around. His unexpected tenderness brought hot tears to her eyes. *Breathe,* she ordered herself as she hurried up the stairs. The last thing she wanted was to break down in front of him again. It would be so easy just to give in. After all, he'd demonstrated how quickly he could assume the role of rescuer. The proverbial white knight—his initial reluctance notwithstanding.

But then, what would that make her? A damsel in distress? The hapless—or worse, helpless—maiden? Blessedly, the ridiculous thought strengthened even as it humiliated her, reminding her of another valuable skill she'd gained, courtesy of her ex-husband. The ability to salvage her pride. And next to physical safety, Anne had learned the hard way that a life without pride, without self-respect, wasn't worth living.

# Chapter Five

After scarcely an hour's sleep, Cole jerked awake, the remnants of a tangled dream still clinging to his mind and his sweat-soaked body, chilling him despite the sunlight flooding his bedroom. It was a dream he'd had many times, especially that first year. Just as it did every time, the nightmare left him shaken.

With few variations, it was always the same dream. A beautiful and startlingly alive Meredith, challenging him to race her to the top of some distant, windswept precipice, her mocking laughter turning to screams as she plunged to her death heart-stopping seconds before he could reach her.

This time, however, instead of Meredith, another woman, a stranger, teetered on the edge of that surrealistic cliff. No less desperate to reach the young woman, Cole experienced the same terror, the same despair, and only by forcing himself awake had he been able to save the beautiful stranger from the horrific fate that had befallen Meredith.

Five minutes later, standing in the shower beneath a needling spray, he was still trying to shake off the effects of his dream, as well as the memories of Meredith it inevitably evoked.

When he reached for a towel, the sound of voices told him Bess and Anne were in the hallway. From the moment he'd introduced them at breakfast, they'd seemed to hit it off, which solved his immediate problem of what to do with

his beautiful houseguest—at least for a couple of hours—
while he made the calls to Drew and Nyguen.

Anne Osborne wasn't the kind of woman to be kept
waiting, and if he didn't have answers for her soon, he had
no doubt she'd start digging for them herself. With luck, by
now Nyguen and his men would have identified the kid
who'd tampered with Anne's car. Cole was still betting on
the kid from the alley—Zach, he remembered her calling
him.

After giving the foggy mirror a couple of swipes with the
towel, he reached for his razor and scowled, remembering
Anne's coddling attitude toward that kid. Just the reaction
he'd expect from someone in the system—a system that all
too often gave suspects the benefit of the doubt.

Wrapping a towel sarong style around his hips, he opened
the door to see his aunt and Anne standing in the middle of
his bedroom.

How Anne Osborne managed to look beautiful wearing
Bess's old flannel robe, he didn't know. But even the faded
flannel couldn't conceal the soft curves beneath, the curves
he remembered too well from last night's embrace.

Bess's bewildered expression melted into a shy grin.
"Oops! I guess I should have hollered at you to give us a
minute. Sorry, hon. I heard the water running and figured
we'd have enough time to raid your closet. Our guest could
use something a bit more suitable to wear into town, don't
you think?"

He noticed one of his sweaters draped over Anne's arm.
"Of course, take whatever you need." It hadn't occurred
to him, until this moment, that the tall, statuesque Anne
could never have squeezed into his diminutive aunt's
clothing. Bess claimed to be five-foot-one, but Cole had his
doubts.

"Sorry for the intrusion," Anne said, wearing an amused
and decidedly unapologetic expression as she ducked out of
the room. With her hair pulled back in a careless ponytail
and her face freshly scrubbed and glowing, she'd somehow managed to look even more appealing than she had

yesterday, dressed in that stylish business suit and expensive tailored blouse.

At the door, Bess said, "We'll be heading into town soon. Will you be joining us?"

"Yes," Cole replied. "But I need to make some calls first. Can you to keep her busy for an hour?"

"No problem," his aunt replied. "I'll give her the dollar tour. But you really shouldn't keep her waiting too long, Cole. Whisking her away with nothing more than a toothbrush was hardly chivalrous." She gave him a teasing smile before leaving him alone with his thoughts.

"Chivalrous," he muttered, feeling just a twinge of guilt. Without question, he'd done the right thing by getting Anne out of her apartment last night, but he could have at least stopped somewhere to allow her to buy a few necessities before they'd left Denver—although, by the looks of her this morning, Anne Osborne was a woman who needed few external contrivances to enhance her beauty.

Unbidden, he remembered again how good she'd felt in his arms last night. "I'll get you for this, Drew," he vowed softly as he dressed quickly and headed for his den, feeling inexplicably irritated and annoyed.


THE RANCH ROAD stretched five miles, ending when it intersected the two-lane blacktop highway that led to Telluride. Sitting between Cole and his aunt in the pickup, Anne tried to concentrate on the scenery. The rutted gravel road, however, wasn't making it easy. Every time they hit a rut, she was jostled against Cole's shoulder, and their thighs, already touching, were pressed even harder together at every turn.

If Cole was aware of her fight to maintain a modicum of physical distance, he gave no indication, but seemed to be extremely focused on his driving. Likewise, Bess seemed oblivious to the situation and chattered away happily, as though this were just any other day.

"Have you ever seen anything more beautiful?" Bess said with a sigh as they turned onto the highway and the distant peaks came in to full view.

"Never," Anne conceded. In every direction, autumn unfolded before her eyes, and it was breathtaking. Golden aspen, ruby red scrub oak and shrubs of burnished copper and variegated green colored the landscape, momentarily distracting her from the details of her situation. "I wish I had my camera," she said almost to herself, gazing out the window at an especially dazzling stand of aspen, which shimmered like liquid gold in the morning breeze.

Bess smiled. "You know, I've lived most of my sixty-five years with the San Juans in my backyard, and every fall I think they put on a better show than the year before."

The twisting road gradually began to straighten, and Anne saw the town of Telluride in the distance. Nestled in what was essentially a box canyon, the resort village bustled with far more activity than she would have imagined, given that the start of the ski season was still a few weeks away. The peaks above town wore snowy caps, but as Cole had informed her last night, the first big storm of the season still hadn't hit.

"Well, here we are," Cole said. "We should be able to find most anything you need in the shops along Main Street."

"If you pick up some film, I'll be happy to loan you my camera to use while you're here," Bess told her.

"Oh, no, that won't be necessary." Anne started to explain that she wouldn't be staying that long, but something stopped her. Fact was, she didn't know *how* long she'd be availing herself of Bess Spencer's hospitality.

"You'd be doing me a favor," Bess pressed. When Anne still hesitated, she persisted. "Listen, honey, I don't know all the details about why you're here, but I get the feeling you could use something to take your mind off..." Her eyes flicked to Cole's. "Well, just to take your mind off things. Promise to make me an extra set of prints, and the camera's yours while you're here." Her smile and goodwill felt as reassuring as a hug from an old friend.

"Thank you, Mrs.—"

"I just go by Bess, honey," she said, directing Anne's attention to a small shop that, judging by the window display, carried only women's clothing. "They should have everything you need in there. I've got a couple of errands to run to get ready for my annual trip to Phoenix, but I shouldn't be long. Where can I meet you two?"

"How about that little bakery up the street?" Cole suggested.

"Great." She turned to Anne. "They serve the absolute best cinnamon rolls and at least a dozen varieties of tea. See you there in about an hour. Behave yourselves, children," she ordered as she turned and walked away.

Anne felt her heart sink. When Cole had said that his aunt would be taking her shopping, she had just assumed it would be without him. "I'm sure I can find everything I need on my own," she told him. "If you'll give me directions to the bakery, I'll meet you and Bess later."

He shook his head. "Sorry. I can't do that. I'm your bodyguard, remember? Where you go, I go."

She frowned. "Is this really nec—"

"Yes. It's necessary. Now, just come along like a good girl and let's get you outfitted."

"A good girl!" she gasped. "Now, look here, Cole," she began as he ushered her into the small, expensive boutique on the corner. One look told Anne that even the most drastically reduced item would far exceed her limited cash supply. "I think we need to keep looking," she said in a low voice.

"Why? Don't you see anything you like?"

Before she could reply, a well-dressed woman came from behind the counter to greet them. "Good morning. Is there any way I can help?"

"She doesn't speak English," Cole put in before Anne could get a word out.

"Oh?"

"No, not a word. She's Dutch. Straight from the Netherlands. That's why it was such a mess when the airline lost her luggage."

"Poor thing," the woman cooed.

"Of course she'll need everything. The works."

Anne found herself flabbergasted by his blatant lies, but the clerk's eyes sparkled.

"Well, let's just see what we can do to help. This way, my dear," she said slowly, loudly.

As she was led into a dressing room, Anne answered Cole's amused grin with a glare, mouthing the words, "I'll get you for this!"

"Let's see," the clerk murmured to her young assistant, "she looks like a perfect size seven to me."

Helpless in the role he'd created for her, Anne could only smile through clenched teeth as the women hauled one outfit after another into the dressing room.

"Oh, and don't forget the underwear," Cole called out. "She's a thirty-four C and partial to black lace."

"Oh! Why, of course." A rush of color rose to the clerk's cheeks, and she fairly tittered, obviously delighted by the tall, good-looking cowboy who not only knew his lady's cup size but preference in lingerie, as well.

If thoughts were deeds, Cole would be the one who needed a bodyguard, Anne thought, fuming.

For half an hour, Anne tried on one expensive outfit after another. Pretending not to understand what the clerk was saying was difficult enough, but her blood pressure really soared each time the women dragged her out to model for Cole. With each smile of approval, the clerks became excited.

When the women finally left her alone and moved to the counter, Anne quickly put on his sweater and the baggy denim jeans she'd worn in and emerged from the dressing room to see Cole standing with his back to her, paying for the stack of clothing heaped on the counter.

Coming up behind him, she stood on tiptoe to whisper in his ear, "Are we having fun yet, cowboy?" But before he could answer, she strode to the door, jerked it open and shouted, "Adios, Señor!" leaving Cole to explain as she bounded onto the sidewalk.

In less than a minute, she found a drugstore and darted inside. Grabbing a sweatshirt, a cheap pair of tennis shoes and a black and purple Rockies cap, she was already paying the cashier when Cole found her.

"All right, I guess I had that coming," he said, moving up behind her. "But when you refused my money last night, I knew you wouldn't make it easy for me to make amends." He wasn't exactly smiling, but his demeanor said he was still feeling pretty smug.

"So you just decided to stack the deck, to make it impossible for me to refuse?"

"All right. I admit it."

She didn't speak to him until they were outside again. "I don't like surprises, Cole," she told him crisply. "And I especially hate being bullied, manipulated..."

"Controlled?"

"Especially controlled," she snapped.

"I'll keep it in mind. And you need to promise me that there'll be no more disappearing acts."

She stopped walking when he did. "All right. It's a deal."

For the first time, she noticed the bulging packages he held in each hand, and her anger dissolved, as they both laughed. "I hope your girlfriend likes black lace," she said. He opened his mouth to reply, but she interrupted. "Oh, Cole, look. There's a pay phone just over there, and I really need to call my office. I know I said you could make all the arrangements, but I really can't wait much longer to check in. Jenetta will be frantic."

"All right."

"Just like that? I'd expected a fight."

"And you would have gotten one, had I not spoken to Drew earlier this morning and learned that he'd checked out your department's phone lines for bugs."

The return of his deadly serious demeanor caused a little shudder inside her.

"We need to find another phone, however. You'd be an easy target from all directions. Let's go. I know a place where we're less likely to risk bumping into someone who might know me and be curious about you."

A few minutes later, Anne was speaking to Jenetta from a pay phone across the street from the funeral home. "You wouldn't believe me even if I told you—which I can't," she replied when Jenetta asked where she was.

"Hey, wait a minute, you're not in some kind of trouble, are you?" Jenetta asked.

Anne smiled at the picture that formed of her assistant leaning closer to the phone, pushing her wire-rimmed glasses up higher on her short, round nose.

"No. It's a personal matter. Nothing I can't handle. But, unfortunately, it means I'll have to be out of the office for a few days—for the rest of the week, at least."

She heard Jenetta sigh.

"I know I'm putting everyone in a bind," Anne said, feeling guilty. "And believe me, if there was any other way... But there isn't."

"You're not ill, are you?"

"No. It's nothing like that," she assured her friend. "It's just that I'm... well, committed to something that I have to see through."

Jenetta's laugh was slightly wicked. "Oh, I see. Well, I just hope he's tall, dark, handsome and crazy about you."

*Three out of four,* Anne thought. "I'll let you know." Obviously Jenetta hadn't heard about the explosion and fire at her apartment, or she would have said something by now. If the incident hadn't made the news, perhaps the damage had been contained to her apartment. Anne could only hope.

"Hey, are you still there?" Jenetta asked.

"Oh, sorry, Jen. What were you saying?"

"I said, Dan and I are here for you if you need us. If you're in some kind of trouble, all you have to do is call."

"I'm all right. Really. I can handle whatever comes along."

Even as she spoke, she couldn't help wondering what Cole's reaction would be to her declaration. She was sure that in his mind, he already considered her completely dependent on him. "But don't worry," she added, "I know who my friends are, and if I get in over my head, you and Dan will be the first ones I'll call."

When Cole held up two fingers, signaling that her time was running out, Anne quickly delved into the details of the appointment changes with Jenetta, noting as she went along which situations could be put on hold until she returned and which clients would need to be rescheduled with another probation officer.

"Ask Frank if he'll find time to schedule a meeting with Christi Montoya. Preferably before the end of the week, if he can arrange it." Although she could already picture the exaggerated frown on Frank Olivetti's face, Anne knew he wouldn't refuse to help out.

She'd decided last night that the sad-eyed fifteen-year-old and the good-natured, grandfatherly Frank Olivetti would get along well. Frank was all heart, and so far, Christi's life had been all heartache. It was a perfect match.

Thinking of Frank inevitably caused Anne to think back to her own experiences as a terrified fourteen-year-old who'd been picked up for shoplifting. A much younger and slimmer Frank Olivetti had been the officer assigned to her case, and from that moment on, her young life had begun to change for the better.

"Frank hasn't come in yet," Jenetta said, startling Anne back to their conversation. "But when he does, do you want me to give him your calendar for the week?"

"That would be a great help. Did he have an early court appearance?"

"No, I don't think so. I just hope he makes it in sometime today."

Jenetta's comment triggered alarm in Anne. "But why wouldn't he? Is he sick?" Everyone knew Frank battled high blood pressure and an unpredictable heartbeat. Since his wife died a few months ago, Anne knew he spent too much time at the office and too little time taking care of himself. Although she'd never share her fears aloud with anyone, she worried that he spent too much time at Mc-Gill's, drinking beer and watching whatever game happened to be on the small screen above the bar.

"Jen, don't you think it's strange that Frank is late?"

"Listen, honey, around here, *strange* is the word of the day. I arrived about ten minutes late this morning, and the lights hadn't even been turned on."

"Where's Marty?"

"No idea."

Anne sighed. Today of all days, she should be there.

"Anne, are you sure there's nothing I can do for you?"

She thought about asking Jenetta to drive over to her neighborhood to try to locate Tabitha, but she decided against putting her friend into a potentially dangerous situation. "If you could just be sure that all my probationers are taken care of—"

"Don't give it another thought. Consider your bases covered." Jenetta's reassurance buoyed her sagging spirits. "I'm just glad you finally called in. I was beginning to think that maybe you'd been hurt in that mess."

Anne's heart sank. "What mess?"

"Hey, you really are out of touch, aren't you?"

She wasn't only out of touch, she was speechless, as the worst scenarios about the tragedy at her apartment formed in her mind.

"It's practically the only news on the radio this morning."

Forcing down choking guilt, she asked, "What are you talking about, Jenetta?"

"Why, the jam-up on the highway, on I-25, that's what! Traffic's been backed up for three hours. It's almost eleven, and people are still trying to get to work."

The breath went out of Anne in a rush as relief flooded her limbs and made her knees go weak.

Cole tapped his watch. "Time's up," he whispered.

"I've really got to go now, Jen," Anne said, trying to control the quiver in her voice.

"Is there a number where you can be reached?" Jenetta pressed. "How about your cell phone?"

"I ... don't have it with me." It wasn't really a lie, Anne rationalized, remembering with renewed irritation how Cole had snatched it away from her last night. "I'll try to call again soon. Thanks, Jen. And don't worry. I'm fine."

"Oh, by the way, before you hang up, what do you want me to tell Marty?"

She'd been mulling the question over all morning, trying to think of a plausible excuse for taking a sudden leave of absence. A white lie about a sick aunt or an ailing relative wouldn't fly—Martin Gartrell knew she had no family. "Just tell him it's personal, and I hope he'll understand," she said. "Tell him I'll explain everything when I come back for Zach's court date on the fifteenth."

"By the way, Zach's been trying to reach you."

Cole reached to disconnect the line, but Anne covered the phone and mouthed, "Just another minute ... please?"

He frowned, but agreed with a curt nod.

"He sounded pretty upset," Jenetta said. "The police went to his house and questioned him. Something about your car?"

A surprise visit from the police would have upset Zach no matter how unjust the accusations—at least she *hoped* they were unjust.

"Jenetta, call him back, will you? Tell him that I said not to worry about the police and to just answer their questions truthfully. Tell him I'll talk to them and straighten everything out." She had to contact Nyguen. He couldn't be allowed to harass Zach. In the past six months, Zach had worked too hard at turning himself around to have it all fall apart now.

"Tell Zach I'll be out of town for awhile, but just as soon as I can, I'll get in touch with him. In the meantime, tell him to leave any messages on my voice mail." Regardless of what Cole Spencer allowed or didn't allow she had to keep in contact with the young man who was so dependent on her. She had to keep him walking a straight line. "I'll check my messages as often as I can. Tell him that, will you, Jen? It's very important that he know I haven't forgotten him."

Jenetta promised she would get the message to Zach.

"And now I've really got to go, Jen."

She had enough on her mind without having to contend with Cole's reaction to her deliberately defying his orders. *Orders,* she thought bitterly as she hung up the phone. That was something else she needed to clear up before a bad situation got worse—before Cole got too used to giving her orders or she started to get too comfortable obeying them.

"Everything all right?"

"For the moment, at least," she replied. "But I'm worried about the effect my absence is going to have on some of my clients." She was thinking specifically of Zach. If this situation pushed him back into the life he'd worked so hard to leave behind, she'd never forgive herself.

She'd seen a lot of kids come through the system in the past three years, and she'd acquired a sixth sense when it came to judging which ones wouldn't make it no matter how many breaks the system allowed them. She'd also become adept at identifying which of the twenty or so juveniles she worked with each year possessed the inner courage and strength of character to start making good choices. And which ones could benefit from a second and sometimes even a third chance.

From their first meeting, Anne had sensed that Zach was one of those special kids who would respond to her efforts. He was unusually bright and starved for positive adult interaction. He was the kind of young man who could have been a class leader and a role model under different circumstances.

Zach could come out a winner, and Anne wasn't about to let him fall through the cracks the way she might have had it not been for Frank Olivetti. She would be there for

Zach, she told herself with renewed resolve. Regardless of what Cole Spencer would or would not allow.

FIVE MINUTES LATER, Anne and Cole walked into the bakery. "I'll be right back," she said, heading for the ladies' room where she changed into the clothes she'd purchased at the drugstore. She couldn't help smiling as she removed the cap Cole had insisted she wear and settled the new cap on her head, threading her ponytail through the opening in the back. Her meager purchases could hardly be called a shopping spree, yet she'd used up all but a couple of dollars.

She hated feeling broke, feeling dependent upon Cole—upon anyone, for that matter. Although she had no reason to doubt him when he said her credit card purchases could be traced, deep down she couldn't help wondering if he had just been trying to scare her into compliance.

Living out here in the middle of the high country, the man was practically a hermit. What could he know about high-tech crime, anyway? "More than you," she muttered as she adjusted her new cap once more and walked into the bakery.

The mingled aromas of fresh-baked bread and savory soups caused Anne's stomach to growl, announcing the return of her appetite. After a glance at the bakery case, she spotted Cole sitting alone at a corner table, studying a menu. Bess was nowhere in sight.

"I like the hat," he said without lifting his eyes from the menu. "But the one I gave you was less conspicuous." One thing for certain, Cole could never be accused of mincing words.

"I like your hat, as well—even if it is a bit conspicuous," she added, her voice dripping sarcasm. "Where's Bess?"

"She dropped by to say she had more shopping to do. She makes an annual trip to Phoenix, and it's the one time of year she indulges in a few frivolous purchases—mostly gifts for the nieces and nephews she'll be visiting. Anyway, she said not to wait for her. She ran into a friend who'll be driving her home."

Anne picked up a menu.

"I guess that means you're stuck alone with me for a little while longer. Sorry."

"I've survived worse," she said, studying the menu while fighting to affect indifference. "Cole, did you mean it when you said Stan's killers could have the capability of tracing a credit card purchase?"

Slapping the menu closed, he leveled his dark gaze on her, willing her by the sheer heat of his glare to look at him. "You didn't—"

"No, I didn't," she answered defensively. "But I might need to if this situation drags on for very long. I know you said it would be dangerous, but I need to be able to get at least get a cash advance or a—"

"You *know,* but do you really *understand?*" He didn't give her the chance to answer. "No, of course you don't. But please try to understand this, Anne—I need your cooperation to do my job. I thought the episode at your apartment last night would have convinced you of the risks."

She lowered her eyes to momentarily regain the breath his intense stare seemed to have stolen. How could she tell him that last night she'd been scared spitless, that the stomach-churning fear had come straight out of her worst nightmares? And how could she explain that from that moment on, she'd become convinced of her need for his help, for his protection?

It should have been so easy to admit. *Damn you, Gregg! Damn you for what you did to me! For what I'm still allowing you to do.*

"I just hope you didn't inadvertently give your assistant any clue as to where you were calling from."

She answered him indignantly. "Of course I didn't!" Could he really imagine she'd be so stupid?

An uneasy truce prevailed while the waitress took their orders. Anne remembered Bess's suggestion and ordered a

cinnamon roll. Cole ordered the same, along with a cup of
coffee. He turned his cup upright and the waitress filled it
with steaming coffee. When the young woman moved the
pot to Anne's cup, Cole stopped her. "Bring the lady herbal
tea with lemon and honey."

Anne's reaction was a startled blink. How was she supposed to deal with this guy, anyway? A man who issued
orders with all the finesse of a Marine drill sergeant, yet
remembered her preference for herbal tea.

"Thanks," she murmured. Keeping an emotional equilibrium around this unpredictable and unreadable man was
turning out to be more difficult than she'd first thought.

When the waitress left them alone again, he said, "You
can write a check."

"What?"

"You can write a check to me for cash and I'll hold it
until this ordeal is over."

The idea came out of nowhere, surprising her, but she
couldn't find any fault with it.

"As for the phone calls, how often do you need to check
in with your office?"

"Once a day."

"No way. Once a week."

"Three times a week," she countered.

He sighed and stared at the ceiling as though searching
for patience. "Twice, and that's as high as I'll go. You'll
have to call from a different pay phone each time, of
course, but I think we can manage that."

She nodded, knowing when to relent, sensing that it
hadn't been easy for him to come even this far. "Fine.
Twice a week, and musical phone booths." Before their
deal could be sealed, she added, "But that's only if nothing unusual comes up that requires me to check in more
often."

His dark eyes narrowed.

"But I will try to stick to our agreement." Although she
had no intention of allowing him to dictate how she should

do her job, his offer of compromise was heartening, a small concession that seemed a big enough victory for one day.

"I spoke to Nyguen before I left the ranch." He couldn't have said anything that would have grabbed her attention faster. "It wasn't Zach who tampered with your car."

Despite her insistence yesterday that it couldn't have been Zach, she felt secretly relieved to know that her trust in her young client hadn't been misplaced. "Did they find out who did?"

He shook his head. "No, but the officer gave the police artist a detailed description, and Nyguen will be faxing us a drawing this afternoon."

"We could get lucky," she said. "I've seen a lot of young faces over the past four years. I just might recognize this one." In her heart, however, she hoped she didn't know the boy who'd tried to disable her car. As unrealistic as it might seem to someone as streetwise and wary as Cole Spencer, she still longed to believe that none of her former clients would want to hurt her.

"You don't want to recognize the kid, do you, Anne?"

She blinked, startled by his accurate assessment of her thoughts. "Why would you say that?"

He reached for his coffee. "Just a hunch." He took a sip before he said, "You really like that job of yours, don't you?"

"Yes, I do," she answered simply. What she didn't tell him was that she loved having the opportunity to affect young lives, to see a kid turn his life around the way she prayed Zach was trying to do. Judging by what she'd seen of him, Cole would probably dismiss as unrealistic the notion of changing a punk into a responsible adult. His reaction to Zach yesterday in the alley, his willingness to believe that Zach had tampered with her car, had given Anne the distinct impression he'd find little sympathy for the kind of young people she worked with, the kind of kid she'd once been.

For guys like Cole, the world came in two shades—black and white. Right and wrong. Anne, however, knew better.

Her view of the world, the one she'd learned to accept as a pretty decent place to live, came in endless varieties of gray.

They ate in relative silence, each avoiding the other's eyes. Anne felt as though she were on some kind of bizarre blind date. The only difference was that she was going home to spend another night under this darkly handsome stranger's roof.

"When you need to call your office again, I'll drive you to Ridgeway," he said as he stood and reached for the check. "It isn't that far, and you'll enjoy the scenery. Have you seen Mount Sneffles?"

"Only on countless postcards."

"You'll understand why it's so photographed when you see it." He walked close behind her until they were out of the restaurant. "Right now, I think we should head to the ranch to see if that fax has arrived."

His words brought reality back with a cold vengeance, and even the beauty of the afternoon sun reflecting autumn's splendor in the high country couldn't permeate the thick, gray dread that enveloped her heart.

EVEN BEFORE he'd killed Stanley Lewellyn, he'd resented having to work with a partner. Having to contend with someone as inept and cumbersome as the man walking beside him made the situation even worse.

"You can't blame me for what happened," his partner reminded him for the second time in ten minutes. "I did what you told me to do, waited just like you said I should. She never showed, I swear she didn't. I don't care what that punk told you."

"Why can't you just admit that she slipped past you?" he asked, grabbing his partner's sleeve and directing him toward the crosswalk. The sky had turned a gritty gray, matching his mood perfectly. How long, he wondered, could he stand living in a city where winter began so early and stayed so late? Of more immediate concern, how much longer could he endure his partner's lame excuses?

"She was there, in her apartment, for at least five minutes," he said. He knew it for a fact because he'd been there
himself, across the street in a van, checking up on his partner and listening to every word she'd said.

"But how—"

"How the hell do I know how she managed to escape?"
he snapped, cutting off his partner's question. "She just
did, all right? She got out of there, and now we have to find
her."

He'd waited just to be sure. Despite the risk, he had to
know if the kid would do what he'd been paid to do. He
knew he might have to use the kid again, and he wanted to
be sure his money wouldn't be wasted. Against his better
judgment, he'd waited until he heard the muffled blast and
saw the flash of flames. He'd even waited until the ambulance arrived, watching transfixed as it drove away empty.
Later, just to be sure, he'd checked out every hospital
emergency room in the city. Anne Osborne had cheated
death and cheated him. His only consolation was that the
situation was temporary. Sooner or later he'd catch up to
her. He couldn't rest until he did.

"Okay, so she was there," his partner muttered. "And
she got away. But even if she wasn't hurt, she had to have
been scared half out of her mind. She knows we're onto her.
Maybe that's enough, huh? Maybe she got the message?"

"Yeah, maybe." It was a lie, one he didn't believe for
even a minute. He knew better, knew all about what she'd
been through with that maniac ex-husband of hers. Anne
Osborne didn't run scared anymore, and that presented a
huge problem.

"This way," he told his partner.

"Well, what about that pickup?" his partner asked as
they hurried toward the small bar on the corner. "The kid
swears it was the same truck he saw downtown when he
fixed her car."

"I checked out the numbers he gave me, but the tags were phony." He jerked open the padded metal door and stepped into the dark anonymity of the dingy neighborhood bar.

Except for a couple of young, long-haired, bearded guys at the bar, the place was empty. His partner followed him to a booth at the back of the long, narrow room, as far as possible from the monster-truck competition that roared out of the small TV mounted over the bar. The bartender, a middle-aged woman whose hair was swept up on top of her head like some kind of peroxide turban, came around from behind the bar to take their order.

When she'd left them alone again, he said, "What have you found out from your sources?"

"She didn't show up for work this morning. And no one knows where she stayed last night. She's in hiding, all right," he said morosely. "Now what are we going to do?"

"We have to find her, and this time we have to do more than frighten her."

"If only we could have caught up to her sooner, talked to her," the older man said wistfully. "Maybe we could have offered her something, money or something."

"We're not offering her anything," he snapped. The waitress brought their drinks, but he was absorbed in re-living the events of the other night, berating himself for not acting when he'd had the chance, when he'd seen that pickup circling the block. He'd had his gun ready. It would have been a clean shot. It wouldn't have been any riskier than using that punk Paxton had sent over with the explosives. Unfortunately, at the time, he had no idea the boy in the front seat had really been Anne Osborne.

"What about the cowboy? Do you have any idea who he is?"

"Now how the hell would I know that?" he snarled before downing another fiery swallow. "He's no one she knew before Friday, at least we know that much." He'd checked out her friends himself, driving past their houses, checking their garages while they slept and their parking lots and office buildings while they worked. Using his well-placed and high-priced connections, he'd run background checks on everyone she was associated with. No brothers. No current lovers. No pickup trucks. And no cowboys.

## Chapter Six

Bess Spencer came up behind Anne on the redwood deck that opened off the dining room. "I made some tea."

Anne smiled and accepted the mug Bess gave her, then held it with both hands, coaxing into her fingers the warmth radiating from the nubby pottery mug. The day had been clear and bright, but this evening the air had a nip to it, a reminder that winter was waiting just over the next ridge.

Bess held her cup between both hands, as well, as she leaned with her elbows on the rail. "I've always loved the view from here," she said, gazing out at the ring of jagged peaks in the distance.

"It's beautiful. Almost too magnificent to be real." What a thoroughly likable person Bess Spencer was, Anne thought as they sipped their tea and enjoyed the view in comfortable silence. If not for her easy companionship, this past week would have been unbearably lonely.

With her eyes still trained on the view, Bess said, "Times like this, it's easy to see why the Utes call them the Shining Mountains."

Anne's gaze traced the highest peaks in the distance, most of them already snowcapped. She'd brought the camera onto the deck, hoping to catch a few shots of the sunset. Bess made a setting suggestion, and for a moment Anne became so caught up in capturing the golds, mauves and pinks of the San Juan sunset she almost forgot the dilemma that had brought her to Cole's beautiful high-country ranch.

"Take a couple more, just to be sure," Bess suggested.

Anne obliged, taking care to set the camera's controls the way Bess had taught her. Even as she took three more pictures, she realized that each one would be slightly different from the shots she'd taken only seconds before.

If anyone had told her she could be happy spending an entire day taking pictures, angling for the best shots, she'd never had believed it. Even more remarkable was the number of shots she found she could take of the same subject, and yet no two would ever turn out exactly the same. Like life, the beauty and the mystery of the San Juans was ever-changing.

She'd been delighted by the first roll she'd taken. As a way of thanking Bess for her technical advice, she'd decided to have one of the best pictures enlarged and framed. Remembering how much Zach loved the outdoors, she'd sent him several pictures, including some shots of Mount Sneffles and the world's highest waterfall, which she'd photographed one afternoon when Bess had introduced her to a wonderful hiking trail just outside Telluride.

"Oh, get that!" Bess exclaimed, pointing to a bank of purple clouds on the horizon. Anne took aim, but as she made the adjustments for the fading light, a sudden movement caused her attention to shift to someone moving across the yard toward the house. One glance and she recognized immediately that the tall cowboy in the distance was Cole.

One would have to be blind to have confused him with the other two men who spent time on the Spencer ranch each day. She'd met Seth James and Pete Hawthorne her second day on the ranch. The two men worked full time for Cole, arriving every day around six in Seth's cherry-red pickup. Pete, a former jockey turned trainer, was all of five-foot-two. Seth, on the other hand, with his thinning gray hair and slightly stooped shoulders, stood out in a crowd for his height, and even loomed over Cole at six four or five.

No, there was no mistaking Cole, she told herself, as she studied his movements and thought about how he, too, stood out among any of the men she'd ever known. And not just because of his physical traits.

Over the past seven days, she'd come to realize what a true individualist, how strong, self-sufficient and capable he was. And yet, watching him deal with people and animals, she'd been struck by his surprising gentleness. Observing him now, she felt a stirring awareness of the total package that was Cole Spencer. His fluid grace and confident stride held her nearly transfixed.

"That should make a good picture," Bess said, startling her. "The sunset, I mean," the older woman added with a quirky smile that told Anne she'd been caught staring.

Glad to have the camera to hide behind, Anne made a noise of agreement in her throat and quickly snapped a picture of the barn that she doubted would turn out.

"He's not so bad once you get to know him," Bess said quietly.

Because she couldn't meet Bess's eyes, Anne fiddled with the camera, trying even harder to appear absorbed in her pursuit of the perfect angle.

"You're from Denver, aren't you, Anne?"

She nodded.

"Lived there long?"

"All my life, except for the four years I attended school in Boulder."

"Then you no doubt remember reading about Meredith Hackett."

Anne thought a minute and then lowered the camera to turn and stare at Cole's aunt. "Yes, of course I do." Anyone who read a newspaper or owned a TV knew all about the beautiful socialite who had taken her own life after a brutal attack had made her the source of tabloid fodder. "Why do you ask?"

Bess studied Anne for a long moment, obviously trying to decide whether to share a confidence. "She was one of Drew and Cole's clients, although you might not remember hearing their names, or the agency's. The press seemed intrigued by the fact that she'd been trying to find her missing half sister, but the reports seldom referred to either of them by name, or the agency." She sighed and turned to stare again at the meadow. "Cole took it hard when she died. Real hard. I don't know what he would have done had he not had this ranch to turn to. Sometimes I think those horses of his saved his life."

Anne felt an uncomfortable tightening in her chest at the thought of Cole grieving for Meredith Hackett.

After a long stretch of silence, Bess said, "I'm not sure he would appreciate me telling you about Meredith. But this week, seeing him with you . . . Well, anyway, I thought it might help you understand him a little better." Her smile was kind. "I guess I never have been very good at keeping secrets. John, my late husband, used to tease me something awful about that. 'Telephone, telegraph and tell Bess,' he used to say."

When Bess launched into another anecdote about her late husband, Anne's mind drifted to thoughts of Meredith Hackett, and a hazy mental picture formed of the gorgeous heiress whose perfect face had been featured if not once a day, at least once a week on the pages of Denver daily newspapers following her tragic death. Trying to fit Cole, the rugged, independent cowboy, into the picture wasn't that easy. How he must have hated all the publicity.

Anne strained to remember, but she could only recall snippets of the things that had been written and said about Meredith Hackett's lover, the private investigator. No wonder he'd left town after her death.

Meredith Hackett had been a regular on the society page, hitting the headlines when she suffered a brutal attack upon surprising a burglar in her Cherry Hills mansion. Anne remembered that the attack had stunned the elite community, where that sort of random brutality was unheard of.

The incident took a bizarre twist when it was revealed that Meredith somehow managed to get to a gun and kill the intruder. The young woman wasn't charged. In fact, Anne recalled that she'd become something of a media darling.

Anne remembered, also, how after her ordeal, Meredith Hackett had become an advocate for tougher sentencing and victims' rights, speaking at social functions and fund-raisers, turning herself from victim to champion in the eyes of her community, and especially the media.

Remembering how the lovely heiress turned her tragedy into triumph, Anne cringed. Then she recalled how the story took a final twist that ended in yet another tragedy. How stunned the city had been when the truth about the death in the Hackett mansion hit the headlines, when the real Meredith Hackett, a woman who had been paying money to a blackmailer for five years, was revealed to have killed her tormentor in cold blood.

Because the incident had occurred around the time she'd left Gregg, Anne hadn't been as tuned in to the sensational newspaper coverage as her friends and co-workers. She did remember, however, how Meredith's story had been covered in detail. If Cole Spencer had been mentioned by name, she hadn't known it. Anne tried again to remember, but most of the details escaped her. Only one in particular came to mind. Meredith Hackett had committed suicide just hours before the police came to arrest her.

"It was a horrible time for him," Bess said, her words penetrating Anne's thoughts, echoing exactly what she'd been thinking. "It's something he never discusses—not with me, anyway. And not with anyone else, as far as I know."

Anne could only nod. Bess's revelations left her speechless.

"It was because of her that he left the agency," Bess said. "And until last week, when Drew called him, he hadn't gone back."

"He must have loved her very deeply," Anne said, her conjecture turning to words almost before she realized it.

Bess opened her mouth to answer, but before she could form the words, her eyes shifted to the door and Anne realized, to her horror, that they were no longer alone. When she turned around she felt ashamed and deeply embarrassed that Cole had caught them discussing the intimate details of his past.

"Anne," he said, his dark expression even more unreadable than usual. "Would you come with me, please?"

"Sure." Her voice would have been steadier if she'd known just how much of their conversation he'd overheard.

AN ARM OF COLD AIR snaked through the door when the redneck stumbled out of the bar. Stanley Lewellyn's killer huddled in a corner booth, downing shots of liquid fire and mourning the end of summer.

The sooner he could collect his money from Renfrow and make tracks out of Colorado, the better. The guises he'd made to land his position would be discovered sooner or later. After all, a bogus law degree could so easily be exposed, and he had no intention of hanging around to find out how it happened. Let Webster buy himself another judge or a department full of cops. He'd done all he felt he could safely accomplish, and by the time Webster hit the streets again, he meant to be a thousand miles away, lounging around in the sun someplace where it never snowed, where he could live like a king. He'd been thinking about Mexico, Costa Rica or maybe Panama City.

California would be nice, too, but as far as he knew, the case of the judge they'd left for dead in the desert was still open, as was the file on the banker who'd died in the house fire in Phoenix. Thinking it over, he realized his chances for escape lay outside the country, especially after he'd eliminated his partner. After he took the old man out, it would be only a matter of time before the police put all the pieces together. It wouldn't be all that difficult to arrange for his partner's demise. In fact, it would be one of his easiest hits. Timing was the important thing. But first, he needed the old man to help him find the Osborne woman. After that, he'd be history.

He had no intention of assigning something as important as silencing Anne Osborne to a partner whose nerves were ready to snap. His first mistake had been depending on him to stake out the County Annex building that night. He couldn't afford another mistake of that magnitude, not if he hoped to live long enough to enjoy the money they were only days away from collecting.

So far, he'd been incredibly lucky. Luck had been with him that afternoon when he'd walked into Assistant D.A. Lewellyn's office and spied the Renfrow file lying open on the desk. Thinking how close that hotshot prosecutor had come to the truth made him shudder. He still marveled at how easy it had been to loosen Stan's tongue that day at lunch.

Of course, the double shots of twelve-year-old Scotch had helped, but even without the booze, Stan had been carrying around his secret investigation for so long that he seemed more than ready to talk, to brag about how he'd kept the case secret, how he was just days away from single-handedly exposing the corruption in the department. How he'd kept his secret for nearly a year, not even sharing his investigation with his wife, and how he'd been too paranoid to even enter the evidence on his computer.

"Everything's in a single file," he'd bragged after downing his fourth double. "The informer answers only to me." Even as Stan had outlined how cracking this case would assure a win in the November election, the killer was plotting his crime.

And except for the woman, the plan had worked nearly perfectly.

The next day, the informant had been eliminated, but not before he'd made a call, at gunpoint, to arrange a meeting to turn over the final piece of information for Lewellyn's case—the name of the inside player, the name of the man who made the whole scam work. *His* name.

Lewellyn, so greedy for personal gain and so eager to pull the political rug out from under his boss, hadn't suspected a thing. The meeting had been set for the Friday night before the long weekend, when the offices in the County Annex building would be empty.

At least that's what the killer had counted on. What he hadn't counted on was a witness.

FOLLOWING COLE through the house and out the back door, Anne tried to imagine the effect of Meredith Hackett's death on a man as confident and proud as Cole Spencer. As they walked across the yard toward the large red barn behind the house, she stole a few surreptitious glances at him. In the dying light, she studied his face and wondered if his lover's horrible death had created those hard lines on either side of his full mouth. Had his dark eyes once been softer, less cynical, before tragedy broke his heart?

Against her will, her thoughts drifted again to the newspaper photos of the lovely heiress. Had they planned marriage? Children? Had he known about the past that led to her downfall?

Without warning, she experienced a strange twinge of unreasonable and unfathomable jealousy as she tried to imagine Cole in love with the exquisite Meredith Hackett, as she pictured his rugged face and his hard expression softening at the sight of another woman.

"In here," he said, shoving the heavy barn door open. Once inside, he slapped the wall switch, and a series of overhead lights blinked on all the way to the end of the enormous structure.

Before proceeding, Cole closed the door behind them, and as he did, a disturbing awareness of his physical presence caused a noticeable hitch in Anne's pulse rate. Suddenly, the soft denim shirt with the sleeves rolled up seemed to reveal too much of the well-defined muscles of his tanned forearms. Tonight, the fit of his faded blue jeans seemed too perfect, emphasizing his narrow hips and the lean, long line of his legs, the corded muscles of his thighs.

"This way," he said, directing her to walk with him down the hay-strewn corridor that divided a dozen individual stalls on each side.

As they walked together toward the end of the paddock, she noticed that he moved with the controlled grace of a natural athlete. There seemed to be something distinctly feral and dangerous about Cole, something so deeply compelling it stirred her own primal instincts.

"Have you spoken to Nyguen lately?" she asked, partly because she wanted to know but mostly to distract her wayward thoughts.

"Briefly, this morning."

"I take it there are no new leads."

They stopped walking, and he turned to face her. "No. I'm afraid not. I guess we were all banking on you recognizing the kid in the sketch."

Something about the young man's mouth had seemed familiar, but not familiar enough. "I studied the sketch again this afternoon, and something about him still seems familiar, but I still can't put a name to the face."

"The original sketch is bound to be clearer than the fax copy," he said. "I asked Nyguen to mail it to us."

She nodded. "Good idea. What else is Nyguen doing to solve this case?"

"The normal routine. Analyzing and reanalyzing the physical evidence found at the scene. Nyguen is a by-the-book investigator. If a procedure isn't in the rule book, he won't use it."

She tried to envision what the investigation might be like if Cole were in charge. No doubt it would be moving faster, and she knew instinctively that Cole would follow the rules only when they served his purpose. She'd sensed his innate defiance of convention from the first moment, and she hadn't needed a full week of observing to know that he lived by his own rules, by his own moral code. Cole Spencer was a man who took his cue from no one, gave orders instead of obeying them. Simply put, he could be nothing but trouble for any woman crazy enough to care for him, to think she could tame him.

And yet, each time their gazes met—or collided, depending on the situation—Anne felt her attraction for him growing. Sometimes, when she caught glimpses of the incredible tenderness that seemed to lie just beneath his rough exterior, she wondered what it would be like to be loved by this man.

Belittled and demeaned by her ex-husband, Anne had smothered her intuition, even when it had begged her to leave him. Since her divorce, however, she'd learned to trust herself again, to rely on her natural instincts, and so far they had not led her astray.

What she'd felt in Cole's arms that first night she had never felt in any other man's embrace. And her feelings for him, instead of fading, seemed to be growing stronger by the day. His touch that night had seemed so gentle, belying the impervious facade of the self-contained, untouchable man. The man was a walking contradiction. Harsh and gentle, tender and rough. A man not easily understood. Not easily touched. But definitely worth knowing. Every instinct demanded it.

No wonder Meredith Hackett, a woman who could have had any man, had chosen the darkly compelling Cole Spencer.

A velvety muzzle protruded from the open half of a divided stall door, interrupting Anne's deep conjecture.

"They're curious about you," Cole explained.

The sleek-coated, bright-eyed horses were bedded down for the night in their stalls, but that didn't keep them from expressing their interest in their visitors.

"The feeling's mutual," she said.

As they passed, Cole smiled and murmured to each horse, calling them by name, taking a moment to stroke each long silky neck before moving on.

When they finally reached the last stall, Cole lifted the latch and swung open the top half of the divided door. Anne followed his gaze to the shadowy interior of the stall.

And what she saw left her wide-eyed and staring.

Surprise didn't come close to describing the expression on her face when she spotted the small, butterscotch ball of fur peering up at her from inside the cardboard box, which Cole had lined with a couple of old flannel shirts.

"Tabitha!" she cried, dropping onto the pile of clean hay he'd arranged around the box to keep the kitten warm. "Oh, Cole! How did you find her? How on earth did you manage to get her here?" When her voice cracked, his heart rolled over.

"I didn't do much, just made a couple of phone calls. Drew did all the legwork. It was you who put those tags on her collar." He knelt beside her to run a hand over the kitten's silky back.

Gathering Tabitha as gently as she might have handled a newborn, Anne cradled the animal in her arms. "Oh, Cole, how can I ever thank you?"

He shook his head. Nothing she could say could match the Christmas-morning sparkle in her pretty blue eyes—and that was thanks enough.

The enthusiastic purring noises coming from the feline seemed much too loud to be coming from such a small package.

"I think she's happy to see you."

"Poor thing! I can count almost every rib!"

"Cats are pretty resilient. Nine lives, you know. A few days of TLC, and I imagine she'll be as fat and sassy as she always was." He hadn't felt this optimistic a few hours ago when he'd picked Tabitha up at the baggage claim area at the Montrose airport. Amazing what a little milk and a can of tuna fish could do.

"Hey, Tabby, are you ready to eat again?" he asked, pulling a can of tuna and a can opener out of his jacket pocket. The moment he pierced the tin, Tabitha's ears perked up, and she skittered out of Anne's arms long enough to rub her gratitude against Cole's leg before leaping back into her box to wait beside the saucer Cole had placed there earlier.

After he'd filled the saucer with tuna, they stood together and watched Tabitha attack her food.

"I think you've just made a friend for life," Anne said, laughing. Then, before he knew what had happened, her laughter died and she threw her arms around his neck and hugged him. "I didn't think I'd ever see her again," she murmured against his shoulder. "Thank you, Cole."

When she tilted her head and looked at him, neither of them breathed. For an uncertain moment, he felt riveted by her gaze, and then, almost without realizing it, he dipped his head and kissed her. To his astonishment, she kissed him back. Her lips were soft and warm and irresistibly inviting.

His hands slid up her spine and cupped the back of her head, and he reveled in the silky feel of her golden hair. He slanted his mouth across hers, continuing to kiss her, deeper and harder. When she responded to his urging by pressing herself more fully against him, he tightened his embrace. Like a man dying of thirst, he drank in the sweet, soft feel of her body molded against his and the honey taste of her mouth.

The sound of the barn door slamming jerked them out of each other's arms, and they stood staring at each other, astonished, flushed and breathless.

"Hey, Cole. Are you in here?" a male voice called from the front of the barn.

"That's Pete," he told her. "I'd better go see what he wants."

She nodded and gave him a shaky smile as he turned to go. He wondered if she felt as flooded with regret as he did. Problem was, he didn't know which he regretted more, kissing her or being forced to stop.

# Chapter Seven

After talking to Pete for a few minutes, Cole rejoined Anne at the back of the barn. Tabitha was nestled in the crook of her arm, sleeping, and as Cole stared at the cat, he experienced a strange mix of irritation and relief. Whether he liked it or not, the distance the small feline's presence put between them effectively cooled the emotionally heated atmosphere that had existed only moments ago.

"I wonder how long she was lost and if she escaped during the fire, or if she slipped out when whoever wired my phone and my apartment came in." She stroked the kitten's head. "If only you could talk."

"I spoke to Drew this afternoon, before he put Tabitha on the plane. According to what he said, it looks as if Tabitha isn't the only one not talking." He watched his words paint a worried line across her pretty forehead. The line deepened when he told her that although Nyguen had been interviewing officers, trying to find the link to Stanley Lewellyn's murderer, as of yet, he still hadn't made any headway.

"Jenetta told me they questioned Zach again."

"Drew told me the same thing. He also said they weren't ready to clear him."

"I just couldn't imagine that he'd be involved in anything to hurt me. Zach's no angel, and he's been in some trouble in the past, obviously. But he's basically a good kid."

Cole found himself biting back a retort. If he'd ever been that idealistic, he couldn't remember when.

"What else did Drew tell you, Cole? Is he working closely with Nyguen?"

He gave her a general accounting of how the investigation was proceeding, how Nyguen was personally sifting through all of Lewellyn's files in hopes of finding a motive or a link that might lead to the killer. He stopped short, however, of telling her that he had argued with Nyguen when he'd asked Cole to bring her back to Denver. Nyguen had an idea that involved smuggling Anne into some sort of concealed listening situation to overhear officers in their daily routines. Drew had thought it a great idea, but Cole had flatly vetoed it.

"You know, I remember something about that night. I don't know if it has any significance... but I found it odd that Stan's desktop was completely cleared. There were no file folders or papers...."

"Go on, Anne."

"Well, I don't know if it means anything, but I know Stan had been working on a big project. A case he'd alluded to earlier that evening."

"Did he give you any details?"

She shook her head. "No. I just remember him saying he had enough work to keep him busy straight through the holiday. I guess that's why I noticed the lack of any paperwork on his desk that night."

"Could it be that he was preparing to leave for the night, that he'd cleared his desk before the murderer came in?"

"I don't know. It's hard to guess anything at this point." She sighed, and he noticed the faint shadows beneath her eyes that attested to the strain she'd been under.

Once again, he cursed the fact that he had to drive her to Denver tomorrow. As far as he was concerned, the hearing she insisted on attending just wasn't worth the risk. And Nyguen's idea of trying to smuggle her into the police station—the same station that, if their hunches were right, was the headquarters for some very dirty and very dangerous cops—was, in Cole's opinion, completely out of the question.

"They don't really have any leads, do they?" she asked wearily.

He shook his head. "None that they'll talk about. I'm sorry, Anne." He knew what she was thinking. With Nyguen no closer to making an arrest than he'd been a week ago, she was still stranded. Removed from her job and her friends, stuck in a situation she loathed, with a man who had, by virtue of their stolen kiss, drawn her with him over the boundary wall they'd both so carefully constructed.

Until Nyguen and his special task force found a suspect, Anne would need to stay here, safe and sequestered. The boundaries they'd crossed tonight would need to be rebuilt.

As for himself, Cole viewed the lack of progress in the Lewellyn murder case as maddening on more than one level. First, it meant that he'd have to try even harder to fight his growing attraction toward his lovely client. But, more importantly, it meant that her life was still in danger, a thought that he found increasingly disturbing on every level.

And lastly, he couldn't help thinking that if he was there, working with Nyguen and Drew on the investigation, he could be making a real difference.

"Are you ready for the hearing tomorrow?" he asked, hoping, but not expecting, her to say she'd changed her mind about going.

"I think so. The phone calls to my office this week have helped me pass on information to Zach that he'll need to make a good showing."

"Are you nervous about going back?"

"I'd be lying if I said I wasn't at least a little leery. I just think about the explosion and I start to feel frightened all over again."

"In a way, that's good," he said.

"I've never considered fear a positive emotion." A fleeting expression told him she'd just revealed more than she'd intended. "What I mean is, I don't believe in letting fear get in my way when I want something."

"But it has in the past, hasn't it?" It had been an impulsive remark, but the look on her face told him he'd hit a nerve, dead center.

"I guess you could say that," she admitted cautiously. "In my *ancient* past," she added emphatically.

"I'll be with you tomorrow. I have no intention of letting you out of my sight or of giving anyone a chance to hurt you."

Her head jerked up. "But the hearing is confidential. I don't think—"

"It's all been arranged. I'll be there with you. You'll be safe."

The silence stretched uncomfortably between them before Anne said, "I suppose I ought to go in. I still have a few notes I need to make for the hearing."

"If you want to take Tabitha to the house, I'm sure Bess won't mind. She loves animals as much as you do."

"Thanks. I don't know how Tabby would adjust to life in the barn, even if it is only temporary. She's a spoiled little city cat, I'm afraid." But even as they discussed her fate, the scruffy-looking feline seemed to have other ideas about life in the country, and she sashayed off Anne's lap and began pawing at a spot in the hay. After a few moments of arranging and rearranging, Tabitha curled into the little nest she'd built and promptly fell asleep. "On the other hand..."

"Come on," he said, reaching for her hand to help her to her feet. "I have something else I want to show you before you leave."

With their shoulders almost touching, they retraced their earlier steps down the long corridor of stalls. At the first stall, Cole opened the top half of the divided door and pointed to the small, spindly-legged colt inside.

"Oh, Cole! She's beautiful!" Anne exclaimed. Her sheer delight at the sight of the newest addition to the Spencer ranch pleased Cole more than he had expected. "She's so small!"

"He," he corrected.

Her smile was sheepish. "Sorry, fella," she apologized to the velvety brown, hours-old colt.

Cole found himself captivated by her delight and her smile, an honest expression that warmed him down to his toes. Even the rush of pride he felt for Belle's first colt paled when compared to the intense emotion this woman evoked in him more and more every day.

While she studied the colt, murmuring to him and trying to coax him to her, Cole stole another delicious look at her, and his brain told him he was headed for trouble. From the moment he'd stopped kissing her, all he could think about was kissing her again.

His heart begged him to enjoy the moment, to drink his fill of Anne Osborne for as long as he could.

"His mother is gorgeous, as well," she said, forcing his attention back to the colt.

"Belle was the first filly ever born on this ranch." As if on cue, Belle pitched her head and emitted a low, tremulous whinny.

"No wonder her baby's a beauty, just look at her! She's the most beautiful animal I've ever seen." Belle pitched her head again and brought her small, soft ears together in a perfect peak. "You know, I think she understands me. Do horses bond with people the way dogs and cats do?"

"I never knew a horse lover who thought otherwise. But in Belle's case, it's even a stronger argument. Her mother didn't survive her birth, and for awhile, it looked as though we might lose Belle, too. We hand-fed her. Although we all took turns, I seemed to be the one with the most time to spend with her."

In truth, no one could force the fifteen-year-old Cole to leave the young foal until he was convinced she was going to survive. For three weeks, he'd taken up residence in the barn, feeding Belle around the clock with an oversize baby bottle.

"Are they Thoroughbreds?"

He smiled at her misuse of the word. "If you mean *purebreds,* yes. All the horses on the Spencer ranch are AQHA registered. Thoroughbred is a breed of its own."

"Racehorses, right?"

"Right. But more and more quarter horses are bred for racing, as well." As he fielded half a dozen more questions about the breed, he remembered a time not long ago when such questions from a certified greenhorn would have irritated him. In this circumstance, however, he was enjoying sharing his knowledge with her, and he found her eager curiosity endearing. The more questions she asked, the more she wanted to know, the more he longed to share every aspect of his passion with her.

When she asked him about the disposition of his high-bred beauties, he found himself revealing more about himself than he'd intended. "As high-strung and unpredictable as any of my yearlings can be, I'd still rather deal with the worst of them than with most people." The sudden look of sadness his response evoked in her big blue eyes caused an almost overwhelming feeling of protectiveness to swell up in him. "What I mean is—"

She held up a hand. "I think I know what you mean, Cole," she said quietly, turning to pet the bay gelding in the stall behind them. "Everyone's been hurt at one time or another."

The way she said it told him she knew about real hurt from firsthand experience.

For a moment, neither of them seemed to know what to do to break the silence that went on too long. At last, Anne said, "You know, I used to want to learn to ride, but I've always lived in the city."

"I could teach you."

"Really? Would you?" Her eyes lit up, and Cole wondered how he'd managed to hang on to his heart this long when at every turn Anne Osborne seemed to be staking a larger claim on it.

"Do you really mean it, Cole? You'd really teach me?"

"Sure."

"When?"

"As soon as we get back from Denver." He thought the mention of the city, of the hearing she was scheduled to attend tomorrow afternoon, might remind her of her dislike for him, might remind her how he'd practically dragged her kicking and screaming to his ranch, and that tomorrow, after the hearing, he'd be bringing her back to what Nyguen had termed her "house arrest."

But if she'd been reminded of any of those things, she wasn't letting it show. Instead, she smiled again, and Cole found himself completely disarmed. In fact, he caught himself holding his breath as he reached past her to close Belle's stall. When he brushed her shoulder with his fingertips, she didn't move away, and for a long moment his gaze rested on her pretty mouth—a mouth so soft, so inviting he wondered how he'd resist tasting it again. For an irrational moment, it seemed to Cole that the air between them trembled.

"We should be getting back," she said in a voice that told him maybe he wasn't the only one struggling with an impulse.

"Right." The need to distance himself from Anne's charm was almost a physical force. "Bess said something about a peach pie."

Inside Cole, a battle raged. His feelings for Anne were growing stronger every day, yet his common sense reminded him how easily an involvement with a client could turn to disaster.

Once inside, he told Bess he'd take a rain check on the pie and tried not to notice the look of disappointment that doused the lively spark his promise of a riding lesson had ignited in Anne's eyes.

"We'll need to get an early start to make your meeting tomorrow. Is five o'clock too early for you?"

"I'll be ready when you are," she said.

He nodded and strode toward his office in search of the emotional breathing space he needed so desperately.

"Hey, Cole," she called after him. "Thanks for rescuing Tabitha and for introducing me to...hey, what are you going to name Belle's colt?"

At his office door he turned to face her. "I guess I really hadn't given it much thought." Of course the colt's registered name would be drawn from a combination of his lineage on both sides, but Cole hadn't come up with a pet name yet. "Any suggestions?"

She thought for a moment. "Let me work on it. A horse that special deserves a very special name."

He closed the door, but not before he heard her say, "Good night, Cole," and the sound of her voice wrapped around his senses like a velvet chord, pulling him closer to that dangerous territory he'd sworn never to explore again.

THE NEXT MORNING, they left the ranch later than planned, due largely to the fact that a fitful night's sleep had left Anne feeling uncharacteristically lethargic and disorganized.

Luckily, the roads were clear and dry all the way to Glenwood, with only light snow here and there between Vail Pass and Loveland Pass. From Loveland Pass to Denver, Anne realized that Cole was exceeding the speed limit. But despite his best efforts, by the time they reached the city and turned onto Seventeenth Street, she had less than ten minutes to spare before Zach's two-o'clock hearing.

"You can let me out at the curb and pull around to the employee's lot to park. My space should be empty. Three eighteen." Her hand was on the door, ready to jerk it open when he stopped her.

"You'd be an open target alone on the sidewalk," he explained. "Anyone who took the time to check knows you're scheduled to attend that hearing."

Anne realized he was right, of course, but the clock was pushing her. Often a hearing could be swayed by something as frivolous as one party showing up late. She hated the thought of Cole's extra precaution on her behalf sabotaging Zach's chances. "Then pull over to the curb and go with me," she suggested. "We'll worry about a parking ticket later."

"I didn't want to worry you by springing this earlier, but there's been a change of plan."

"You can't be serious? Cole, don't even kid about something like that. Zach's future hinges on this hearing."

He flashed her a look that told her he'd never been more serious.

"The judge's representative who's scheduled to preside over this hearing is a stickler for details. If I show up late, we could be at a distinct disadvantage no matter how well prepared we are." There was even a chance the hearing could be postponed, which was always a blow to the probationer. "Please, Cole, just let me out anywhere. I can't be late!"

"You won't be," he assured her as he turned onto a residential street and drove east for three blocks before pulling the pickup over to the curb.

Why was he deliberately trying to make her late? "You're not parking here?"

"I already have."

"But I'll never make it in time!" She glanced at her watch again, exasperated. "It's ten to two now." She'd have to race just to make it to the building, and then there was the elevator and the long corridor on the third floor, leading to the hearing rooms at the end of the hall.

"You have plenty of time," he said calmly.

Anne jerked her door open and sprang out onto the sidewalk, half running, her anger propelling her.

When he grabbed her arm, she almost stumbled as she jerked away from him.

"What do you think you're doing?" A sudden and unbidden memory of Gregg and his not-so-subtle physical intimidation sprang to her mind. "Let me go!"

He released her immediately. "This way," he said, his dark eyes sparking with an impatience that matched her own.

"But the County Annex building is that way."

"I know," he said firmly. "But your hearing is in there."

Anne stared uncomprehendingly at the stately three-story home in front of her. "What? What are you talking about?"

"There was a last-minute change of venue," he said. "Now, come on. You don't want to be late."

Feeling angry and disoriented, Anne followed him up the walk, across the wide porch and into the entryway of the large, native stone structure.

Once inside, Anne was stunned to see Zach sitting on a narrow bench against the wall in a richly paneled hallway. Her shock was complete when Russell Nyguen walked out of the room at the end of the long hallway and motioned for them to join him.

Anne's questioning glance flicked between Zach and Cole.

"Don't ask me," Zach said with a shrug. "When I showed up at your office that guy—" he pointed to Nyguen "—brought me over here."

"And *that* guy," Anne said, indicating Cole, "brought *me* here. Believe me, buddy, I'm as much in the dark as you are." Seeing the uncertainty in Zach's eyes, she draped her arm around his narrow shoulders and said, "It doesn't matter, okay? Right now, all we need to focus on is what we came here to do. Let's just think about your hearing and not worry about the small stuff. Okay?"

Later, she would demand answers from Cole, she promised herself, although she couldn't imagine any excuse for why he hadn't told her about the change, except one. Cole Spencer was the arrogant control freak she'd pegged him to be from the beginning. And it would take more than a stolen kiss and a rescued kitten to change her mind about him this time.

ANNE HAD PARTICIPATED in enough probation hearings to know when one was going well, and as far as she was concerned, Zach Turner's hearing was off to a great start. Some of the officials who sat on this board had been present at his first hearing. Anne had dealt with most of them in the past and found them, as a group, to be sympathetic to probationers who were making a real effort at a fresh start.

Although she hadn't had a chance to talk to any of them before the board convened, no one seemed put out by the change of venue—a change Anne assumed had been arranged at Detective Nyguen's request.

An officer of the court, who'd been appointed to Zach's case at the time of his sentencing, opened the hearing. Gilbert Pembrooke wasn't known for his warmth or his lenience. His prematurely silvered hair and impeccable manner of speaking lent an air of authority that most young people found daunting. Even Anne found him a bit intimidating, especially when his icy blue eyes were trained on her.

At Pembrooke's instruction, Ted Alverez, the juvenile crime representative from the D.A.'s office, gave a brief summary of the charges that had landed Zach in Mountainview in the first place. Anne still simmered every time she thought about how the neighborhood pushers enticed their young runners to do their dirty work.

The next report came from Zach's guidance counselor, Victor Redding, who spoke fondly of Zach. Anne could tell Redding wished his young charge well.

When Sue Ellen Yardley, the social worker assigned to the Turner family, gave a brief overview of Zach's home life, including a short summation of how Zach's mom was progressing in her detox program, Anne noticed the effect on Zach. He hated hearing about his mother's weaknesses.

Mrs. Yardley finished her report by adding, "Oh, and by the way, Karli's teachers credit Zach with her improved attendance. And Mrs. Rieman, Karli's math and science teacher, says that since Zach started working with Karli on her math, she's brought her grade up two letters." Everyone smiled, even Zach, before dipping his head, apparently self-conscious and embarrassed by the unexpected praise.

Anne spoke last, giving her report of Zach's employment situation and general compliance with the terms of his probation, rounding out a hearing that, at least to Anne, seemed all positive.

The mood in the room—which, upon closer inspection, appeared to be a sparsely furnished dining room—was decidedly upbeat. The only one who seemed less than pleased by the proceedings was Zach himself.

While the educational and social reports were being read, he'd kept his wide brown eyes lowered, and for some reason, he still seemed unable or unwilling to look Anne in the eye.

Although she tried to tell herself he was just suffering from a case of nerves, a nagging inner voice said something else was wrong. Having worked with him for six months, she knew Zach pretty well. For the most part, he'd always displayed a happy, positive attitude, which the adults in his life admired and his peers responded to, making him a natural leader.

Today, however, all those positive characteristics seemed to be hiding behind a subdued, almost sullen mask. Although Anne couldn't help feeling disappointed, she wasn't really that surprised. She'd seen this reaction before, even from some of the most self-assured kids, ones who'd been through the process more than once. The toughest street kid could lose confidence during a hearing. In a life filled with too many disappointments, they seemed to expect the worst from these hearings. Most couldn't bring themselves to believe that the system could work in their favor.

Although why Zach thought he had to prepare for disappointment today, Anne couldn't guess.

At first, she attributed Zach's disturbing demeanor to Cole's unexpected presence. Kids like Zach didn't respond well to strangers, especially ones with whom they'd had an unpleasant encounter.

*Sorry, buddy,* she thought, *but you're not the only one who's walking a thin line today.*

Just knowing that Nyguen stood like a sentinel on the other side of the door served as a grim reminder that her own life could be changed merely by her having taken the risk of attending this hearing. The individuals responsible for tossing that explosive through her window had come heart-stoppingly close to hitting their target. By now, they had to know she'd survived. Whoever had tried to kill her was still out there. Somewhere. If they'd tried once, it made sense that they'd try again.

The extreme measures that had been taken to rearrange this hearing reinforced the morbid message that, even in the county building, in her own office or in a hearing room, she wasn't safe. Every time she thought about going to her office, her thoughts stopped cold with the image of Stan's lifeless body, cut down in cold blood in his own office.

"Ms. Osborne?" Pembrooke's voice broke into her thoughts, and she blinked.

"Sorry," she said, before answering the question about Zach's job at the Burger Barn and the possibility of a full-time job next summer at Discount City.

Finally, after all the reports had been given, the room lapsed into silence while Pembrooke took a few minutes to study his notes. Zach was seated between Anne and Cole, making it impossible for her to look at her young client without meeting her bodyguard's eyes. As she whispered a few last-minute reminders to Zach, she knew Cole couldn't help hearing. "Remember, whatever they ask you, just answer honestly," she advised him. "Everyone here is on your side. Remember that."

Anne knew it wasn't easy for the fifteen-year-old to confront all these professionals who had gathered for the sole purpose of assessing his chances of rehabilitation.

The week before her own life had been turned upside down, she'd done everything she could to prepare Zach for what to expect. Now it was up to him. All she could do was hope he had enough confidence to be himself, to show Pembrooke and the others what kind of person he really was—who and what he was made of. That he was a young man who'd made a mistake, but for the past six months he'd been trying to prove how willing and able he was to make the most of the second chance he'd been given.

As she tried to catch Zach's eyes, to somehow communicate her confidence in him, she and Cole exchanged glances. His eyes, as dark and unreadable as ever, gave her no clue to his thoughts. What did he think of this procedure? she thought. Of the role she'd played? Of the way she'd performed? Of the advice she'd given the nervous young man who sat between them?

*Wait a minute.* She stopped herself cold, astonished. *What difference does it make what he thinks? What do I care? And more importantly, why?*

"All right, Zach," Pembrooke said. "Now it's time to put all the pieces together." He picked up a file and read Zach's midterm grades aloud. "It looks as though you've been attending school regularly. And your grades come out to a solid B average."

Zach almost smiled, and without realizing it, Anne held her breath. Although the final outcome of this hearing would be decided by a vote of the board, Pembrooke could, as the personal representative of the judge who'd sentenced Zach, influence the board's ultimate decision.

"Your caseworker says you're getting along well with your mom and your sister, and I have a signed statement from your boss—" he picked up a file and flipped it open "—a Mr. Jenkins, who says, 'Zach is a hard worker. Dependable, willing and smart.' It would appear you've been keeping your nose clean, working on that fresh start we discussed last year."

Anne exhaled quietly, allowing herself a measure of cautious relief.

"All right," Pembrooke said. "If no one has anything else—"

Ted Alverez leaned forward in his chair, and Anne felt the proverbial other shoe ready to drop. "There is just one thing," the man began, his face grim. "I was given a report yesterday that concerns me greatly." He paused and adjusted his glasses, skimming the papers in his hands with agonizing slowness. Finally, he lifted his eyes from the file, trained them on Zach and asked, "Zach, what connection do you have to Webster Renfrow?"

Anne could feel the shock, which jolted her straighter in her seat, vibrating around the room, and the look on Cole's face said that he, too, was fully aware of Webster Renfrow's reputation. Everyone knew Webster Renfrow.

# Chapter Eight

"Zach, we're waiting for your explanation."

The young man didn't say a word, seemingly frozen where he sat, staring at his hands. Refusing to look up, to offer any explanation, he sent a wordless admission of guilt rippling around the conference table louder than a scream.

"For those of you who don't already know," Alverez explained, "Webster Renfrow is a major player in this city's drug and gang activity. Even from behind bars, he somehow seems to keep a controlling hand in these crimes."

Victor Redding's large, round face reddened. "Zach, do you know this man?"

"Everyone knows him," Zach mumbled without looking up.

The adults exchanged disappointed glances, and Anne's heart sank. If Webster Renfrow had somehow managed to draw Zach in, it had to have happened in the past week. Otherwise she felt sure she would have sensed some change in her young client's behavior sooner.

*Damn it, what does it take to reach these kids?* she wondered. What parent, caseworker or probation officer was strong enough to combat the influences of a kid's own backyard? Could a neighborhood code of silence ever really be broken, even by the most well-intended outsider's effort?

Alverez tried again. "Zach, if you have anything to say, anything that might help us understand . . ." But Ted's plea went unanswered and he could only shake his head before leaning over to say something in a low voice to Redding.

When Pembrooke spoke, his voice had a distinctly hard edge. "If you hope to receive any kind of positive recommendation from this group, you'd better say something, young man."

When Zach finally looked up, his face was devoid of color. "I—I...that is, I mean...I don't really know him." His voice was tremulous and reed thin.

"This visitor's log from the county jail says that you do." Alverez held the damning papers up for everyone to see before passing photocopies to Anne, Pembrooke, Redding and Mrs. Yardley. "You'll note Zach's name is listed as one of Webster Renfrow's visitors on September third." He leveled his gaze at the young probationer. "Why would you go to the jail to visit someone you don't know?"

The young man's head shot up, and his eyes blazed. "I don't do drugs!" he said. "I never have." His voice cracked, and Anne knew he was close to tears. For a moment she didn't know which impulse was stronger, the one that urged her to throttle him or the one that pushed her to protect him.

When she glanced past the young man whose head was bowed again, her eyes met Cole's, and she sensed that he, too, had been moved by the young man's emotional outburst. If Cole Spencer, a tough, street-wary bodyguard and former cop, had been touched by Zach's sincerity, perhaps the others in the room had been touched, as well.

"Just tell us why you went to see the man, Zach," Redding prodded, leaning forward in his chair in an obvious attempt to telegraph his support to the young man across the table. Anne empathized with the counselor's need to reach Zach. They were all pulling for him—surely he could feel that support.

"You've got to give us something," Mrs. Yardley prodded. "Some explanation for going to see this man. Is he a friend of yours?"

Zach responded to their questions in exactly the way Anne feared he might. He shrugged. Anne could see the wall going up between Zach and the adults he'd already decided were against him and would disappoint him in the end.

After a lengthy silence, Pembrooke shook his head and sighed. "All right. I think we can move on now." He aimed his remarks at Anne. "Under the circumstances, I'm sure you realize we can't vote on an early end to Zach's probation."

She could only nod. Pembrooke was just doing his job, Anne reminded herself, merely putting into words what would be the inescapable outcome of a formal vote.

"In fact," Alverez said, "based on what has transpired this afternoon, I wonder if we shouldn't be considering Zach's return to detention." Ted Alverez's words hung in the air, a hammer poised to crush Zach's hopes. But still the young man continued to stare at his hands, which were clenched in fists in his lap. Anne could almost feel the stinging waves of disappointment slapping him.

"I think we shouldn't forget an otherwise stellar report," Pembrooke said. "And I, for one, am prepared to consider a compromise." His declaration shocked them all. "I don't think it would be in Zach's best interest to return to the detention center at this time. What is your opinion, Ms. Osborne?"

Anne cleared her throat before quickly reviewing all the reasons Zach's chances for success at home and in school during the remainder of his probation period still seemed quite good. "But before we make a decision," she concluded, "I think we need an explanation from Zach as to what kind of relationship he has with Mr. Renfrow."

She heard Zach suck in a sharp breath of startled air, and she wasn't surprised when his head shot up and his dark eyes branded her a traitor. What did surprise her was the subtle change in Cole's expression. A change that said she'd shocked him, that he, too, had been as stunned as Zach by her tough demand.

*Sorry, fellas,* she wanted to inform them, *but trust works both ways.* Anne prided herself on being a loyal friend, on being the kind of friend who would go to the mat for someone she loved. But the lessons of her young life, and the advanced degree in survival she'd earned as Gregg's wife, had taught her that friends sometimes needed to be called to task for the things they'd done.

"I agree with Ms. Osborne, Zach," Alverez chimed in. "If you can't, or won't, give us any explanation, we'll be forced to draw our own conclusions."

Once again, all eyes turned to the slender young man in blue jeans, flannel shirt and the blue-and-orange windbreaker he'd reclaimed from Polly the day Anne and Cole had met. Despite the fact that he measured a good three inches taller than she was and would be getting his driver's license within the year, Anne thought Zach more nearly resembled a six-year-old who'd just broken his mother's favorite vase.

"I went to see him for a... friend," he said, his voice so low and hollow that Anne wondered if Mrs. Yardley, Alverez and Redding, who were seated on the other side of the wide oak table, had heard him. "Somebody wanted to know... how he was... getting along. That's all."

"A friend?" Anne asked, skeptical. "What friend?"

Zach still didn't look up. "Just a friend."

Every instinct told her he was lying. But she also sensed that if she tried to back him down now, in front of everyone, she'd lose any chance of reestablishing the rapport she would need to help him in the future. What she knew Zach couldn't imagine right now was that life went on after this hearing, and like it or not, she would still be his probation officer.

Anne shifted her gaze to Pembrooke, asking him without words for understanding on Zach's behalf, to give her just a little more time to reach a kid who still might deserve a second chance. Pembrooke's nod was almost imperceptible, but it told her what she needed to know, that he'd decided to give Zach a break.

"All right," he said. "I think that's all we need from Zach for now." He motioned for the uniformed bailiff at the door to escort the young probationer into the hallway.

Cole rose and left the room, much to Anne's surprise.

"Under the circumstances," Pembrooke began, "my recommendation is that Zach's probation period be extended another three months."

Anne had expected much worse. Unfortunately, Zach would be devastated by the decree—to a fifteen-year-old, three months was an eternity. But under the circumstances, Anne could hardly justify asking the members of the board to reconsider.

When they finally voted, the outcome was unanimous to extend Zach's probation period and to meet again in four weeks to assess his progress. Before they adjourned, Alverez moved that a formal statement be included in Zach's files, indicating his reluctance to answer their questions about Renfrow.

Again Pembrooke surprised Anne when he said, "I disagree. I don't think we need to belabor the Renfrow issue. As far as I know, visiting someone at the county jail is not a crime."

For a moment everyone seemed too surprised to speak.

"After all, we don't want to push the boy into trouble where there is none," Pembrooke explained quickly before he adjourned the meeting and rose to leave the room.

"I'm as disappointed as you are, Anne," Ted Alverez said. "I thought Zach was different."

"I wouldn't count him out yet, Ted," Anne said, gathering the paperwork that had been distributed during the hearing into a folder.

"Hmm. Well, maybe not. But this Renfrow character is bad news. If Zach's hooked up with him, no telling what else he's into."

"That's what we have to find out, isn't it?"

Alverez merely nodded. "See you in thirty days." At the door, he seemed to remember something. "Oh, by the way,

I'd like to get together to discuss the situation with Shannon Browers.''

The name didn't ring a bell, but Anne assumed he was referring to a new probationer. "I'm sorry, but I don't believe I've seen her file yet."

Ted seemed surprised. "Really? I'm sure Marty said she was part of your caseload."

"Well, I've been out of the office for a few days."

He shook his head. "Her file would have come across your desk at least a month ago. Shannon Browers," he said again.

Anne tried to remember. "I'm sorry, Ted, but I'm still drawing a blank." Which wasn't like her, and they both knew it.

"When you get back to your office maybe you could check your files. I'm sure as soon as you do, you'll remember this kid. On her fifteenth birthday, she and a girlfriend went joyriding in her mother's car. When they hit a utility pole, the girlfriend went through the windshield. The D.A. didn't press the issue, and Shannon got off with a pretty light stay at Mountainview, despite the fact that the girlfriend didn't survive."

Anne shuddered. It wasn't a new story, but such a waste of a young life always hit her hard. "What's her latest situation?" Anne asked, hoping some detail would trigger a memory of the girl's case.

"My office got involved last summer. Since then she's been identified with a group of juveniles suspected in a drive-by shooting. Then, last month, Shannon moved on to even bigger trouble. We've identified her as one of the three individuals on a tape from a security camera at a convenience store that was robbed. The clerk was found shot to death in the alley, and the videotape clearly shows Shannon with some kind of weapon."

Anne sighed. "Sounds like this kid is definitely headed for hard time." There'd be no way she would have forgotten a juvenile in this much trouble.

Ted stared at her a long moment.

"What is it, Ted?"

"Well, I was just wondering why your office recommended that she be tried as a juvenile. And why you recommended her release into the custody of her aunt while she's awaiting trial."

Anne could only stand and stare. "My office?" Based on just the bare facts Ted had shared, she couldn't imagine putting Shannon Browers back on the street even if she had been placed in the custody of a responsible relative. "Ted, I can assure you I haven't recommended anything with regard to this kid."

Ted flipped open his date book. "Clearly we've got a problem here. Can you meet with me tomorrow morning? Say, around ten?"

Anne shook her head. "I—I don't know—"

"What is it, Anne? Problems in the department?"

She hadn't thought so until now. "I'm not sure. But it sounds like I need to ask a few questions before I can answer any of yours."

Cole appeared in the doorway. "Ready?"

She nodded.

Alverez wouldn't be put off. "We need to straighten this out, Anne."

"I know we do, and I'm as concerned as you are, believe me, Ted. I'll get back to you as soon as I can. Unfortunately things are in kind of a jumble right now, but I promise I'll get some answers and call your office to schedule a meeting."

"By tomorrow?"

"I'll do the best I can," she promised.

"I hope so," Ted replied, clearly irritated by what he obviously took as her brush-off. "This kind of bureaucratic foul-up doesn't wash well with the public when one of these kids jumps bail or decides to gun down another innocent victim."

"I'll do what I can," she said again.

"You'd better," Ted shot back. "The D.A.'s office is bogged down with enough trouble right now—" he ran a hand through his hair ''—what with Stan's murder right there in the building. Anyway, this kind of screwup from your department just adds to the heat.''

At the mention of Stanley Lewellyn, Anne felt the blood drain from her face.

''She *said* she'd get back to you,'' Cole said, stepping in between them. His voice and demeanor were ominous, just short of threatening. But Ted wasn't backing down easily

For a long minute the two men glared at each other before Ted finally blinked. ''I'll be waiting for your call,'' he said quickly before leaving.

''Was that really necessary?'' Anne asked when they were alone in the hearing room again.

''I thought so. What was he so incensed about, anyway?''

She gave him a terse outline of the Shannon Browers situation.

''Do you have any clue what's going on?''

She shook her head. ''Only that someone is either signing my name or representing a decision as originating in my department, about a client I've never heard about or seen.''

''Do you have any idea who or why?''

''Neither,'' she said wearily. ''But you can bet I'm going to try to find out.'' They walked together into the hallway. ''But in the meantime, I've got to try to get a straight answer from Zach about this Renfrow thing.''

Again she saw the darkening of his expression at the mere mention of the name. At some point she'd confront him, ask him point blank what, if anything, he knew about the man. For now, however, she had to concentrate on Zach, on getting the answers he'd avoided giving to the board.

She hated to push the kid, but her own predicament left no time to finesse the situation. On the one hand, she'd worked too hard to help Zach turn his life around to give him up to the streets. But on the other hand, if he was involved in some illegal activity with Renfrow, she had to know.

If helping him meant discovering something that might well send him back to the detention center he despised, then she'd have to risk it. Whoever had killed Stanley Lewellyn had forced her hand and limited all the choices, robbing her of precious time that might be needed to regain Zach's trust.

If Zach really was involved in some significant way with Webster Renfrow, he was playing with fire, and Anne knew that if someone didn't step in to save Zach now, there might never be another chance.

When Anne told Cole she needed to talk to Zach privately before leaving town, he'd surprised her by offering to buy them a late lunch. As they drove to the restaurant, Cole and Zach engaged in a conversation about Cole's pickup, and Anne found herself listening in wonder as the two of them chatted like old friends.

"You know, this is the kind of rig I'm going to have someday," Zach said.

Cole smiled. "Oh, yeah?"

"Yeah. Only I doubt if I could ever afford one like this."

"Well, maybe not now," Cole replied. "But if you set your mind to it and save up, I bet you could find a good used one. My first truck wasn't much to look at, but it got me where I needed to go. The important thing is to keep working toward your goal."

Anne could have hugged him for giving Zach that piece of sound advice.

"I intend to do just that," the young man said earnestly.

Inside the small diner on the west side of town, Cole amazed her again by leaving them alone to talk in a corner booth. He positioned himself in the booth next to them, however, where he sat ostensibly reading the paper while he ate. Although she hadn't actually caught him staring, Anne could feel his eyes on her, which made it difficult to concentrate on the things she needed to discuss with her young client.

"Jenetta tells me you've been questioned by the police."

Zach nodded as he salted a huge stack of fries and squeezed a pool of ketchup beside them. "Yeah. They came around a couple of times, talking about your car."

"What did you tell them?"

He shrugged. "Nothing to tell. I didn't know what they were talking about." He popped a couple of fries into his mouth and took a long drink of soda. "They asked me if I'd seen you that day, and I told them that I had. I told them how that guy—" with a jerk of his head he indicated Cole "—had tried to bust me for stealing my own jacket."

Anne almost smiled, imagining how Zach's retelling of that incident must have sounded to Nyguen. "What else is going on, Zach? What's the deal with you and Renfrow?"

His eyes fell away from hers, and he toyed with his food. "I already told you. A friend of his asked me to drop by and see how he was getting along. That's all."

She didn't believe him any more now than she had when he'd evaded the Renfrow question during his hearing. "Zach, you've got to tell me the truth. If you're in some kind of trouble, I'll find out sooner or later."

"I'm not in any trouble," he said defensively. "Why won't anyone believe me?"

"I want to believe you, Zach. I really do. I know how hard you've worked to turn things around."

"It hasn't been all that tough," he said.

She sensed his embarrassment and regretted that Zach hadn't had enough praise in his young life to know how to handle it. "All the same, I'm proud of you, and I don't want anything to spoil your success."

His eyes fell away from hers, and he seemed to be unduly concentrating on his meal.

"He's trouble, Zach. But I don't have to tell you that, do I?"

"No, ma'am," he said softly.

"And you also know that sooner or later if you get involved with him, he'll take you down to his level."

"I know." For the first time since before his hearing, Zach lifted his chin and looked her squarely in the eye.

"Don't worry. There's no way I'm going to mess up again. I'd rather die than go back to Mountainview."

His impassioned assurances should have made her feel better, but they didn't. "All right, Zach," she said quietly. "I have to believe you. I'll prepare a statement for your records and count on you to have a clean slate at your next hearing. In the meantime, just remember the things we've talked about, about taking control of your situation and making good choices."

He nodded solemnly.

"So far, you're doing great. Your grades have improved, and if you keep up the hard work, college can still be a possibility for you." He'd shared with her his dream of someday teaching high school math. "You're on your way, Zach. The next three months will pass quickly, I promise. Just don't let anyone spoil it for you."

In his eyes, she saw that he longed to believe her.

"I'll be out of the office again next week," she continued. "I'll call you on Wednesday, and we'll conduct our weekly meeting by phone." She made a mental note to tell Jenetta to take Zach off next week's schedule.

"So, does that mean you're still on vacation?"

"Well, yes. I guess I am." To distract him from asking more questions she couldn't answer, she said, "Hey, did you get those pictures I sent?"

His expression turned blank for a second and then he jammed his hands into his jacket pockets, as though searching for something. "Oh, man," he groaned and smacked his forehead with his palm. "I must have left them with Jenetta."

"Jenetta? Why would you have given them to her?"

"I brought them with me when I went to the County Annex building this afternoon. I showed up early for my hearing, just like you said I should, but when no one was in the hearing room, I decided to go up to your office to wait for you. I was showing the pictures to Jenetta when that cop came for me."

Anne knew Jenetta didn't invite conversation with every probationer who passed through the department, but she liked Zach, and she often engaged in good-natured banter with him when he came to the office for his weekly appointments. "She'll hang on to them for you, I'm sure."

"Yeah, I hope so. If she remembers to get them back."

A vague, nameless warning went off inside Anne. "What do you mean, if she gets them back?"

"Well, they were all looking at them, you know? Passing them around."

"They?"

"You know, the other people in the office—your boss, that Marty guy and the woman who works down the hall. And Jenetta's husband."

"Dan was in the office when you were there?"

"Yeah. Is he a friend of yours?" When she nodded, Zach frowned. "Well, I think he's a jerk!"

His declaration stunned her. For reasons Jen had only hinted at, she and Dan had never had a family of their own, but Anne knew for a fact that Dan liked kids. He volunteered his time to referee basketball at the YMCA, and he played Santa every year for his nieces and nephews. "Why would you say something like that, Zach? What did he say or do to make you feel this way about him?"

He shook his head. "What he said to me wasn't that bad, but he was really letting Jenetta have it when I walked in, yelling at her, you know? When I walked in, she looked ready to bawl. And then he jumped all over me for not knocking when I came in. Hey, I never knew I was supposed to! The office door is usually open, and even if it isn't, it's never locked."

"It's all right, Zach. You didn't do anything wrong. Maybe you just caught him in a bad mood."

"Hmm, maybe," he said, though obviously still unconvinced.

She had no intention of pumping Zach for information, but she couldn't help wondering what Dan and Jen had been quarreling about and why Dan had turned his anger on Zach.

"Anyway, he backed off when your boss came out of his office to see what was going on."

"And that's when you showed them the pictures."

"Yeah...hey, now I remember! Frank Olivetti and Jen's husband were looking at them when that cop came for me."

"Nyguen?"

"Yeah. When he showed up I kinda forgot everything else. Sorry. I promise I'll get your pictures back for you."

"They're not my pictures, Zach. I had those copies made for you."

His expression brightened. "Cool. I've only been to the mountains once, on a field trip when I was a kid."

She smiled. "Such a long time ago," she teased.

He grinned, and Anne felt relieved to see the Zach she knew best, the happy, upbeat kid, full of dreams and promise despite his situation.

"Hey, you know, I was just thinking that maybe I could get one of those pictures blown up...like a poster to hang on the wall. My mom's birthday is next week. Maybe I'll surprise her with a poster for our living room."

"That's a great idea, Zach. I think she'd like that."

Cole cleared his throat, and Anne turned around to read the message in his eyes that said it was time to go.

A few minutes later, they drove up in front of Zach's building.

"Remember what I said about Renfrow," Anne warned before he got out of the truck.

"I'll remember," he promised.

"Take it easy, kid," Cole said.

"Always. And, hey, take good care of that truck. I might want to take it off your hands someday."

Cole's smile was wry. "I'll keep that in mind."

"Be careful, Zach," Anne said solemnly.

"Hey, no problem. I know what I have to do."

"You'd better know," she muttered when the door closed behind him. The board had given him a break, but

Anne knew all too well that guys like Webster Renfrow didn't give second chances.

AT THE FIRST TRUCK STOP on the westbound interstate, Cole pulled over so Anne could call Jenetta.

"I'm glad you called," Jenetta said, and her voice sounded strained. "You know I love my job—and most of the time I can even put up with the hectic pace and the short tempers—but today was just too much! I swear, sometimes I don't think it's worth it."

"What is it, Jen?" Anne asked patiently, rolling her eyes at Cole where he stood leaning with his back against the building sipping a Coke.

"Marty might fool the rest of the staff with that laid-back Southern California crap, but not me. The rest of you don't have to deal with him when he's ready to pop, but I'm trapped right outside his door, you know?"

Anne thought about what Zach had told her, that Dan and Jen had been quarreling earlier in the day. "I'm sorry, Jen. It sounds like things have been pretty tense around there."

"Tense?" Jen blurted. "Yeah. You could say that. Marty's been putting in long hours, and his mood swings from bad to worse. When he came in this morning, he looked just awful, his eyes all red-rimmed, and he needed a shave. I almost felt sorry for him until he started chewing me out for a misplaced file. And then, come to find out, the file he'd been searching for was on his desk the whole time."

The frazzled assistant had gone on to explain how from the moment he walked into the office this morning until the time he left for lunch, Marty had been growling like a grizzly bear.

"If he asked me once, he's asked me half a dozen times if I've heard from you. When he came back from lunch, he almost blew a fuse when he thought you'd missed Zach's hearing. Then, when I explained that the hearing had already taken place, I thought for sure he was going straight into orbit."

Jenetta drew a deep breath. "He told me I didn't know what the hell I was talking about. He said he'd waited outside that room for almost an hour and neither you nor Zach nor Pembrooke had showed up."

"Jen, why didn't he know the hearing had been moved?"

"How would I know?" Jenetta answered with uncharacteristic defensiveness. "I'm sorry," she added quickly.

"It's all right," Anne said. "I know you're tired and stressed out. I'm sorry for the load I've put on you."

Jenetta sighed. "No, it isn't you. You're doing what you can. It's just that with everything else going on, I'm overreacting."

"Everything else?"

"Nothing. Forget it. None of this is your fault."

"Jenetta, I've got to go, now," Anne said, relenting to Cole's prodding. "The reason I called was to tell you to take Zach off the schedule for next week. I'll deal with him by phone. And please tell Marty I'm sorry, and that I'll explain everything when I can. Take care of yourself, okay?"

"Oh, I'm all right," Jenetta assured her. "Today I even amazed myself. You know, that assertiveness class my sister talked me into taking a few years back must have done some good, after all. Marty backed down when I confronted him, and even offered to file Zach's paperwork when the courier from Pembrooke's office sent it over."

After thanking Jenetta again for taking up the slack her absence was causing, Anne hung up the phone and sighed.

"Tough day at the office?" Cole asked.

"Yeah." And mulling over the things Jenetta had said, Anne couldn't help wondering just what was going on there.

The sun was low in the sky, but the long, lazy Indian summer day seemed endless as they headed back to Telluride. Since her conversation with Jenetta, Anne had been lost in thought.

"You really like that kid, don't you?" Cole asked without taking his eyes off the road. "You believe in him."

She jutted her chin. "Yes, I really do."

"It shows."

She glanced at him to see if he was baiting her and decided he wasn't.

"I hope you know he's lying through his teeth about Renfrow."

"Oh? And just when did you become an expert on juveniles?"

He shrugged. "It doesn't take an expert to spot a liar, no matter how good that liar is."

"If you're saying Zach's a con artist, you're wrong. And if he lied, it's because that's how he's learned to cope with his crummy life, how he's learned to survive."

"And that excuses him?"

"Of course not," she replied. "But it does help to explain him, to understand him and to maybe help him change."

He didn't respond to that, but the skeptical slant of his mouth spoke his disapproval louder than words.

"I know how to do my job, Cole. I know about kids like Zach." Why did she feel compelled to explain herself to him? Why should she care what he thought, or if he approved of her?

After a taut silence, he said, "I wasn't criticizing. Only making an observation about the kid—"

"He has a name, you know."

"Right. Sorry. Like I said, I was only making conversation. I wasn't putting you down or demeaning the job you do. As a matter of fact, I was impressed as hell at the way you handled yourself, as well as Zach, today."

He'd shocked her with his completely unexpected compliment. "Really. At one point during the hearing, I thought you seemed as upset with me as Zach was."

He glanced at her and then back to the road. "Well, you gotta admit, you did jerk the rug out from under him."

"Is that what you thought?"

"It doesn't matter what I think."

But it did, she realized, much to her chagrin. "It's called tough love, ever hear of it?"

He nodded and his smile was almost wistful. "Grew up with it. My folks didn't know any other kind."

"The young people I work with make a big issue of trust, of fairness, and I couldn't agree more. What they don't always understand is that in any relationship it's got to go both ways. I do everything I can to prove to Zach and kids like him that they can trust me. Some of them aren't particularly trustworthy, you know."

His frown said he knew.

"Anyway, when I point out that I need to be able to trust them, they sometimes act as though I've betrayed them or sold them out." For some reason she didn't even attempt to hide the exasperation she felt, exasperation that had been building inside her for months.

"Zach strikes me as a kid who has been betrayed more than once."

"He has. But when you think about it, we've all been betrayed, haven't we? Lied to, hurt by people we've trusted the most," she said, staring straight ahead to avoid his eyes.

"Who hurt you, Anne?"

"Huh." It came out a dry chuckle. "I don't think you've got that much time, cowboy," she said flippantly. They rode in silence for a few moments before she added, "And besides, it doesn't matter anymore. I've moved on with my life and accepted the fact that the world is an imperfect place, filled with imperfect people who at times can be really wonderful." Her thoughts drifted to yesterday, when Cole had done a pretty wonderful job of proving that point by surprising her with Tabitha.

"I've been thinking of leaving the department," she said. "Sometimes I think I'd be more effective as a high school counselor." She surprised herself by confiding in him.

"I think you'd make a difference wherever you are," he said without hesitation. The reassuring note in his voice gave her spirits an unexpected lift. "You were great with

Pembrooke," he said, surprising her again. "The guy seemed like a real hard ass at first. The way things were going, I thought he was going to send that kid—" he smiled, almost playfully "—Zach back to jail. If you hadn't given such a strong and realistic opinion of the situation, I think he might have."

She was completely taken aback by his remarks. Maybe Zach wasn't the only one who needed to learn how to accept compliments. "So, you think I did the right thing by vouching for Zach but not throwing him to the wolves when I knew—everyone knew—he was lying?"

He shrugged. "I don't think I know enough about him to pass judgment."

"But based on what you saw today," she pressed. "If you'd been on that board today, what decision would you have made?"

An unexpected and inexplicable sadness flickered momentarily in his eyes. "I don't think you want to know, Anne," he said quietly before lapsing into silence and his own thoughts, deeply private thoughts, she sensed, that had little to do with Zach.

After a moment he said, "I guess Zach's record since he's been on probation proves his sincerity about turning his life around, but his involvement with this Renfrow character bothers me, to say the least."

She'd been waiting for an opening, and she seized it. "What do you know about Renfrow, Cole?"

He hesitated, glanced at her and then back to the road. "I don't know anything about the man, personally. It's the type I'm all too familiar with."

The type of character who'd been involved with Meredith Hackett, she finished for him silently. The reaction she'd seen today had nothing to do with Renfrow personally and everything to do with what the man represented.

They both allowed a long stretch of contemplative silence before Cole said, "Someone very much like Renfrow once hurt someone I cared about a great deal."

"Meredith Hackett."

He glanced at her and then away, and the ensuing silence was filled with his departed lover's name, so that Anne felt as if the woman had somehow managed to insinuate herself between them physically.

"I remember reading about her," she ventured softly.

"Then you know what happened."

"I know she took her own life."

He winced. "Yes."

After several minutes of silence, she said, "Tell me what happened, Cole."

"He was blackmailing her. Evidently they had a long history. I don't know all the details." His expression said he'd never wanted to.

"I'm sorry."

"Yeah. Well, anyway, she killed him. I'm not saying it was right, but I don't think the world's worse off for his passing." Deep cynicism echoed in his voice. "When the truth came out, she couldn't handle it."

She sensed there was much more to the story than he was admitting, and yet she felt deeply moved that he'd shared this much.

"I'm sorry," she said again softly, her heart aching for him, for Meredith, for the hell the young heiress must have endured before she opted to end it all. Cole's pain must have been unbearable, incomprehensible to anyone who hadn't been through the loss of a loved one. So many unanswered questions. Anne felt compassion for the young beauty, but she couldn't help resenting the woman's selfishness.

For miles, as the sun set behind the mountains in front of them, they rode in silence, a silence that seemed to take on a life of its own, wedging itself between them, the way memories of Meredith would always divide Cole from any other woman. The thought saddened Anne more deeply than she ever imagined it could.

Feeling road-weary and depressed, Anne almost jumped out of her skin when a long while later he finally spoke. "When I left the hearing room, I spoke to Nyguen and called Drew. I'm afraid they haven't made much headway in discovering the source of the leak in Nyguen's department—if there is a leak. Several cops have been questioned.''

"And?"

"And nothing.''

Why did she feel as though he was holding back. "Please don't try to protect me, Cole." He laughed. "Oh, all right, but you know what I mean. I hate to be kept in the dark. Like today. Why didn't anyone tell me about the change of venue?"

At least he had the good grace to look sheepish. "Sorry about that. The decision to move the hearing out of the County Annex building happened this morning. Nyguen called while you were in the shower. I should have told you. No excuses.''

"All right." Though hardly appeased, she accepted his apology. "But from now on, whatever has to do with this case has to do with me. All right? I have the right to know everything you know. It is my life, after all. It was me in that office that night. And it was my home they ruined.'' Emotions came out of nowhere to gather in a knot in her throat.

He didn't say anything, but for some reason she felt he understood the impact of her admitting for the first time to him—and maybe even to herself—the deadly seriousness of her situation.

Fumbling with the handle, she lowered the window, suddenly desperate for fresh air.

He signaled and pulled the pickup over to the shoulder and stopped. "It's all right," he said, turning to her and draping his arm over the back of the seat. "Nothing in your life could have prepared you for what you've been through. It's only natural for you to feel angry, overwhelmed." His voice, so soothing and low, began to dissolve the barrier behind which she'd stored too much emotion in the past twenty-four hours.

"I am angry," she admitted. "Did you know that Stanley Lewellyn was only thirty-four years old? He had a wife and two kids. The baby, Cherise, just turned two. He was so proud of those kids." For the first time she remembered seeing their pictures on the corner of his desk that night, and suddenly her eyes filled with stinging tears. "It—it wasn't like we were especially close or anything, it's just, well, just so unfair!"

His fingers moved through her hair to the back of her neck.

"He was just a nice guy, you know? Just a regular guy, doing a not so regular job."

She realized she was crying when he handed her a tissue.

"He wasn't perfect—" She gave a short hiccupy little laugh "—in fact, sometimes he could be a jerk, especially when he knew he was losing a case." She dabbed her eyes again. "But to die that way, to just have his life...stolen." She shuddered. "It's just so horrible."

He put his arms around her, and for some reason she wasn't ashamed to let him see her cry, or even to let him comfort her.

Gregg had hated it when she cried. In fact, he'd ridiculed any display of emotion. By the time they divorced, she'd learned out of self-defense how to steel herself, how to bridle her natural emotional reactions.

"Go ahead, Anne," Cole whispered against her hair. "Cry it all out."

In a few moments her tears subsided and she lifted her face. "You're shirt's all wet." She sniffed.

His smile was warm. "It'll dry." A wonderful sense of well-being seeped into her heart. "Let's get out for a minute," he suggested. "I think we could both use some fresh air."

For the first time, Anne realized he'd pulled into a turnout that overlooked a long, lush mountain meadow, ringed by distant snowcapped peaks glistening in the dying sunlight of late day.

She opened her door when he came around to her side of the pickup.

"Let's walk down to that stream."

He took her hand as they negotiated the gentle embankment, and he kept his fingers closed around hers until they reached the grassy banks of the clear, cool stream.

Inhaling slowly, deeply, Anne drank in the crisp mountain air, letting it cleanse and renew her. Once again, she felt nature's recuperative powers.

"Tell me what we can do to find Stan's killers. I want to help. I was there, and maybe that's not much, but it sounds as if it's all we have."

He frowned. "You're an enigma, Anne Osborne. One minute you seem as soft and vulnerable as a kitten. The next minute you're in complete control."

"If I really was in control, I'd be at my desk right now, trying to figure this whole thing out."

"Really, and miss all this?"

She followed his gaze across the meadow to the jagged peaks beyond before she said, "Don't try to change the subject."

His smile was wry. "Okay. Let's get down to business." He patted the ground beside him and Anne sat down. "Do you have any idea what Stan was working on the night he was murdered?"

She blinked. "Wow, that one came out of left field."

"I know. But Nyguen is convinced Stan knew his murderer. The police found the side door to the building unlocked and wedged open. It could be that Stan was expecting a visitor."

"If he was, he didn't mention it when we spoke earlier that evening."

"Do you know if the killers took anything with them when they left?"

Anne shook her head. "I didn't see them leave, remember?"

"Right. Well, Nyguen and Drew think some of Stan's files are missing, and the natural assumption is that the murderer took them, or that Stan may have been killed for whatever was in them."

"As I mentioned the other day, I did notice Stan's desk had been cleared that night. And I remember thinking how odd that seemed for someone who was preparing to work through the weekend. I just wish I'd seen whomever was in there, instead of merely hearing the voices."

Cole's expression turned grim, and he started to say something, then seemed to think better of it.

"Spill it," she prodded.

Even in the dim light, she sensed his amused expression. "You don't give up easy, do you?"

"I can't afford to."

"All right," he said. "You're going to find out soon enough. Nyguen wants you to listen to some tapes he made. I have the cassette with me. Tonight, when we get to the ranch, if you're up to it, I'd like you to listen to them."

"Tapes? Of what? Voices? Cops' voices?"

He nodded.

"Well...yeah. I guess that makes sense. Sure. Why not?" It wouldn't hurt to try, but Anne doubted that it would do any good. To her that night loomed as one big shock. Even when she tried to imagine the voices, to somehow recreate the sounds in her mind, she came up empty. When she went back to that night in her mind, all she could see was Stan's body, the bullet wound in his head, the lifeless, bewildered expression on his waxen face.

In a way, the thought of the tapes frightened her. What if, in her eagerness to find a lead, to find some direction in this dead-end case, she identified the wrong man?

As if she'd voiced her private concerns, Cole said, "I know, it seems like a long shot. The chances that you'd match a voice on tape to the voices you heard that night seem pretty slim to me. I think if we work instead on trying to piece together Stan's last movements, we'd be getting closer to finding a motive."

She felt gratified by his use of the pronoun *we*. It implied that he considered her an active partner rather than a helpless victim. "Stan did sometimes tell me a little about what he was working on. I remember he was really excited. He planned to run for D.A. in November. Did you know that?"

"We'll go over all of what Stan said and what you remember when we get to the ranch." He surprised her when he added, "And, by the way, I've asked Nyguen to give me a full report on Renfrow."

"Based on what?"

"I want to know if Zach's involvement with Renfrow has anything to do with you."

Now he'd really shocked her. "What? But that's incredible. What happened to innocent until proven guilty?"

"I'm not drawing any conclusions or passing judgment," he said. "But I used to be an investigator, Anne. Some would even say a pretty good one. And every good investigator knows that not even a long-shot connection can be ignored in a case this scrambled."

"But to suspect that Zach is involved in Stan's murder—"

"Hold on. Now you're the one jumping to conclusions. All I'm trying to do is gather the widest possible circle around you. Everything that affects you has to be taken into consideration. When someone as dangerous as Webster Renfrow has any connection to my client, I need to know everything about him."

Anne felt herself drawing back from the intimate atmosphere that had prevailed between them for the past several minutes. She was his client, he'd reminded her and himself.

Obviously, he was as eager as she to get both their lives back to normal. He'd made it clear from the beginning that he didn't want this case, had only taken it as a favor to his brother. Well, at least they understood each other. Cole had been hurt deeply by the woman he loved, and he felt burned by the system she represented. His lover had been involved with the type of individuals who filled the files of Stanley

Lewellyn's office and filled the courtrooms where she spent most of her days.

Cole's pride, his confidence and maybe even his heart had been severely damaged in the process of losing Meredith Hackett. She'd been a client of the Spencer Agency, Bess had told her. Had he been her bodyguard? she wondered. Was that the reason he so despised the job now? Did that account for the wall she sensed he'd erected around his heart, for the wariness and skepticism?

If it did, she couldn't really blame him. In fact, she'd reacted in much the same way, protecting herself, building barriers around her heart in order to shield herself from again succumbing to the kind of confidence-destroying relationship she'd endured with Gregg.

*We make quite a team,* she thought with grim amusement as they walked together back to the road. *A couple of veterans so wounded by the past we dare not risk the future.* Well, at least she knew where he stood.

Then why, with all of that so firmly in mind, did she have to stop herself from fantasizing about what it would be like to be the object of Cole's affections? And why was the memory of his kiss always just a heartbeat away? And why, when she knew enough of his past to know better, did she bother wondering what kind of woman could make him take a chance on love again?

And why, when she caught him looking at her in the moonlight, did her heart beat double-time?

*Because you're a fool,* an inner voice answered, *a fool on the verge of falling in love with the wrong man. Again!*

# Chapter Nine

The next morning, Cole was out of the house at first light to say goodbye to Bess before Seth drove her to the airport. By the time he'd finished talking with Pete about their day's chores, it was almost nine. He worked a bit with a yearling he planned to show in California in November before grooming the eleven-year-old mare he'd decided would be the perfect mount for Anne's first riding lesson.

When he led the mare into the training ring, he spotted Anne coming out of the house...and couldn't take his eyes off her. How many women looked as elegant in blue jeans as they did in silk?

Only one other, he remembered, as, unbidden, the image of Meredith Hackett drifted out of his memory. To his surprise, however, the jab of bitterness that normally accompanied any thought of her seemed curiously absent. In fact, for the first time in two years, he felt almost nothing at all, and out of nowhere the old saying about indifference being the opposite of love came to him.

"He's beautiful."

"She," he corrected.

"Sorry, girl." Her smile was as welcome as sunlight after a rain. "I'm not sure I'm ready for this," she admitted.

"You'll be fine. Come in and get acquainted."

She hesitated.

"Penny's the most dependable horse on the place." When she still seemed dubious, he added, "Trust me. I'm

your bodyguard, remember? It's my job to keep you safe."
He was rewarded with another smile, this one even sunnier.

"Well, if you say so." With a quick motion, she pulled
her long hair into a high ponytail secured by a tortoiseshell
barrette. A few blond wisps swirled softly at her nape and
around her pretty face, a face that glowed with a generous
mix of excitement and fear. As she bent to slip through the
rails, Cole couldn't help noticing how her blue jeans fit her
curves. Somehow, she even managed to make the baggy,
one-size-fits-all Telluride sweatshirt she wore look good.

"Okay." Taking a deep breath, she shoved her sleeves up
to the elbows and muttered uncertainly, "Here goes nothing."

"Penny, meet Anne," he said.

As she reached out a tentative hand to meet the mare's
inquiring nose, Anne's face reflected her trepidation.

"That's right. Go ahead. Touch her. She loves to be babied. Talk to her and let her get used to the sound of your
voice. I promise, she's user friendly."

As she cautiously stroked the mare's neck, she murmured, "Okay, Penny. Just remember, I'm new at this."

Half an hour later, Anne was guiding Penny around the
small, enclosed training ring with what appeared to be
growing confidence. "This is wonderful," she exclaimed.
"But when do I get to try the real thing?"

Cole had positioned himself in the center of the ring,
where he could get to her quickly if she needed him. "What
do you mean? This is the real thing—Penny's a real horse,
and you're a real rider." As a matter of fact, a very balanced rider, with much more poise and athleticism than
most beginners possessed.

"But when do I get to go out there?" She motioned to
the grassy carpet that led to the hills that ringed the
meadow.

"Not today," Cole said, shaking his head. "Controlling
a horse, even one as dependable and even-tempered as
Penny, within the confines of a training ring is a far cry
from maintaining your seat on the diverse terrain."

"Come on, Cole," she pleaded. "You said yourself I was a quick study. Penny will take care of me, won't you, girl?" When she leaned forward to stroke the mare's neck, she dropped the reins. He read the panic on her face when she grabbed for them and lost her balance. When she lurched forward, Penny broke into a choppy trot, throwing Anne sideways in the saddle.

Cole's response was automatic. "Whoa!" he shouted, running up alongside Penny. The mare obeyed immediately, but not before she stumbled on the dragging length of leather. When the horse stumbled, Anne rocked back in the saddle with a gasp, and before either of them knew what was happening, Cole had hauled her out of the saddle.

"Damn it, Anne, don't ever let go of your reins like that."

"Let go of me!"

He released her immediately, stunned to see the strange expression on her face.

"Don't ever grab me like that again," she warned, her cheeks flushed red and her breath coming in short gasps.

Her outburst shocked him, but before he could form the words of an apology or attempt to explain how many accidents he'd seen due to a horse stumbling on a dangling rein, she'd turned on her heel and stalked out of the ring. For a second, all he could do was stand speechless and watch her go.

By the time he called, "Wait a minute, Anne," he had to shout for her to hear him. "Wait," he called again, hurrying to catch up to her. "Wait just a damn minute, will you?"

She ignored him. He caught up to her just as she reached to open the gate into the yard. When he clamped his hand on top of hers, preventing her from leaving, she pulled her hand back as though his touch had shocked her.

"Listen, I'm sorry, okay? I overreacted when I thought you were falling. I didn't mean to frighten you."

"You didn't." Taking a deep breath, she turned around to face him. "I'm sorry, Cole. I'm the one who's overreacting. But if you don't mind, I think I'd like to call it a day." Her tone was icy and distant.

"It's my fault. I should have tied the reins before we even started," he said. "I should have known better."

"Forget it," she said. "It's all right." When he took a step closer, she winced and wrapped her arms around herself. The involuntary reaction, when coupled with her response to him grabbing her, triggered a flash of insight that made Cole seethe.

As an investigator and even as a cop, his experiences with domestic violence had been limited. He'd seen enough victims, however, to recognize the obvious signs—the wince, the retreat, the wariness. The immediate recoiling from anyone who posed a physical threat.

The stunning realization that Anne had been hurt in some way hit Cole with a surge of unimagined anger. All he could think about was getting his hands on the son of a bitch who'd hurt her. In all likelihood, it had been someone she'd trusted, maybe even loved.

"Thanks for the lesson," she said as she turned and pushed through the gate and started up the walk toward the house. He didn't try to stop her.

"I would never hurt you, Anne," he said to her back. "I only grabbed you because I thought you were falling."

She stopped but didn't turn around.

"Please don't go. If you're still interested, we could take a short trail ride. You were right. You did catch on quickly, and I'll be riding right next to you, just in case something unforeseen should happen."

She stood rooted for what seemed like several minutes before slowly turning around. Her eyes were wide and dry—the hurt Cole saw shimmering there went way beyond tears.

"I think I'd like that," she said. "If you're willing to give me another chance."

He was the one who needed that second chance, he thought. "Give me a minute to pack some food, and we'll make it a picnic."

She nodded and forced a smile. "Sounds good."

He moved with her across the porch, careful to keep a measure of distance between them. At the front door she stopped and looked at him, and for a long, cautious moment they stood face-to-face in silent communication before he said, "I meant what I said, Anne. I would never hurt you. You can trust me. I'm here to protect you." But with his arms suddenly aching to hold her and his heart begging to let her in, Cole couldn't help wondering which of them needed protecting more.

AN HOUR LATER, Anne guided Penny to where Cole's mount, a powerful black gelding named Shadrach, had stopped on a high, flat grassy knoll. "How's this?"

She turned in the saddle to gaze at the ridge where jagged and snowcapped peaks decorated the southwest horizon, creating a majestic backdrop that seemed close enough to touch. "I couldn't imagine a more perfect spot."

Cole swung out of the saddle, then held her reins while she dismounted.

"This has always been one of my favorite places," he said, handing her the basket he'd strapped behind his saddle.

"I've never seen anything more beautiful."

While she spread out the blanket Cole had tied behind her saddle, he unsaddled their horses and tied them with a long line of rope, which allowed them room to graze.

Anne unpacked the basket and smiled to herself as she set out the delicious assortment of foods he'd chosen—perfect slices of lean roast beef, fresh vegetables, homemade bread and cookies. Again, he'd surprised her. The hard-edged bodyguard and cowboy had shown more of his sensitive side by thinking to include honey-Dijon mustard and a butter knife.

When he dropped down on the blanket beside her, she became all too aware of his sexy presence, of the pleasantly male scent of him—soap and leather mingled with the earthy scent of horse. Busying herself with filling their plates, she stole a surreptitious glance at him and admitted to herself that the attraction she felt for him went beyond his good looks. The confidence he exuded assured her, and the athletic grace of his movements fascinated and intrigued her.

Even when relaxed, as he was now, half-reclining on the blanket beside her, he seemed to radiate power, a pure animal power, tempered with innate tenderness and the gift of genuine empathy. That potent combination of sensuality and sensitivity aroused in Anne an attraction stronger than anything she'd experienced before. It tightened around her heart and made it suddenly difficult to breathe normally.

He smiled when he caught her looking at him, and she handed him a sandwich to distract them both. Despite the appetite induced by their three-mile ride, Anne found herself more interested in their conversation than the food. For almost an hour they ate and talked. Their conversation ran the gamut from the trail they'd taken to the dispositions of the horses grazing contentedly nearby to the weather, which they agreed had turned cooler in the last few minutes.

"By the look of those clouds, we could get some snow tonight," he said.

For a fleeting moment, Anne toyed with the idea of being snowed in with Cole. The thought stirred a concoction of battling emotions that were instantly scattered by a cracking sound in the distance.

Before she could ask, he said, "Probably one of my neighbors target practicing. Hunting season opens soon."

She listened for another shot, and when none came, she said, "It should be against the law to disturb all this peace and quiet."

He poured hot tea from a thermos into two metal cups. "It is peaceful," he agreed. "But if you really listen, you'll realize it's anything but quiet."

It took a moment, but soon Anne understood what he meant. The gentle rustling of a breeze through gold-tinged aspen trees, the murmur of the nearby stream and the chatter of birds overhead created the score for the mountain's natural music. ''I see what you mean,'' she said.

He smiled, obviously pleased by her new appreciation of his world. She couldn't help wondering how much more of his world he'd share and hoping this was just the beginning.

LATER, WITH THE REMNANTS of their meal still spread around them, their conversation shifted into more personal areas. She'd found Cole Spencer intriguing from the start. But now, watching his expressions grow animated and almost boyish and listening to the affection in his voice when he described what it had been like growing up with his brothers on the Spencer ranch, she found him irresistibly endearing.

The clearer the picture he drew of his idyllic childhood, the more sharply Anne saw the contrast to her own experiences. And slowly, almost without realizing it, she began to reveal larger bits and pieces of her own past. Her childhood, her experiences as a foster child and what it had felt like to be caught up in a dismal cycle of unhappy foster homes and temporary relationships.

''It wasn't always grim,'' she told him. ''When I was a teenager, I was placed in the custody of a woman who eventually adopted me. She helped me take control of my life.'' *At least for a while,* Anne added to herself.

''Is she the reason you decided to work with troubled kids?'' Cole's gaze was intent, and Anne couldn't remember conversing with a more thoughtful, careful listener.

''Probably. Although at the time, I don't think I realized it. Max—'' she smiled ''—her name was Maxine and she pretended to hate that nickname when we used it.''

''We?''

''Oh, yes. I inherited quite a few temporary siblings during the four years I lived with Max.''

''That must have been tough.''

''It was. Figuring out where you belong in the world is a tough assignment for every young person. But Max taught me how to face the truths in my life, no matter how ugly or unpleasant. She taught me that as long as people keep running from what frightens them most, they're only pretending to live."

*No one can live your life for you, honey,* Max would always say. *People can make you feel pretty happy sometimes, and sometimes they can make you feel horrible. But your life, your real life, is the one you make for yourself. It's all up to you. Where you came from, the things you've done in the past, are only as important to who and what you are as you decide to make them.*

"Until Max came into my life, I carried my background like a giant chip on my shoulder, blaming it for everything."

"Your Max sounds a little like my dad," he said wistfully. "Taking responsibility for your life and then living with your choices was one of his favorite themes. Climbing back onto the horse that had thrown you was another." He laughed, but something in his voice hinted at a deep sadness.

"Max didn't let anything keep her down for long. Although I never saw her ride a horse, I have no doubt she'd have climbed back on no matter how many times she was thrown."

"Do you still see her?"

"No." What she wouldn't give just to have been able to say goodbye. "She died in an accident while she was driving to my college graduation ceremony." No single event before the murder of Stanley Lewellyn had affected Anne as deeply as the wreck Max didn't survive, the collision with the drunk driver that had taken her life.

It had been only three weeks after the funeral, while still deeply immersed in her grief, that Anne had relented to Gregg's pressure to marry him. Looking back, she realized that even as they stood exchanging vows, she'd been running from the pain of losing Max. In hindsight, the link between that loss and her abdication of her life to Gregg's obsessive need for control never seemed clearer.

Longing to shrug off the depressing thoughts of the past, she said, ''Anyway, I think Max would have approved of what I'm doing now.''

''Your job?''

''Yes. She'd approve of how I see something of myself at that age in each one of the kids I work with.''

''Sounds horrible.''

She laughed. ''Believe me, it can be pretty scary. You know, in a way I think it's easier to forgive others than to forgive ourselves, don't you?''

''But why would you need forgiving? You didn't make the mistakes that put you into that life-style and through all those difficult situations. Your parents were to blame, not you.''

''Yeah, that's what I used to tell myself. I blamed them every time I stole a tube of lipstick or lifted another wallet.''

Anne would always credit Frank with turning her life around when he'd taken her to Maxine Barbour's home that dismal Christmas Eve after she'd been picked up for shoplifting in a downtown department store. Because of Frank's personal intervention and Max's love, Anne had been given the kind of support necessary to turn her young life around. Under their influence, she'd attended college and ultimately chosen a career where she could use not only her education but her experience to try to make a difference in troubled kids' lives, just as Frank and Max had made such a big difference in hers.

When she'd landed the job at the county probation office, Frank had been her mentor and father confessor. When the system seemed creaky and inefficient, Frank had always been there to pull the strings and grease the wheels. When he wasn't instructing, Frank was sharing his well-tested techniques for negotiating the bureaucratic haze, which too often descended over the juvenile justice system.

After relating all this to Cole, Anne said, "Between Max and Frank, I learned I had choices, no matter how insignificant it might seem at the moment."

He grew quiet for a bit before he said, "You were married once." It wasn't a question.

She nodded. "Right out of college." For some reason the defenses that normally kicked in at this point in any conversation were absent. "I met him in my last year at CU. He'd finished his M.A. in business a year earlier."

"You were young."

"Too young." She sighed, remembering how overwhelmed and flattered she'd been to think that someone as competent and successful as Gregg would really want to marry her—*her,* the kid with no real home or family, from the wrong side of the tracks. "But being young wasn't our only problem. Most of those came from me thinking that the woman Gregg had married was a fraud and that one day I'd slip and reveal my true self, the shoplifting delinquent who, but for luck and a couple of incredible adults, would still be pilfering makeup from the local drugstore." She smiled, but Cole's expression was one of intense solemnity.

"I'd convinced myself that someday Gregg would discover the mistake he'd made marrying me." Trying to explain to Cole how she'd felt, she realized that she was finally putting into words feelings she'd never discussed with anyone.

More amazing, she felt herself longing to tell him even more, to pour the rest of her heart out. Even as she tried to figure out why, she kept talking.

As she opened her heart to him, she remembered thinking that she'd never be able to trust anyone again—especially a man. But here she was confiding in Cole, a man who, in so many ways, was still a virtual stranger.

"In the end," she said finally, "I guess it came down to a matter of survival. My pride was long gone, but somehow I knew if I could just find the strength to walk away, I might find it again." She swallowed hard. "When I left him for the last time, it was in the middle of the night, with nothing but the clothes on my back and a few dollars in my pocket." That night, something inside her had clicked, a door had closed even as another one opened.

After a bitter argument, Gregg had launched into one of his tirades. "Nothing physical," she told him. *At least not that time,* she added to herself. "But his verbal abuse could be nearly as devastating. It all started over a dress." A dumb dress that, ironically, he'd convinced her to buy for a dinner engagement with one of his clients. "A lousy dress. I remember he asked me to model it for him and when I did, he went into a rage, accusing me of all kinds of things—of buying the dress to attract the advances of his client, a man I'd never even met before." She could still see that dress lying in shreds on the bedroom floor. "Anyway, when it was all over, Gregg fell into one of those exhausted sleeps that always followed his tirades. I just sat there beside the bed. I didn't realize it at the time, but I was waiting to be sure he wouldn't wake up. Then, I simply got up, opened the front door and started walking. Before I knew it, I was on a bus headed east."

Three hundred miles and a couple of days later, she'd walked into a women's shelter, numbed, cold, broke and alone, and yet feeling stronger than she had in years.

"I stayed at the shelter for about a month and then one day, I felt strong enough to leave. I filed for divorce the same day."

"Why did you decide, after all that time, to finally leave him?"

"I don't know," she said. "It just happened. That night I guess I must have decided it was time to get on with the life I was meant to live. I hated running, but somehow I knew that when I had enough strength, I would come back. And I did. I came back to Denver to reclaim my life, or at least what was left of it."

He looked in her eyes, and she felt a stirring kinship. Cole obviously knew what it was like to run, to be ready and willing to give up anything and everything to be free of the pain. When would he be coming back? she wondered.

For a few minutes they sat in silence, both absorbed in their own ruminations. Anne felt oddly relieved, unburdened, exactly the opposite reaction she'd supposed she might have experienced after confiding to anyone the most disturbing events of her life.

As for Cole, she couldn't guess what he was thinking. Was he remembering Meredith Hackett? Still missing her, maybe?

"I heard from Drew this morning," he said, startling her to their present reality with an almost physical jolt. "And I've decided to go back to Denver tomorrow. I believe I can help with this case, but I need to be there, working with them as leads develop."

Anne could hardly believe her ears. "Oh, Cole, that's exactly how I've been feeling! I just know that if I'm there, working with them, helping to sort out leads, I believe the chances of finding the murderer will be greatly increased. But why do we have to wait until tomorrow? Let's head back tonight. We can take turns driving—"

He reached for her hand and closed his fingers around it. "Whoa, hold on a minute. You can't go back to Denver, surely you know that."

She jerked her hand away from his. "I don't know any such thing. Look," she began again in a more conciliatory tone, "I'll even wear that stupid outfit and cap if it makes you feel better."

He didn't return her smile.

"Oh, come on, Cole. Those tapes were a joke. With all the background noise, I could hardly tell what was being said, much less recognize anyone's voice. Maybe Nyguen can set up a situation where I can listen to the officers he suspects without them knowing, like a lineup, you know?" When he didn't respond, she pressed him harder. "Besides, with you and Drew and Nyguen looking after me, what can happen?"

He looked past her, his mouth set in a hard line. "Tomorrow morning I'm putting you on a plane to Phoenix. You'll be safe with Bess. When this is all over, I'll come down and get you myself."

For a moment, all she could do was stare at him in stunned silence before she got to her feet and stood over him with her arms wrapped around herself to quell the anger that made her tremble. "Have you heard one word I've said in the past hour?"

In one fluid motion he was standing in front of her. His dark eyes bored into her intently. "This is different."

"Oh, really? And just how is this so different? Explain to me the difference between you giving me orders and running roughshod over my life and what Gregg tried to do?"

"I can't let you go back to Denver, surely you can see—" His sentence was cut short by an explosion of bark from the pine tree directly behind them. A cracking sound splintered the calm again, and Anne realized someone was shooting at them.

With speed that left her gasping, Cole grabbed her hand and dragged her into the shadowy shelter of a stand of small aspen trees. When he dropped to the ground, he took her with him.

"Stay down," he ordered, his arm pinning her to his side and his body half covering hers. Another crack and shattered branches rained down on their heads. Two more quick shots and then silence for what seemed like an eternity.

Anne strained to hear any sound and stared into the distance until her eyes ached. But the only noise, other than the drumming of own heart, was the rustling of the leaves, stirred by the air that was steadily becoming cooler.

"Cole...those shots. They were aimed at us, weren't they? That wasn't your neighbor sighting his gun or target practicing, was it?"

The grim set of his full mouth and the dark worry in his eyes gave her his answer. And like it or not, Anne knew her stay at the Spencer ranch had just come to an end.

By the time they reached the barn and unsaddled and fed the horses, the sun had set and the afternoon breeze had turned to a cold evening wind. A freezing drizzle, which drove a chill through even the warmest layers, was turning quickly to snow.

They'd ridden to the house through the trees instead of retracing their path across the open meadow. Even in her shaken state, Anne had realized that the path they'd taken, while more rugged and longer, provided lifesaving cover from the gunman.

Even with Cole riding beside her only an arm's length away, Anne had felt more afraid and vulnerable with each step. They'd ridden in taut silence through the woods, with every sound spooking her, causing her to wonder if her next breath would be her last.

Finally, inside the warm, musky-smelling barn, Anne began to feel less afraid.

"Do you think he followed us?" she asked Cole as he set their saddles on wooden frames in the tack room.

"I don't really think so. If he had a scope on that rifle, which I suspect he did, he could have picked us off anytime as we rode back."

"Then you're saying he shouldn't have missed the first time."

"We were open targets."

A chill traced the length of her spine. "Then why?"

"It could have been a warning. It's almost as though whoever fired those shots wants you to know he can find you no matter where you hide."

"But why didn't he just . . ."

"Just kill us?" Cole finished the question she couldn't bring herself to voice.

She nodded, clenching her teeth to keep them from chattering.

"He's already killed once. Lewellyn's murder was intended. At this point, I don't think anyone believes otherwise. His death was planned and executed by someone with a strong motive, I suspect. The murderer, or murderers, as the case may be, left little or no evidence, except for a body and a bullet fired from a garden-variety handgun that could have been found at any pawn shop. You were the only variable that night. Killing you would lead to even more complications. If he can, maybe he'd rather frighten you into silence. Maybe he figures it's worth a try."

A surge of anger, as bright and hot as any flame, flared to life inside her. "Well, he can't frighten me off. I won't let him intimidate me, Cole. I can't. I'm going back to Denver, and if I have to sit in Nyguen's office twenty-four hours a day, listening to every voice on the force, then I will." She'd stopped being a victim years ago. "I want my life back, Cole. *I'm not running anymore.*"

By they time they emerged from the barn, snow was falling in large, heavy flakes. Hurrying toward the house in the cold, wet darkness, Anne couldn't shake the feeling of eyes on her back.

Once inside, Cole shrugged out of his jacket and walked straight to the large stone fireplace at the end of the room and began to build a raging fire. In a few minutes, reassuring flames danced in the hearth. Anne stood before the flames willing the heat to penetrate to the deep inner chill that she was beginning to think might become permanent.

She stayed by the fire when Cole left the room, and when he came back with a mug of hot chocolate, she said, "I think we need to talk."

"Go ahead," he said flatly, taking his hot chocolate with him to the couch.

"I meant what I said earlier. I'm going back to Denver to try to help the police identify whoever was in Stan's office that night." The thought of the explosion in her apartment and the shots on the mountain still terrified her. But the thought of allowing someone to continue terrorizing her, forcing her to sit in the dark shaking with fear, never knowing if or when the next strike would occur, seemed an even more dreadful fate. "I know you probably won't understand this, but, as of now, I want you to accept my release of the Spencer Agency from any obligation to protect me. You tried, but it didn't work out. Obviously, the leak in the department is much more serious than any of us realized. For all we know, Nyguen's closest aide could be implicated. How else could the individual who shot at us today have tracked me this far?"

His eyes bored into her, and she couldn't help shifting her gaze to fire, away from the flame raging in his eyes. No doubt she'd stung his ego. Well, so be it. If the past had taught her anything, it had taught her to trust herself, her own instincts first, and worry about male egos later.

"Fine," he said quietly.

"If you'd like, I'll sign something. And when we get to Denver, I'll explain to your brother, to Nyguen..."

The only sound in the room was the snapping and hissing of the logs as the hungry flames devoured them. Finally he said, "How long will it take you to gather your things?"

Startled by his odd request, she stared at him. "Tonight? We're leaving tonight?"

"We'll start out as soon as you're ready."

"But I thought..."

He didn't look at her but just sat staring into the fire. "Look, they've found you, okay? As of now, you're no safer here with me than you would be in Denver. The best we can hope for is that whoever took that potshot on the mountain will draw the same conclusion you did, that we'll be staying here tonight. Leave the lights on in the bedroom when you come down."

He rose and walked to the fireplace, leaning on the mantel as he gazed down into the fire.

Anne felt the trembling beginning again as soon as she headed for the stairs. At the landing, she turned to see him still standing by the fire. "Cole, please try to understand. I just can't sit by any longer and let someone steal another moment of my life."

"No, I don't suppose you can," he said without turning around, careful not to disturb the wall he'd build between them. "Pack your things, Anne," he said quietly. "I'll do whatever I can to get you safely back to Denver. Once we're there, if you decide you want or need a bodyguard, Drew can recommend someone."

A lump formed in her throat and refused to be dispelled or swallowed. It had never occurred to her that they wouldn't be together in Denver, that he wouldn't be working with her to help Drew and Nyguen solve the case. "So you're quitting?" she asked, her voice sounding as clogged with emotion as it was.

"I believe I was just fired," he said simply.

"But—"

"But what, Anne?" When he finally turned to face her, the reflection of the fire in his eyes glittered like a thousand angry diamonds. "You can't have it both ways. Did you think my bringing you up here was a game? Or maybe you think the world is filled with only those good guys you referred to the day we met?"

Without thinking she'd moved back into the room. "Why are you acting as though all of this is my fault?"

"Well?"

She clamped her hands into fists at her side, fighting to control her temper. "What the hell are you implying, Cole?"

"How many people know where you are, Anne? Two? Four? Your secretary, maybe? How about Zach, that model of rehabilitation and loyalty? Did you think you were so damn indispensable that they couldn't live without you long enough to save your own life?"

The wave of anger that crashed into her left her knees weak.

"How about it, Anne? Who did you tell?"

"No one, damn you!" she blurted. "No one at all!"

Neither of them spoke for a moment. "Aw, hell," he grumbled. "It doesn't make any difference now." He headed for his office. "Maybe it's all for the best anyway. Now, get your things together, Anne. We'll leave as soon as you're ready."

She could only stand and watch him go. Shocked, angry and alone. When he disappeared into his office and closed the door, it felt to Anne as though he'd shut her out of his life forever.

# Chapter Ten

Cole quickly gathered his gear for the trip to Denver. As he packed, his thoughts were back on the mountain, on what might have happened, on how he would have lived with himself if the sniper had hit his target.

Absorbed by that grim thought, he grabbed an assortment of shirts and jeans without thinking and shoved them into his bag, tucking a thirty-eight and an extra box of cartridges beneath his socks.

The rifle he kept under the seat in his pickup was loaded, and a small revolver he used when he couldn't carry a larger weapon was tucked inside the glove box. He had no intention of being caught unaware and unarmed, the way he'd been this afternoon. From now until the police had a suspect behind bars, he intended to be fully prepared for the worst.

Reminding himself to grab a couple of blankets from the closet on his way out, he zipped the bag closed and opened the door to see her standing there, her hand raised to knock.

"I'm ready," she said quietly, her fist uncurling as it dropped to her side.

He couldn't help but stare at her. Even dressed in the ridiculously oversize denim jeans and shirt he'd forced her to wear the night they'd left Denver, she was still so damned pretty he almost couldn't resist touching her. "Let's go."

He followed her down the stairs, fighting to keep his eyes off her sexy backside and his mind off his longing for her. Right now, all he could allow himself to think about was getting her to Denver safely before the predator who'd tracked her to the mountain this afternoon found another opportunity. Just the thought of anyone hurting Anne caused his overworked senses to tighten another notch.

It would be almost impossible for him to walk away from her, although common sense told him that removing himself from her life was the only way to clear the perspective he'd allowed to become blurred by his feelings for her.

The almost deadly mistake on the mountain had been all his fault. Protecting her should have been his only concern. In a way, he'd been waiting for something like this to happen since that first day, when Anne showed him how independent she was. That she had no intention of following anyone's rules. It was bound to happen that she'd inadvertently reveal her location to someone close to her. Why, then, if he'd been prepared for this eventuality, did he feel strangely betrayed?

He didn't know. All he knew for sure was that getting her to Denver and finding someone else to protect her had become top priority. Although he would no longer be her bodyguard, he had every intention of staying with the case. When he wasn't working with Nyguen and Drew, he'd be guarding Anne from the shadows. He figured he owed her that much for putting her life at risk today. But he owed her for something more, as well, for something she'd said today about running.

He had no way of knowing what Anne knew, or thought she knew, about his involvement with Meredith Hackett. The things she'd said this afternoon, those things she'd confided about her past, had forced him to look at his own life and admit to himself that he'd been running from the moment of Meredith's death. Now, thanks to Anne, Cole saw himself for what he really was, a man running from the past, unwilling to confront the ghosts that kept him from living the life he'd once loved.

COLE HAD NEGOTIATED the ranch road in all kinds of weather. So familiar to him was the five-mile stretch of dirt and gravel that most of time he drove it without thinking. On a night like tonight, however, with wind-driven snow obliterating all but the most immediate visibility, every inch of the familiar ranch road became a malevolent stranger, demanding his full attention.

Because his pickup had four-wheel drive, traction wasn't a problem on the back roads. The two-lane highway, however, would be another story, Cole thought. That ice-glazed blacktop would be an equal-opportunity hazard to any vehicle tonight.

He began a mental tallying of the restaurants and motels in the Ridgeway area where he and Anne might be forced to spend, if not the entire night, at least a good part of it, waiting out the storm.

"Did you see that?" she asked, jerking around in her seat so abruptly, he hit the brakes without meaning to.

"What?" he asked, after his heart returned to its normal rate and the pickup stopped skidding.

"I thought I saw something—a light—behind us."

He pushed lightly on the accelerator, but kept his speed slow as he peered harder into the rearview mirror. Seeing nothing but swirling white, he said, "It was probably just a reflection of our taillights off the snow."

"Maybe," she replied, but she seemed unconvinced.

"I don't know what you could have seen. No one uses this road except to travel to and from the ranch."

She acknowledged what he said with a vague nod, but continued to stare out the window behind them, anyway. After a while she said, "I guess you're right. The snow does have a way of distorting things."

The snow pelting the windshield in driving streams of white created an almost hypnotic effect that Cole had to fight to resist. Gripping the wheel with both hands, he pushed the truck deeper into the storm.

Without warning, the truck's engine sputtered.

"What's wrong?"

He didn't have time to answer before the engine cut out again, this time for more than just a hiccup. They exchanged glances when the engine died completely.

Shifting into neutral, Cole turned the key. The engine shimmied to life, only to quickly die again. As the truck rolled to a stop, Cole reached under the seat for the long utility flashlight he always kept there for emergencies.

Anne offered him a sympathetic smile when he pulled the lever to pop the hood, settled his hat firmly on his head and clambered out into the storm.

A cold, angry wind buffeted him as he peered beneath the hood. Juggling the flashlight in one hand and a screwdriver in the other, he leaned closer to get a better look at the battery cables.

"Let me hold the light." She startled him, and he almost banged his head on the hood. He hadn't heard her get out of the truck, and he wouldn't have heard her words over the howling wind if she hadn't shouted. His first instinct was to order her back inside the cab, but she was already reaching for the flashlight.

By the light of the beam she directed onto the battery, Cole inspected the battery cables and gave them each a tug. "I thought maybe one of them might have been jarred loose when we hit that rut a while back," he yelled. "But everything looks fine." He tightened each cable connector anyway, just to be sure. "The keys are in the ignition. Give it a try, will you?"

She nodded and handed him the flashlight.

Once, twice, three times she turned the key, to no avail. On the fourth try, Cole heard the familiar warning tick tick tick, and hurried over to the driver's side and tapped on the window. "It's no use," he said when she rolled the window down. "We'll ruin the starter if we keep at it. Shut off the headlights and turn on the hazards. The cold is hard enough on the battery, we don't want to drain it any further."

He jogged around to the passenger side and climbed in, rubbing his hands together to warm them. Snow clung to his lashes and brows and dripped down his back where it melted and ran off the back brim of his hat.

"What now?" she asked.

"It's a good two miles to the highway."

She frowned. "Which means it's a good three miles back to the house."

"Right." With the engine dead, the heater was rendered useless, and the inside of the cab was cooling off fast. "As I see it, we have a couple of choices."

"I'm all ears." She shivered. "Frozen ears, I might add."

"Cold ears I can fix," he said. He reached into his duffel bag, pulled out a hooded sweatshirt and handed it to her.

"Thanks."

"There's a shack about a half a mile south of here," he said as she pulled the sweatshirt over her head. "It's an old line shack, but we let the local scout troop fix it up and use it as a base camp when they have their jamborees."

She tied the hood under her chin. "I only have one question. Does this hunting shack have a heating system?"

"It doesn't have a furnace, if that's what you mean. And on a night like this, there's liable to be an inch or two of snow blowing in between the cracks in the logs. But it does have a small fireplace and potbellied stove. The scouts always leave a good supply of firewood inside."

She rubbed a circle on the frosty pane and stared out into the storm. "You said something about a choice?"

"We can stay here and hope the storm subsides before we freeze to death."

She wrapped her arms around herself and worked up a smile. "The accommodation with the wood stove gets my vote," she said and pulled on the men's work gloves he dug out from under the seat and handed to her.

In light of the things she'd shared with him this afternoon, her decision to take action, rather than sit and wait for conditions to improve didn't surprise Cole.

"A half mile can seem pretty far in weather like this," he warned.

"I can make it," she assured him. "Besides, we don't really have an alternative."

"I packed some blankets. We can stay here for a while longer to see if the weather breaks."

"What would you do if I wasn't here?"

"I'd probably walk back to the house," he admitted. "But I'm wearing boots. Those canvas shoes you're wearing rule out that option."

"Sorry."

"Don't be. I should have tried to find you a pair of boots before we left the house."

"I'll be fine."

Before leaving the shelter of the pickup, Cole used plastic bags to fashion crude overshoes around Anne's sneakers. He also helped her tie one of the blankets around her shoulders before they headed out.

"One more thing," he said, handing her a length of nylon cord. "Tie this around your waist."

Her eyes grew wide as he secured the other end of the rope around his own waist.

"Is this really necessary?"

"I don't want to lose track of you," he explained. "In this kind of blizzard, it's easy to become disoriented. After all, until we get back to Denver, I'm still your bodyguard, remember?"

Her smile was feeble. "How could I forget?"

Despite her bravado, Cole read the concern in her eyes. "We'll make it," he promised. "Before you know it, you'll be sitting in front of a fire."

"I'll try to keep that thought."

Without thinking, he put his arms around her and kissed her. Her lips were warm and welcoming, but her cheeks and nose were cold, reminding him that he had no time to lose getting her to shelter. Lifting his mouth quickly from hers, he said, "Ready?"

She only nodded, probably as surprised as he'd been by their kiss. When they were standing on the side of the road with the storm howling, she found her voice. "Are you sure you know where you're going?"

It was a good question. One he'd already asked himself. "Sure," he said, shouting to be heard over the wind. If he'd guessed right, they'd be sitting in front of a cozy fire in just a few minutes. On the other hand, if he'd guessed wrong… "Let's go," he said, to keep from finishing that grim thought.

"Lead the way," she said, pulling the fleecy hood tighter around her face and hugging the blanket around her shoulders. "I'll be right behind you, cowboy."

IF ANNE HAD EVER BEEN colder or more miserable, she had no memory of it. The wind, frigid and unrelenting, stole her breath and seemed to beat her back one step for every two she took forward. Thanks to the blanket Cole had tied around her before they'd started out, her upper body stayed remarkably warm and dry. Her feet, however, were so cold they were quickly growing numb. Despite the makeshift overshoes Cole had fashioned for her, snow had saturated her shoes. An inner voice told her to keep moving, to keep wiggling her toes.

The going was rough, down over the side of the steep embankment and across what seemed like an endless stretch of swirling, blinding snow. Where it had gathered in drifts, it seemed to suck and pull her down. But each time she stumbled, Cole seemed to be there to catch her before she fell.

"Just a little farther," he shouted over the wind. "We're almost there." He took her hand, and amazingly, even through the bulky gloves, Anne felt his reassurance. Holding tight to his hand and his promises, Anne allowed herself to be led blindly through the storm. After several more long minutes of incredible effort, Anne's legs started to shake, and the muscles in her calves and thighs began to burn. Until tonight she'd always considered herself in fairly good shape. The blizzard, however, taxed all her energy, all her strength.

How could Cole hope to find the cabin in these conditions? It seemed as though they'd been walking for hours. What if they'd passed it already? What if they couldn't find their way back to the road? The defeating thoughts that swirled through her mind with every step seemed almost as nefarious as the storm. "How much farther?" she asked, choking back a wave of near hysteria.

"We're almost there. Just a little farther."

She held tight to his hand and put her head down, trying without success to dodge the pellets of icy snow that stung her face. When she looked up again, the storm's white fury seemed to overwhelm her, and she stumbled and fell.

Cole sank down in the snow beside her. "Are you hurt?"

"I—I don't know . . . my knee," she said, teeth chattering. "I hit my knee on something."

After he helped her to her feet, he put his arm around her waist and urged her to lean on him. "Come on. The cabin's just over there. See?" His breath against her cheek felt warm.

Anne peered through the white and felt her heart leap at the sight of the small log structure straight ahead and just a few feet away. With Cole helping her, she limped up to the door, and he untied the rope connecting them.

A small covered porch protected them at the doorway, offering at least partial relief from the pummeling wind. Anne sagged against the door while Cole searched the ledge above it.

"Damn it!" he shouted.

"What's wrong?"

"It's gone. The spare key we keep for the scouts. They must have forgotten to put it back the last time they were here."

"Maybe it's open," she said even as she reached for the door and turned the knob. A whoop of delight accompanied her success, and a rush of warm air and the earthy smell of wood smoke welcome them, even as it triggered a question in Anne's mind.

But before she could ask, a figure stepped out of the shadows and instantly raised a dozen more.


DREW DIALED the number the information operator had given him and waited through five long rings before he heard the familiar Irish brogue on the other end of the line. When Seth said hello, Drew nodded for Nyguen to pick up the cordless phone he'd carried in with him from Francine's desk.

"Seth, it's Drew Spencer. I'm sorry if I woke you."

"No problem, Drew," Seth replied. "What can I do for you?" Seth had worked for the Spencers for more than ten years, yet the brogue he'd brought with him from Dublin hadn't seemed to fade.

After explaining that he was trying to reach Cole, Drew asked, "Did you see my brother this evening before you headed home?"

"No, sir," Seth replied. "I left the ranch just after five, as is my habit, but your brother and the young woman, Miss Osborne, hadn't come back from their trail ride." Seth told him Cole and Anne had left the barn before noon.

"Did they say where they were going? When they planned to come back?"

"No, sir," Seth replied. "But they took a picnic basket, and before he left, your brother said he'd see me tomorrow and then asked me to take care of the evening chores before I left." Seth went on to suggest that Drew was worrying needlessly, if he was concerned about Cole still being out on the mountain. "I know few men more capable on horseback than your brother. And that Miss Osborne seemed to be getting along just fine with Penny."

The hired man was right. There wasn't anything Seth could tell Drew that he didn't already know about his brother's ability to take care of himself on horseback—or on foot, for that matter. Under normal circumstances, Drew wouldn't have wasted a moment's concern about his brother's excursions, much less resort to calling Seth in the middle of the night. But this was no ordinary circumstance, he reminded himself.

Drew was thinking aloud when he commented that Cole would never plan an overnight trip in the mountains without checking the weather forecast first.

"This storm's a real doozie," Seth said. "According to the weatherman on the television, it was supposed to swing south of us, but the wind changed and she snuck up on us and hit when we weren't looking."

Nyguen sank down on the leather couch, holding the phone between his shoulder and his cheek.

"Cole had been watching the sky all morning," Seth said. "Before he took off this afternoon, we'd talked about bringing the mares into the barn for the night, just in case. Pete and I did just that before we left, and it's a good thing we did. It looks like this storm will go on all night."

Nyguen yawned and Drew slumped down in his chair, the effects of this long night beginning to take a toll.

"I tried calling Cole myself a little earlier," Seth volunteered, "to tell him about a mare with a swollen leg. But I also wanted to tell him about the officer who came to the ranch looking for him this afternoon. Maybe if you get hold of him, you could tell him about the mare for me?"

Seth couldn't have said anything that would have grabbed Drew's attention faster. He came to immediate attention in his chair, and Nyguen bolted to his feet. "An officer? Do you mean a policeman?"

The older man said that's exactly what he'd meant. "Seth, are you telling me a policeman came to the ranch looking for Cole?"

"Well, he claimed to be a policeman, but he didn't look like any cop I'd ever seen before."

"But he told you he was?"

"Yes, sir, he did. But I didn't exactly believe him, not with him dressed like he was in that suit and tie. And he was a big man, with a belly almost too big for his belt."

"Did he say why he was looking for my brother?"

"He wouldn't say, and he all but called me a liar when I told him I didn't know where Cole was or when he'd be back." Seth was as easygoing as an old house cat, but Drew had seen him with his back up a time or two, especially when his Irish pride was wounded or he felt slighted or insulted.

"So what *did* he tell you?"

"Not much. He was too full of his own questions to answer any of mine."

"What questions? What did he ask you, Seth?"

"Like I said, he wanted to know where Cole was, and did I know if he was still an investigator, and had we had any out-of-town visitors lately."

Drew felt the muscles in his neck and shoulders tensing. "What did you tell him, Seth?"

The Irishman's laugh turned into an indignant snort. "Well, sir, seeing as how the man wouldn't give me more than a last name, I didn't feel obliged to give him the time of day."

*Good old Seth.* Ten years on the ranch had convinced him and everyone else that he was part of the Spencer clan. "You say he gave you his name. What was it, Seth? Do you remember?"

"Hannigan," Seth said. "But he didn't have a badge that I saw. Said he was from Denver, and that he was here to help Cole."

Nyguen shook his head and shrugged in reply to Drew's questioning glance.

When Drew asked him, Seth tried to give a description of the cop and also a description of his car. "Like I said before, he was a big man. What hair he had left was gray, and he had the nose of a man who enjoys a pint on a regular basis."

Drew could see Nyguen's mental wheels churning.

"The car was a rental," Seth continued. "That much I'm pretty sure of. You know, we see a lot of them around town these days. It was a big car. One of those big Fords, I think. A four-door, it was. Dark blue, and brand, spanking new."

After jotting down the word Ford, Drew said, "All right, Seth, I'll let you go back to bed. Sorry again for disturbing you at this hour. When you see my brother, ask him to call me, would you?"

"I'll tell him," the older man promised. "Though I wouldn't figure on him returning that call any time soon, if I were you." Seth reminded Drew that the last time a major storm had hit the area, the phone at the ranch house had been out of service for a week.

"Pete and I will start clearing the ranch road at first light, but it will take some time to make it to the house. I put the blade on my Jeep tonight, but we might need to borrow something bigger to get the job done. There's easily two feet of snow already on the ground, and so far it shows no sign of stopping."

Drew thanked Seth again and hung up.

"You know anyone by that name, Russell?"

Nyguen shook his head. "Hannigan. Not off the top of my head. But I'll drop by my office on the way home and pull up personnel listings." He stopped pacing long enough to ask, "If Cole and Anne didn't make it back to the ranch before the storm hit, what are their chances for survival?"

Drew leaned forward in his chair and steepled his hands in front of him on the desk. "They'll make it," he said with more resolve than he felt. "My brother won't take chances with her safety, which means he wouldn't be out on a night like this without a good reason."

"Such as?"

"If he knows someone's located Anne, he's working on getting her out of there. Otherwise, he'll keep her on the ranch, snug and safe until this storm breaks. My guess is, the phone lines are down, and as soon as service is restored, we'll be hearing from him."

"So what do we do in the meantime?"

Drew slumped back in his chair and sighed. "Unfortunately, there isn't much we can do except wait to hear from them and try to find out who this Hannigan character is and what he's after." *And trust Cole's instincts,* he finished to himself.

"You know," Nyguen began, "if someone has managed to track Anne to your brother's ranch, we might just have our first real break."

"Yeah," Drew replied without enthusiasm. That break, as Nyguen put it, could be defined in various ways, depending on one's perspective. Cole certainly wouldn't see this as a stroke of luck. If Anne's safety had been compromised, Cole would more than likely come back to Denver to regroup. Unfortunately, that strategy might be just the move Stanley Lewellyn's murderer was waiting for.

Drew thought about what Nyguen had said, running all the facts through his mind over and over again. They'd been playing off each other for days, tearing at every scrap of information, desperate for a lead.

"Maybe this Hannigan, or whatever his name is, was just fishing, trying to confirm or deny his own hunch," Drew said. "Obviously, they've put Anne together with the agency, but if they really knew Cole was working the case, why would this Hannigan reveal himself, just step out into the open and question Seth that way?"

"Maybe the guy was someone trying to warn Cole. Maybe an old friend from Cole's days on the force. It could be someone on the inside, close to the murderer, but not fully implicated in the crime."

"A witness, or maybe a cop who knows too much about his buddy, maybe even his partner?"

"Could be. And it could be that, with the right bait, we can reel this guy in, make a deal with him and get him to play for our side."

"What kind of bait did you have in mind, Russell?"

Nyguen stopped pacing, but he didn't answer right away. He didn't have to. Drew knew exactly how Nyguen planned to reel his suspect in. The only question was how to break it to Cole, how to approach him with the news that Nyguen intended to use his client, the woman Cole had spent two weeks keeping out of harm's way, as bait to lure a murderer.

"I'll be waiting for your call," Nyguen said at the door.

"When I hear from Cole, you'll be the first to know."

After Nyguen left, Drew picked up the phone and dialed the ranch again. On the tenth ring, he hung up, sank back down in his chair and exhaled a worried sigh. He'd been the one who'd convinced Cole to take this case. He'd been so sure that the only way to reclaim his brother's confidence, to convince him to come back to the agency, was to present him with a case he couldn't refuse. He'd felt so sure of himself, convinced that what he was doing was the right thing for Cole and for their client.

Now, sitting alone in the middle of the night, with only his thoughts and a phony hip cast leaning against the wall in the corner, Drew Spencer wondered if he'd made a mistake. He wondered how he'd find a way to live with his mistake if anything happened to Anne Osborne or his brother.

# Chapter Eleven

A sickening thud announced the attack, which came without warning, without any chance to fight back. It happened so quickly. One minute they were relieved to be out of the storm, and the next, Cole was on the floor. Anne found herself being shoved viciously aside by whoever or whatever charged past them. Sitting with her legs sprawled where she'd landed on the floor, the back of her head aching from where it had made contact with the rough-hewn logs, she felt momentarily paralyzed, too shocked by what had just transpired to even move.

The sound of Cole's groans jerked her out of her stupor immediately. Instinct took over in a rush of adrenaline-charged action. *The door!* an urgent inner voice screamed. *Get to the door before he—it—comes back!*

Scrambling to her feet, Anne slammed the door closed and fumbled with the cold metal lock. With the storm suddenly shut out, the interior of the small, dark cabin seemed unnaturally quiet. Dropping down beside him, she cried, "Cole! Cole, can you hear me?" His skin felt icy when she touched his cheek, and she was immediately filled with the terrifying thought that she'd lost him. "Oh, Cole, please, please, wake up!"

Pushing aside the lock of unruly hair that had fallen across his forehead, she saw in the dim light from the fire a trickle of blood just above his right temple. Unbidden, the horrifying image of Stanley Lewellyn's lifeless body formed in her mind, and she had to bite her lip to keep from crying.

She tried again to rouse him, settling his head in her lap and stroking his hair. When his eyelids fluttered open, she almost dissolved into relieved tears. "Oh, thank God." Her heart pounded as she hovered over him. "Cole, it's me, Anne."

"Wh-what happened?"

"Someone hit you. Your head's bleeding. Just stay still." Easing his head off her lap, she rose and surveyed her surroundings for the first time, her eyes searching the dimly lit room for something to clean and bandage his wound. Her gaze stopped on the bed in the corner opposite the native rock fireplace. "Do you think you can walk, Cole?"

"Yeah. S-sure." His speech was slurred, and he was trying to sit up, without much success.

She bent beside him and put his arm around her shoulder to help him to a sitting position. "Come on. Let's get you up off this cold floor." She grabbed his right hand where it dangled around her shoulder. Sliding her other arm around his waist, she laced her fingers through the belt loop at the back of his jeans and said, "Okay, on the count of three."

When he nodded, the lock of dark hair fell across his forehead again. In a dreamy, half-drunk voice, he said, "If I could count to three, I could walk." A lopsided smile curved his lips. How chalky his face seemed in contrast to the inky blackness of his hair.

His solid weight pushed down on her, and for a minute she thought her knees would buckle. But somehow, between them, they managed to get him to his feet, where he stood for an uncertain moment, trying to regain his equilibrium.

"Great," she said breathlessly. "Now all we have to do is get you into the bed."

He looked down at her, his smile lazy and incredibly appealing. "That's the best idea I've heard all day." His attempt at humor, despite the grim reality of their situation, made her feel immeasurably better.

"Don't go getting any ideas, cowboy," she muttered as she struggled under his weight to help him across the room. "You're in no shape for those kind of games tonight."

His smiled faded. "Yeah, well, you can't blame a guy for trying."

With his arm around her shoulders effectively pinning her intimately against his hard, warm body, she felt herself responding to him despite their terrible predicament. *Get a grip,* she told herself. *Cole's the one with the lump on the head, and the only one who should be feeling giddy.*

The bed was made of pine, with a simple headboard and a single bare mattress. Anne eased his arm from behind her neck and helped him sit down with his back to the headboard. After quickly fashioning a pillow out of her jacket, she eased his head back. He winced, and a surge of sympathy washed through her. "Sorry."

"No problem," he said, his voice uncharacteristically thin. With a half smile, he attempted to prove to her that he was all right. His eyes, however, with their overly large pupils and glassy sheen, undermined his effort.

Anne had never been around anyone suffering from shock, but her instincts told her Cole was a prime candidate and that he needed to be kept warm. "Do you keep any blankets or bedding here?" she asked as she spread the blanket she'd worn as a coat over a straight-backed chair near the fireplace to dry.

Cole's eyes were closed, but he pointed to the large pine chest at the end of the bed. "Should be something in there," he muttered. He was shaking so hard, his teeth chattered.

Anne found two sleeping bags, rolled and stuffed into plastic bags and smelling faintly of mothballs. She unrolled the first one and eased it under him, then unzipped the other one and put it over him flannel side down.

"There should be some bandages . . . a first-aid kit in the kitchen." His whole body seemed to shiver down deeper into the bedding.

The word kitchen, Anne soon discovered, was an over-statement for the space designated by a wood-burning stove and a narrow countertop running the length of one wall. Above a deep, single sink, however, she opened a metal cupboard that held a surprising variety of supplies. "Well, at least we won't starve." A dozen or more cans of pork and beans, tuna fish and soup shared the shelf with a stack of metal plates and cups. A couple of saucepans and a large cast-iron skillet were stacked beside a smoke-blackened coffeepot. *Where there's a percolator, there has to be coffee,* she thought. If she could get a cup of strong coffee down her patient's throat, maybe the jolt of caffeine would help his body combat shock.

Upon further inspection of the kitchen, Anne found the first-aid kit in the only drawer, alongside a can opener, some mismatched silverware, battered utensils and a web of tangled fishing line.

When she went to the bed, she saw that Cole's eyes were still closed. Using the flashlight they'd brought with them, she examined his wound carefully, and to her relief discovered it wasn't as bad or as deep as she'd first thought. The bleeding had all but stopped.

He opened his eyes and fixed an intent gaze on her face as she swabbed the cut with iodine and covered it with gauze.

"You're very pretty, Anne Osborne." It took some doing to ignore the seductive note in his lazy speech. "I like it when you wear your hair down." When he reached out to toy with a long blond strand that had fallen over her shoulder, Anne had to work to concentrate on bandaging his head, to ignore glancing at his sexy, crooked smile. When his fingertips grazed her cheek she told herself that if he was suffering from a concussion, as she guessed he must be, he wouldn't remember a thing he'd done or said tonight. What harm could come of allowing him to flirt a little?

"How are you feeling?" she asked, standing over him after she'd secured the dressing with a couple of adhesive strips.

"Like I've been kicked by a mule."

"You were out cold for a few minutes."

"Probably a mild concussion," he muttered. "I'll be fine."

"It sounds like you speak from firsthand experience."

He smiled before his lids drifted closed again.

"Cole," she whispered. "I don't think you're supposed to sleep."

He opened his eyes. "Then we'll just have to think of something to keep me awake, won't we?"

She felt a rush of heat spreading across her cheeks and blessed the shadowy room that allowed her to hide her ridiculous reaction to his teasing. "I—I need to see to the fire."

Hurrying away from his bedside, she took her time gathering several logs from the stack beside the door. Thank goodness for the scouts, she thought as she placed several larger logs near the fire. Returning to the doorway, she spied a small, clublike piece of kindling and quickly surmised that it was probably the weapon their attacker had used to render Cole helpless. Angrily, she tossed it into the flames.

She found bottled water stored beneath the sink. She made coffee and set the pot on the grate above the fire. In a few minutes the fire was snapping enthusiastically, and the smell of percolating coffee wafted through the air. At last, she felt her limbs beginning to thaw. Even her feet were warmer. Shrugging out of the hooded sweatshirt, she tossed it on to one of the straight-backed chairs by the fireplace to dry. When she turned around and glanced at the bed, she saw that Cole was awake. He didn't see her watching him, nor did he notice that she saw him wince when he touched his head.

Remembering the bottle of aspirin she'd seen in the first-aid kit, she retrieved it and shook out three, then poured water into a metal cup and brought them to him. He accepted the cup and the pills without protest.

"I made some coffee. It should be ready in a few minutes."

He nodded his thanks and downed the pills. "What the hell happened, anyway? What hit me?"

"Not what, *who*," she corrected. "It all happened so fast, I'm not even that sure what happened. All I know is that one minute we were in the doorway, and the next thing I knew you were on the floor. Whoever it was couldn't get out of here fast enough. He ran me over getting out the door." She clasped her hands in front of her to keep them from shaking.

"We must have given him a hell of a scare, barging in like that from the storm," Cole said in a voice that, to Anne's mixed relief, seemed to have lost its half-drunken tone. "Did you get a look at him?"

"No. All I saw was a blur of black. I think he must have been wearing one of those ski caps that covered his face. He was big, I can tell you that much. And tall." Or maybe he'd just seemed that way, lunging out of the shadows the way he had. "Do *you* remember anything?"

He ran a hand through his hair and sighed. "Trust me, if I'd had the time to see him, I wouldn't be laying here nursing the world's biggest headache. All I remember is opening the door. And then the lights went out."

"I don't understand how he could have just happened upon this place. From the minute we left the road, my biggest fear was that you wouldn't be able to find the cabin in the storm."

"He either has incredible luck or he knew about the cabin before the storm hit."

"Could it have been someone you know?"

"I can't imagine any of my friends or neighbors reacting the way our mysterious guest did."

"How did he get in? The windows aren't broken, and when I locked the door, it seemed to be working fine." The only windows, two small panes centered on opposite walls, were without curtains. She let herself imagine what might be standing in the dark on the other side of the glass, and goose bumps sprang up on her arms.

"He used the key to get in, just like I was trying to do when you discovered the door was unlocked." He went on to explain how they left a spare key above the door in case the scout troop wanted to use the cabin or a hunter became lost in a storm and needed emergency shelter, much the way he and Anne had tonight. "Now that I think about it, leaving the key in such an obvious spot probably wasn't such a good idea."

"I can assure you, whoever hit you was no Boy Scout." She shivered when she glanced at the door and then to the black-eyed windows still staring ominously back at her. If Cole's attacker was still out there, he could be on the other side of that darkness even now, watching them.

As if he'd sensed her alarm, Cole said, "He's gone, Anne. And if he's dumb enough to come back, I promise you I won't be caught off guard again." He withdrew the handgun from his jacket pocket and laid it beside him on the bed. "Ever shoot one of these?"

"No. Until now, I guess I've never needed to."

"And with any luck you won't need to now. But just in case, you need to know the basics." She listened intently as he explained how to load and unload and how to release the safety. "The rest is pretty simple." He pointed the gun at the door. "Just pick your target and squeeze the trigger."

"For some reason, it doesn't seem all that simple to me."

"The hard part is knowing when to shoot." Once again it seemed he was speaking from experience, some dark experience that had left an indelible impression.

"Do you think it's possible that whoever hit you could be the same person who shot at us this afternoon?"

"I think it's a distinct possibility."

"But if it was the sniper, why did he run? Once he hit you, he could have killed us both if he'd wanted to. He certainly had the element of surprise on his side. Why run back out in the storm? He could have stayed, told us anything, made up any kind of lie about how he'd ended up in the cabin in the middle of the night. If he is Stanley's murderer and he's gone to all the trouble to track me to the ranch, why leave when he had his chance to finish what he started the night he destroyed my apartment?"

"I think it would be a mistake to assume that whoever shot at us this afternoon and Lewellyn's murderer are one and the same. The sniper might only be an accomplice, maybe the second man in the room."

"The other voice."

"Right. And if that's the case, the accomplice, although still afraid and desperate, isn't a murderer."

*Not yet, anyway,* she thought.

"Even though he's deeply implicated and facing the possibility of hard time, he isn't a murderer. But he still can't let you identify the murderer. From the killer, it's only a short step to him. Maybe he's thinking he still has options, and maybe one of those options is trying to frighten you."

It seemed a plausible explanation to Anne, and at least it offered some hope.

"Of course, there could be other reasons for him not wanting to hurt you, reasons maybe even more compelling than his own safety."

Until then, she'd followed his logic, but now he'd lost her. "I don't get it. What reason could there be for not wanting to eliminate the biggest threat to his freedom?"

"Did you ever consider that the murderer or his accomplice could be someone familiar to you?"

"What?" His simple supposition shocked her, and she rose and paced across the room. "You're not back to suspecting Zach, I hope."

He shook his head. "Of course not."

"Then who?"

"Sit down, Anne," he said. "Hear me out."

Reluctantly she sat on the edge of the bed after he'd scooted to a sitting position. "You and Stanley Lewellyn worked on the same floor of the County Annex building, right? But you weren't the only ones. For all we know, the killer could be a colleague, someone who knew you both. I know Nyguen and Drew have already begun to explore that possibility. It's a known fact that most murders are committed by acquaintances of the victims. Sometimes very close acquaintances.''

Even as he made the suggestion, Anne began to mentally construct a list of co-workers and associates in both departments. ''In Stan's case, that list would be huge... twenty, maybe even thirty people who were our mutual acquaintances, people who might have worked with one or both of us on occasion.'' She stopped short of taking the thought further, of allowing herself to seriously consider individuals by name.

Cole, however, seemed strangely energized by the course his conjecture and their conversation had taken. ''Lewellyn prosecuted adult criminal cases, right?''

''Yes.''

''But there were times you worked together, weren't there?''

''Sure, although that didn't happen often. When it did, it usually had to do with a decision about whether to charge a juvenile as an adult. In those cases, our offices worked very closely. Stan's office always needed our input, especially if the kid had a record, and even if he didn't, we're supposed to be the juvenile experts.''

''When was the last time that situation occurred?''

Anne had to think a minute before the answer came to her, and when it did, the implications it brought with it staggered her. ''Oh, my God,'' she gasped, bringing her hand up to cover her mouth.

''Anne? What is it? What's the matter?'' He sat up straighter and stared hard into her eyes. ''Tell me. What did you just figure out?''

''The case,'' she said, her voice barely audible over the beating of her heart. ''I remember now. It was Renfrow, Cole. The last time our departments worked together it was Renfrow!''

DROPPING his soiled apron into the hamper beside the back door, Zach called out, "I'm leaving, okay? The grill's clean and I mopped both bathrooms."

"Good night," came the preoccupied voice of the night manager from his office. "See you tomorrow, Zach."

Zach grabbed his jacket, pushed open the back door and stepped out into the night. His breath misted in front of him as he fumbled to unlock his bike. It wasn't the cold so much as the night that he minded. In this neighborhood, anything could happen to someone out alone at this hour. Even someone with his reputation, a guy who'd done some time in Mountainview and had been known to hold his own in a fair fight. But that was the problem. In this neighborhood, at this hour, chances were good the fight wouldn't be fair.

Telling himself to stop psyching himself out, Zach stood up on the pedals and forced the bike around the corner. The street was virtually empty at this hour—too early for the bar crowd and too late for most kids.

Just a couple more blocks, he told himself, thinking how good his narrow bed would feel tonight. He hoped the apartment was warm. If Karli was still up when he got home, he thought maybe he'd make them some hot chocolate and popcorn, if there was any.

The limo was the first thing he saw when he turned onto his street. From the day Paxton had forced him to deliver the message to Webster Renfrow, Zach had dreaded this moment. When the hundred dollar bill had mysteriously shown up in his mailbox, he knew Paxton would be back. If only he'd gotten to it first, maybe things would have been different. As it was, he'd had no choice. He wished he'd had a picture of Karli's face when she'd come charging up the stairs, waving that bill around. She'd looked so happy. Too bad he'd felt so dirty he couldn't help her celebrate.

He took a deep breath and brought his bike to a slow stop in front of his building. The pale light of a dome lamp inside the limo came on when Paxton climbed out.

"Hey, Zachy-boy. Working late, huh?" The big man was dressed in shiny black pants and a white shirt that showed above the collar of a long fur coat that almost reached his calves.

Zach nodded numbly, cold, scared and feeling utterly hopeless against this powerful street king.

"That's good. I like a kid who knows how to work, especially since I just so happen to have another little job for you."

To protest would have done Zach no good. He was in too deep. Even though he had no idea what was in the message he'd delivered to Webster Renfrow that day, the fact that he'd delivered it and then accepted Paxton's money would make him as guilty as sin in the eyes of every single member of that probation board—especially Anne Osborne, he thought sadly, knowing that their relationship was ruined.

"All right, kid. I don't want any mistakes. Understand?"

Oh, Zach understood, all right—understood that he had no choice but to do what Paxton asked. To ignore him or try to double-cross him would bring horrible consequences. He could handle whatever Paxton did to him— hell, maybe he had it coming. But it was his mom and Karli he had to think about now.

"What do you want me to do?" he asked, wrapping his arms around himself to try to stop his shivering.

"Step into my office, kid, and we'll go over it."

Zach's heart beat faster and his palms grew sweaty as he climbed into the back seat of Paxton's car. The sudden rush of heat, though welcome at first, quickly became overpowering, and Zach started to feel nauseous.

"Renfrow asked especially for you for this job. You know what that means?"

Zach didn't answer. How could he with his throat as dry as chalk dust?

"It means he's counting on you to show him what you're made of."

*What I'm made of,* Zach thought miserably. Wasn't that what Anne Osborne had said during one of their first meetings, that someday he'd be tested and he'd find out what he was really made of? He remembered her telling him that, and he remembered how, just listening to her telling him that his life could change, he'd started believing her. The job. The pickup. The home away from the city for his mom and Karli. He'd really wanted to believe everything she'd said was possible.

Now, however, he was finding out she'd been wrong. That just wanting something badly enough doesn't make it happen. He'd known at the back of his mind that his dreams couldn't come true, but still he'd wanted to believe. Unfortunately, Paxton was his reality now. And tonight Paxton was showing Zach what he'd always suspected about himself, that what he was made of wasn't worth a whole hell of a lot, after all.

"Brian Renfrow needs a place to stay put for a while," Paxton said, jerking Zach out of his miserable thoughts.

"No way," Zach blurted before he could check the impulse. "I don't want anything to do with Brian, with any of the Renfrows."

In a flash, Paxton had him by the shirtfront, yelling, "Damn it, kid! Don't give me your crap. I ain't in the mood for it." He shoved Zach back against the seat like so much dirty laundry. "Now you just shut up and listen and I'll tell you how you can help your old friend."

*Friend?* Zach thought bitterly. Webster Renfrow's younger brother was no one's friend. Even for Zach, who'd grown up fast and hard on the streets, Brian Renfrow had always been too wild, too unpredictable and dangerous. Brian had always been bigger than Zach—and meaner, with a reputation for hurting people for no good reason. Head case, they used to call him behind his back. Brian's fascination with explosives and fire had scared even his roughest friends.

When Zach heard that Brian had been arrested for assault, he hadn't been surprised. Deep down, although it broke every code of the neighborhood, secretly Zach had been relieved when they'd locked Brian up.

And when he'd heard that Brian had escaped, Zach had felt even more elated, thinking that Webster's mental-case brother would probably never be seen in the neighborhood again.

"What do I have to do?" he asked, forcing himself to sound much more calm and assured than he felt.

"Brian needs a place to stay. He'll be in the neighborhood tomorrow, and he won't have time to stand at the door waiting to be let in. You get my meaning, Zachyboy?"

Zach's mind raced. Tomorrow he was scheduled to close again, and Mr. Jenkins was counting on him. But how did he tell Paxton no? In a contest between the safety of his family and his obligation to Mr. Jenkins, again Zach had no choice. But something deep down urged him to try anyway.

"I can't help him. You don't understand. I'm in enough trouble already with Anne...that is, with my probation officer. They know I went to see Renfrow," he said quickly. "They're watching everything I do right now. It—it wouldn't be smart for Brian to come to me, of all people."

For a moment, the look on Paxton's face said he might be considering what Zach had said, that he might let Zach go without pressing him into this awful corner. But suddenly the big man's expression brightened, and he smiled his sneering smile again. "Don't you worry about that lady friend of yours."

Zach stared at him, stunned and confused. *Lady friend?*

"You know who I mean. That Osborne woman."

Zach's personal nightmare seemed to be growing more horrible by the moment. Every evil tentacle Webster Renfrow controlled seemed to be coiling around him and everything he cared about.

"Don't you worry about it, kid. She's going to have more trouble than she can handle. She won't have time to be worried about you."

"I gotta go," Zach said, scrambling for the door, suddenly consumed with the need to flee.

He didn't know what hurt more, the hand on the back of his neck that was cutting off circulation to his shoulders or the cold metal of the gun barrel jammed into his ribs. "Now you listen to me, you little scum sucker," Paxton hissed. "You'll be waiting for Brian Renfrow tomorrow. You'll give him whatever he needs. Do whatever he asks you to do. You take care of Brian, and Webster will take care of you."

The last thing Zach wanted or needed was the kind of help Webster Renfrow offered. He'd been walking the straight and narrow long enough to know that dealing with Renfrow was like Russian roulette with no empty chambers. He felt trapped by Paxton and trapped by Renfrow. Not for the first time, the neighborhood seemed to Zach to be a long dark tunnel with walls that were constantly closing in and an air supply that was slowly and surely being siphoned off.

Paxton spun him around and shoved him against the door. The handle dug into his back, and with his shirt bunched at his throat, he couldn't breathe. The big man's pale eyes sliced through him like a blowtorch through tin. "You take good care of Brian. Understand? Keep him outta sight. If he wants something, you get it. Money, food, a woman or any other damn thing he wants. You got that, Zachy-boy? Or do I have to make a bigger impression?" He dragged Zach closer before slamming him against the door again.

When Zach's head made contact with the metal strip above the door, his senses spun. As if to punctuate his demands, Paxton drove a fist like a hammer into Zach's stomach before he opened the door and shoved Zach into the street.

Even as he lay on the cold pavement, folded in pain and gasping to catch his breath, Zach told himself he was getting off easy. This was just a warning, the beginning of a situation that could only get worse.

# Chapter Twelve

"Webster Renfrow? But how can that be? At the hearing, Alverez said Renfrow was in the county jail. He isn't a juvenile."

"You're right, Webster Renfrow isn't a juvenile. By now he must be at least twenty-four or five."

Cole looked confused. "But you just said—"

"I know what I said. The last case Stan's office worked on with ours was the Renfrow case—Brian Renfrow, Webster's younger brother." A sick feeling settled in the pit of Anne's stomach as she began recounting for him Brian Renfrow's crimes. "In front of all those kids, in the middle of the day." She stopped to take a steadying breath. "He shot the kid right there on the high-school lawn. The young man died before the ambulance arrived. The victim was no saint. He'd been in and out of trouble since he was twelve. But to be shot down at fifteen, no matter what the situation, is beyond all reason." She sighed, remembering the year-book picture she'd seen in the newspapers. "He could have been any kid, anywhere." Still a baby, really, with big eyes that looked as though he'd just been told a wonderful secret. "Anyway," she said, shifting around to sit beside him on the bed, "Stan was determined Brian would be tried as an adult. And Marty—my boss, Martin Gartrell—was just as dead set against it."

"Who won?"

"Marty. And I can tell you, we were all pretty surprised by that. In a tug of war with the D.A.'s office, juvenile doesn't usually come out on top."

"So where's the kid now? Has his case gone to trial?"

"Not yet. Brian managed to escape from the juvenile detention center where he was being held. I remember Stan going ballistic when he found out. In fact, that day I thought he and Marty might actually come to blows over it. Had Frank Olivetti not stepped in, no telling what their war of words would have led to." She'd never seen Stan so incensed, nor Marty more enraged.

"Have you told Nyguen this?"

Her face must have reflected her shock at the conclusion he'd drawn so rapidly. "Marty is no murderer!"

"All right. I believe you. But this is still something that Nyguen needs to know about."

She knew he was right. "To tell you the truth, I'd forgotten all about their argument, maybe because they seemed to have forgotten about it, too." She remembered Jenetta complaining that they'd asked her to call and reserve a court for their weekly tennis matches.

At Dan and Jenetta's Fourth of July barbecue, she also remembered Marty and Stan taking the lead to gather all the kids for a game of volleyball. "If there was any problem between them, they seemed to have worked it out by the middle of the summer. I don't know how they were getting along just before Stan was murdered." The words caught in her throat. Although on some level she accepted what had happened, emotionally she was still suffering from shock.

"What was Marty's reaction to Stan's death?" he asked.

"Hey, wait a minute—" she sat up straighter "—Marty couldn't have had anything to do with Stan's death. I just remembered, he was on vacation that whole week."

Cole absorbed that information without comment. "There's something I don't understand," he began. "From everything you've told me, Lewellyn was a real profes-

sional. Why did he take the Brian Renfrow case so personally?"

Anne felt uncomfortably torn between loyalty to her boss
and respect for Stan's memory. "Stan was a professional,
a top-notch litigator. I believe he really cared about the individuals he dealt with, especially the victims. Anyone
who'd ever worked with him would tell you that no one
worked harder or had more of a presence in the court-
room."

"But?"

She sighed. Why was there always a but? "But...I can't
pretend not to have known that Stan was deeply motivated
by his political aspirations."

"He wanted the D.A.'s job?"

"Yes. And a lot more. Attorney general was one office
he talked about frequently. I don't know if Marty accused
Stan outright, but he mentioned to me that he thought Stan
was trying to make political hay out of Brian Renfrow's
case."

"And did you agree with Marty?"

She stared into the fire a moment before she answered.
"You know, I'm almost ashamed to say that I did. Stan's
ambitions were well known. He made no secret that to him,
the assistant D.A. position was just the beginning. He
wanted to be recognized at the state level for his hard
work." Stan had mentioned more than once his dream of
being the youngest state attorney general. "Juvenile crime
is a hot topic, and Brian Renfrow's case was just the kind
of high-profile trial that might have helped Stan make those
political dreams a reality."

She went on to explain how, at times, she felt steam-
rolled by the ambitious young prosecutor. "Marty made no
bones about how he felt, that Stan was overstepping his
bounds and trying to use our department to make a name
for himself. It was as though he was just waiting for the
right kid and the right case."

"You mentioned someone else...Frank Olivetti. How
did Olivetti get along with Lewellyn?"

At the mention of her mentor's name, Anne couldn't suppress a fond smile. "Frank gets along with everyone. He's been around the juvenile justice system longer than anyone I know, and everyone loves him. Even the most hard-boiled kids respond to Frank."

"What about Pembrooke? He seems like he's a reasonable man. Which side of the issue does he come down on?"

Anne had respected Cole for his abilities as a bodyguard and investigator from the beginning. But now she found herself even more impressed by his ability to draw a large mental picture around each aspect of a complex situation.

"Pembrooke is in an unusual position," she explained. "He works for judges, but he's also been involved with the D.A.'s office from time to time. I'm not really sure how he feels about the issue, but if I had to guess, I'd say he'd lean toward applying the full extent of the law in every case."

"Yet he seemed sympathetic to Zach, didn't he?"

She agreed. "But don't forget, Zach has already done most of his time at Mountainview. There are still some of us who believe in rehabilitation."

She saw in his eyes that her reference to the remark he'd made earlier hit home. "I'm sorry I said what I did back at the house. I was wrong." His apology seemed as heartfelt as any she'd ever heard.

"I'm sorry, too," she said. "If I did or said something that gave away my location, it was inadvertent. Believe me, since the night my apartment was destroyed, I've known the danger I'm in, even if I haven't always shown it."

They talked about the case for a few more minutes, and by the time Cole finished asking her about other individuals within the department who might have had strained relations with Stanley Lewellyn, Anne's head was beginning to ache.

As Cole had predicted, the wind whistled through the fine cracks in the log walls. On the floor opposite the bed, the snow sifted in through the cracks in the walls and formed small white pyramids. The fire had all but died. The room had grown chilly and was steeped in shadows.

Anne stretched and then wrapped her arms around herself when she shivered.

"It's late," Cole said, straining to see his watch in the dim light. "After midnight. We're both exhausted—"

*And there's only one bed,* Anne added silently.

"We've got a long, cold walk ahead of us if we want to get out of here in the morning. We'll call Drew as soon as we can, but I think we should still plan on driving to Denver as soon as we can dig out and make it to the highway. If my car's still immobilized, we'll drive one of the extra ranch pickups into Ridgeway and catch a plane. Nyguen needs to hear all of this as soon as possible."

He intercepted her glance at the bed. "It might be a bit crowded, but we can share the bed."

His suggestion sent excited apprehension curling through her. "That's all right. I'll be quite comfortable over here by the fire."

"In that chair?"

"Sure. The blanket I wore here is dry now. I'll just use that."

He studied her for a moment. "Are you afraid to share my bed, Anne?"

When she found her voice, she said, "Of course not. But you're...injured. Your body needs rest to recuperate. I'll be fine over here."

"But if you—"

"I won't change my mind," she finished for him.

He smiled. "I was going to say, if you get cold, there should be another blanket in that trunk."

"Thanks." Desperate to turn the conversation away from the subject of their sleeping arrangements, she said, "Cole, just one thing I need to know. It could be just coincidence that Zach has some connection to both me and Renfrow, couldn't it?"

He didn't answer immediately, but seemed to be studying what was left of the fire for an answer. "I hope so, Annie," he murmured softly.

No one but Max had ever call her Annie. For some reason, she didn't mind hearing it again from Cole. It sounded natural—even affectionate—coming from his lips.

"I know how you feel about that kid," he said. "And I just hope he's worthy of your trust—or at least that he realizes all you've done for him."

"That isn't the point, really. Not with any of them. I'm not in this profession to try to aggrandize myself. I just try to make them see that they have a chance and choices in life." She sighed, suddenly bone tired. "But I have to confess, it isn't easy thinking that Zach might have betrayed me."

He nodded. His expression said he understood all about betrayal. "Anne, what does Zach know about the night Lewellyn was killed?"

She thought a moment before answering. "I suppose he's heard some things, maybe read about Stan's death in the papers or seen the TV news coverage. He doesn't know I'm involved, if that's what you mean. At least I hope not." If Zach knew she'd been a witness, it only meant one thing, that he was involved in some way with the men who did the killing.

After a moment or two of contemplative silence, Cole swung his legs over the side of the bed. Before he could stand, however, she put a hand on his arm, stopping him. "And just where do you think you're going?"

"The fire is almost out, and it's going to get a whole lot colder before dawn."

"You stay put. I'll see to the fire."

"But—"

"No buts." She enjoyed turning his words on him. "For tonight, like it or not, Cole Spencer, you're the victim and I'm the rescuer. How does it feel?"

He smiled and reached for her hand, brought it to his lips and kissed it. "Not bad," he murmured. "Not bad at all."

Despite the doubts about this man that still swirled as thick as snow at the summit of Mount Sneffles, Anne felt something wonderful happening between them. When he touched her, she felt her heart expanding to take in even more of him.

BLINDED BY a wind-whipped sea of icy white, he pushed on through the storm. His heart hammered a ferocious warning—if he didn't find shelter soon, he wouldn't survive this hellish night.

But which way to go, he wondered, with ice and snow pelting him at every turn, robbing him of all sense of distance, space and time.

He should have stayed in the cabin, he told himself, and he could have if he hadn't panicked. If only he'd had the guts to either finish the job he'd started when he'd smashed Cole Spencer over the head, or had the wits to come up with some plausible reason for being there.

Who knows? They might have believed him, or at least she might have. He could have said he'd come to warn her, to help her or to confess and be done with the lies. Either way, she would have listened. She was like that, she always wanted to believe the best about people. And in the beginning, he'd hoped he *would* be able to help her, to protect her from his dangerous partner.

But maybe it wasn't too late, he suddenly realized. Maybe there was still a chance. If only they gave him a chance.

On the other hand, if he did manage to find his way back to the cabin and they gave him any trouble, if they wouldn't listen, if they forced him, he'd have to kill them. It was a grim reality that he wasn't sure he could face, but then again, what choice did they leave him?

Damn him and his softheaded idea of trying to frighten her away from cooperating with Nyguen. He should have gotten to her sooner, tried to reach her another way. All his life he'd been too trusting. When his partner had said, "No one will get hurt," he should have known better. "A quick and harmless way to make your retirement," he'd promised. "Lots of money with hardly any risk. Nobody gets hurt, and a screwed-up kid gets a second chance."

And wasn't that all he'd ever worked for? To help people, to serve and protect?

What a fool he'd been to think the scheme could work that easily. And how naive of him to think that the kind of kids dirty money helped would be the kind of kids who'd take advantage of a break to turn their lives around. Brian Renfrow! Now there was a rotten kid. If ever they should throw away the key, it should be on that kid.

In the end, the money hadn't been half as good as he'd been promised, certainly not good enough for having turned kids into drug runners. Not nearly as good as he'd been promised in his first meeting with Webster Renfrow. He should have known better. None of his get-rich-quick deals had ever panned out.

Not the Nevada land deal in the seventies that had cost him his savings, or the stock market scam in the eighties that had forced him to start dipping into his lodge's pension fund. And now it was too late.

His father had always predicted he'd die broke, and it turned out the old man was right. Broke, he could live with. Prison, he couldn't.

At least until now, none of his ill-advised business decisions had ever led to murder. And even this time, he couldn't really take the blame. How was he to know that Lewellyn would get hold of enough information to make a case? How was he to know that his partner had a deadly solution to every obstacle? That murder meant nothing to him? That his heart was as cold as this godforsaken night?

Clenching his fists, he thought about his options and decided there was no easy way out. Even the money, which had seemed such a grand amount just a short time ago, now seemed just barely enough to cover what he'd embezzled and provide him a safe and permanent escape.

Cursing himself, his partner and Renfrow, he tramped through the storm, stumbling on the rocks and underbrush lurking beneath the unstable crust of snow. *Why me?* he thought miserably. *Haven't I always been the kind of guy to give a sucker an even break?*

Well, tonight the tables had turned, and with the storm nibbling at his chances for survival like a wolf nipping at a lamb's heels, he felt like the biggest sucker of them all. If he got another chance, things would be different.

Whatever was left for him, he'd figure out a way to make do. He was getting too old for this crap, too old to take orders from this vicious new breed of men who were calling the shots.

He stumbled again and fell hard against the trunk of a dead tree. The gun strapped beneath his arm jammed into his ribs, and like a bear snagged in a steel trap, he let out a roar of pain. Clambering to his feet, he gasped and struggled to the shelter of a huge pine tree, where he sagged, exhausted and angry, against the twisted trunk.

Beneath his jacket, his shirt was soaked. Someone his age and size should have better sense than to go running around like a maniac in the middle of what had to be the world's worst snowstorm.

Though he was standing beneath the branches of the gigantic tree, the storm still buffeted him. Hot tears of regret filled his eyes when he thought about what he could have—should have—done. A man with more guts would have taken his shot this afternoon instead of just trying to warn her away.

If only he'd tried to bring her in on the deal instead of trying to frighten her with those stupid phone calls. If only he hadn't lost his nerve when he'd surprised them in that cabin.

If only... If only things had gone differently, then Anne Osborne would either be dead or cooperating right now, and that old woman who'd walked in on him in Spencer's ranch house this afternoon would be alive and well and soaking up the sun in Arizona, instead of lying bound and gagged in a closet with her head split open. When he called his partner and told him what he'd done, he'd been furious. "Clean up your mess, old man. And call me when you get back to Denver. Don't leave without taking care of the witness. Understand? You're as good as dead if Renfrow finds out she's still alive tomorrow.''

Before today, he'd only had to worry about his hot-headed partner and his cold-blooded employer. What he'd done to the old woman forced the situation to the limit—as if things hadn't already reached the extreme.

Now he was in it as deep as his partner—maybe even deeper. The reaction to a battered old woman was certain to bring down every legal hammer.

With a shudder, he pulled his jacket tighter around himself and stepped a few feet away from the tree, staring into the storm, desperate for a way out. Almost overcome with despair, his fear turned to red-hot anger, and he cursed the day he'd met Anne Osborne.

In his desperation, she became his worst enemy, the target of all his anger.

He'd tried the phone calls, the threats, and finally relented to the explosion his partner had arranged to have that punk kid set up. That alone should have been enough to scare a normal person away, he told himself, his anger mounting to a fever pitch.

But not her. Hadn't he heard her saying how she intended to go back to Denver and spend however long it took to find Stan's killers? Standing there in the darkness of the old woman's room, he'd heard it with his own ears. She wouldn't stop because of threats.

Not Anne. She'd always been out to prove something. Well, she'd proved something, all right. Proved it to him, at least. From his hiding place in the ranch house, in the old woman's sickeningly rose-scented bedroom, he'd had to make the hardest decision of his life. He shuddered to think that he might have been trapped in some sting operation at police headquarters while Anne Osborne and Nyguen sat behind a two-way mirror listening to his every word.

After all he'd done or tried to do to keep her from getting hurt, she was still out to get him. ''Well, you can go to hell, Anne Osborne,'' he shouted into the wind. ''Go straight to hell and take your bodyguard with you.''

He knew he'd never find his car in this storm, and even if he did somehow manage to stumble into it, he'd either freeze to death or asphyxiate himself trying to keep warm. His only chance was to get back to that cabin. He'd found it once, when his car had slipped into the ditch and he'd headed out on foot searching for shelter. He'd find it again.

And when he did, Anne Osborne and Cole Spencer would be in for the last surprise of their lives.

COLE AWOKE SLOWLY, at first not remembering where he was or why his muscles ached as though he'd slept on a bed of boulders. He was half-asleep and still feeling slightly confused and disoriented in the darkness. His fingers sought the tender spot at his brow, found the bandage, and all the memories came flooding back.

The one-room cabin was pitch dark. The fire had gone out, but surprisingly the room was still warm. He listened for the storm, for the howling wind that had buffeted the cabin all night, but instead he heard the gentle rustling of the pines.

The storm was over. Moving cautiously, lest any sudden movement trigger the return of the headache, he rolled on his back. That's when he realized she was curled up beside him, fully clothed and sound asleep, the oversize denim jacket, her only cover, pulled up to her chin.

She must have put in a miserable few hours trying to sleep in that stupid rocking chair. Or maybe she'd been waiting to be sure he was asleep before she'd slipped into his bed. Whatever the reason, he was glad to find her next to him.

Rearranging the sleeping bag she'd tucked around him last night, he covered them both. Without concern for consequences or propriety, he pulled her into the warm cradle of his body. In her sleep, she snuggled closer, cozily fitting her curves against him. Her purely involuntary movement, one living thing seeking the warmth of another, flooded him with a rich mix of desire and tenderness.

There had been no one since Meredith, and it felt good, even under these strange circumstances, to hold a woman he cared for in his arms. And he did care for Anne, he admitted to himself in the darkness. He seemed to be caring for her more and more with each hour they spent together. The feelings he had for her delighted him, even as they disturbed him. Delighted, because she was so easy to care for, so basically decent and good, not to mention beautiful, desirable, intelligent. Yet all those qualities couldn't quite erase his deep feelings of guilt. If not for him, Meredith would still be alive. What right did he have to happiness, when he'd been so largely responsible for her destruction?

"So cold," Anne murmured in her sleep. He drew her closer, enjoying the sweet softness of her hair against his face. He sighed, bracing himself for the image of Meredith and the wrenching guilt. But to his amazement, the only face he saw when he closed his eyes was the lovely face of the woman he held in his arms.

SHE AWOKE, shaken by a dream that had seemed all too real and too close to her waking reality to be easily dismissed. In her nightmare, she'd been running without moving, hiding without cover and then running again, desperate to outdistance a terrible nameless, faceless threat that, despite her frantic scrambling, always threatened to overtake her.

For a moment she lay in the still, gray light of predawn without moving, keenly aware of his arms around her, of the heat from his body pressed against her back. It had been after one o'clock when she'd given up trying to sleep in the rocker and crawled into bed next to the sleeping man. She'd moved cautiously, carefully, so as not to wake him, and she'd stayed close to the edge of the bed. It was a wonder she hadn't rolled onto the floor in her sleep.

Had he held her this way all night, dreaming of another woman? Was he hoping he'd awaken to find Meredith in his arms?

She sensed a change in his breathing, in the stirring of his breath in her hair. "Cole?" She whispered his name without moving.

He murmured something she didn't understand, a soft, sleepy sound that she found irresistibly sexy and which stirred her slumbering senses.

His arms tightened around her. His snuggling was only an instinct, she told herself, even as he urged her to roll over to face him.

"Good morning," he said softly.

"I'm sorry I woke you."

"Really? For a minute it seemed to me you were enjoying this as much as I was."

She didn't answer.

"This isn't such a bad way to wake up, is it?"

"No," she replied honestly, staring into his eyes. "It isn't."

"It's been a long time."

*For me, too.* Long before she'd left him, Gregg had effectively smothered any desire she'd ever felt for him.

"Anne." He said her name softly and touched her cheek, and she wondered if he could read her as easily as she read the desire in his eyes. Could he know how badly she wanted him?

The answer to her unspoken question came almost immediately, when he brought his mouth down on hers and kissed her with exquisite tenderness. For an instant, she thought she might still be dreaming. When his kiss deepened and every nerve in her body responded, she knew that no dream could ever feel this good.

She kissed him back, and shocked herself with the intensity of her hunger for him.

Taking her face in his hands, he pressed his mouth to hers again, kissing her more passionately, more perfectly. Her hands slid up his tightly muscled back and into the thick, soft waves of hair at the nape of his neck.

He kissed her over and over, each kiss more urgent than the last. With his lips and mouth he communicated his intent in a way words could never have expressed. She found herself delighting in his desire for her and reveling in the passion he evoked inside her. It had been a long time, too long, since she'd felt so needed, so deeply desired.

His lips explored where his hands traced a seductive course down the column of her neck. His hands continued to work their magic, and somehow their clothes were discarded with impossible ease. At the first touch of his bare flesh, Anne felt any resistance she might have contemplated flow out of her. Immediately a flash flood of desire swept in, washing away all thoughts of the past, all concerns for the future.

Except for the moment, the world ceased to exist and there was nothing in it—nothing but this man, this beautiful, sexy man, who touched her in ways that thrilled her beyond reason, beyond control.

"How I've wanted you," he murmured as he touched and stroked and caressed her, lovingly lifting her to heights of pleasure she'd never known existed. When their bodies sought the perfect union, they climbed together in a mindless ascent. Higher, higher, moving in harmony to the strains of an ancient melody as old as the mountains and as new as the day. Higher and higher, to that last perfect pinnacle, they climbed to that place where their hearts and minds and bodies met in complete and utter joy.

After, lying breathless and spent in his arms, a delicious sense of well-being seemed to encase her. She sighed against his chest and let her fingers toy with the dark, coarse curls of hair. He kissed the top of her head and stroked her hair.

"You were right," she murmured. "This *is* a wonderful way to wake up."

His laugh was soft and low.

"I didn't know it could be . . . like this," she said, lifting her head to look at him. "With Gregg it was . . . well, it was never like this."

He slid his hand down to caress her cheek. "I hate it that anyone ever hurt you."

"We've all been hurt," she said, and then after a moment she asked. "Do you miss her?" If she'd been walking on broken glass, she couldn't have felt more wary, but she pushed on. After what had just taken place between them, she had to know.

"In a way."

She detested the jealous pang in her stomach. "Tell me about her." She had to know about the woman she could feel coming between them even as they lay locked in each other's arms.

He shifted, and she edged a few inches away from him— a few desolate inches that suddenly felt like miles.

"She was smart," he began. "And funny."

"And pretty."

"Yes..." He hesitated, and a flash of deep inner pain flickered in his eyes.

*And you still love her.* She sat up slowly, reached for her clothes and handed him his clothes. She slipped hers on.

"She was young," he said as he dressed. "Just twenty three. Maybe that was part of the problem."

"What problem?"

"Anne...I—"

"It's okay," she said quickly, fully dressed now and slipping into her shoes. "I shouldn't have asked." When she stood up, he reached for her hand and she turned to stare at him where he sat on the edge of the bed dressed in jeans that were not yet fastened. He'd put his shirt on but hadn't buttoned it. Damn it, he was so darn sexy she couldn't keep from staring. Her desire for him, so recently sated, welled up again.

"I'm glad you asked about her," he said, surprising her as he rose and walked across the room to resurrect the fire. "I've wanted to tell you."

"Tell me what?"

He sighed and rose from his position in front of the small flames he'd coaxed to life in the hearth. Sitting down beside her again on the bed, he said, "I want to tell you about her, Anne. I guess I just don't know where to start."

"Just start wherever you can," she said quietly, suddenly feeling overwhelmed by a rush of tenderness for this big, strong, sexy man whose emotions obviously held him in such a stranglehold.

"She was actually Drew's client," he began. "Her mother had recently died after a long illness. Meredith had learned, after going through some of her mother's papers, that she had a half sister, a child her mother had given up for adoption before she met Meredith's father."

"So she hired you to find her sister."

"It was Drew's case," he said. "But I put in some time on the research. It was a fairly uncomplicated situation. The records on that kind of thing have become pretty easy to access, if you know where to look."

"Go on, Cole."

"Anyway, Meredith and I became . . . involved."

"Lovers?" The word almost stuck in her throat.

"Yes," he said quietly. "It was a mistake from the beginning. I should never have let myself breach that professional barrier. But I did."

His admission stung her, and she reflexively struck back. "Seems you've made the same mistake again."

"This is different."

"Oh?" Her stomach knotted. "So what was the mistake you made with her that you haven't made with me?" Before the words were even out, she regretted saying them. *He loved her, you idiot! That's the difference.*

"She loved me," he said solemnly, surprising her with his response.

Without warning, the cabin door flew open, startling both of them. She hardly caught a glimpse of the figure in the doorway before Cole shoved her to the floor. Before she knew what had happened, he was crouched in front of her, protecting her with his body.

Where he'd found his gun, and how he'd drawn it so quickly, she'd never know.

# *Chapter Thirteen*

"Hey, Cole! Relax, man. It's just me!"

Cole stared in the direction of the familiar voice, but with the morning sun behind it, the figure in the doorway was only a profile in black.

"It's me. Seth. Put that thing down, will ya?"

"Seth! Damn it, man, you almost got yourself killed." He lowered the gun and engaged the safety.

As Seth moved deeper into the room, Cole saw his gaze move to the bandage on his forehead.

"Are you all right?"

Cole nodded and reached for Anne's hand to help her to her feet. "I'm fine, except for you taking ten years off my life by barging in like that. Didn't you ever hear of knocking?"

"I—I . . ." The look on the hired man's face said he was troubled.

Cole moved to where Seth stood just inside the doorway. "What is it? What's happened?"

"When I saw that guy . . . well, I didn't know what had happened. Sorry about the door. I'll fix it. Hey, what happened here last night?" Seth's glance slid between them before coming back to fix on Cole.

"Seth, I know it's early and this lump on my head is probably still scrambling my brain, but for the life of me I can't make any sense out of what you're saying. What are you trying to say?"

With a nervous glance over his shoulder, Seth said, "I think you'd better come look at this."

Cole walked over to the man he'd known for the better part of ten years. He'd never seen him so somber, and until he followed Seth's gaze out the door, he didn't know why.

At first, when Cole glanced at the pile of dark clothing lying in the snow beside the door, he thought it was nothing more than a stack of rags or a bundle of garbage bags. But after a closer look, his mind registered the awful reality. It was a man. A man lying in the snow with a frozen stare locked eternally on the sky.

He spun around when he heard Anne gasp. Her eyes were riveted on the body. Seemingly oblivious to everything but the dead man, she moved woodenly, as if entranced, toward the still figure in the snow.

"There's a big old Ford stuck up to its axles in snow just a quarter mile behind your truck," Seth said. "I figure it must be his."

Cole nodded absently, more concerned about the color that had drained from Anne's face than by Seth's announcement.

He put his arm around her shoulders and said quietly, "Anne. Go back inside. Seth and I will take care of him."

She didn't seem cognizant of his arm around her, and her own arms were wrapped tightly across her stomach. The look on her face was one of horror. For a long awful moment, she stood like that, staring down at the body in the snow.

"I know him," she said finally. "Hagan. Dan Hagan." She swallowed hard. "He's my assistant's... Jenetta's husband." Standing this close to death for the second time in three weeks seemed like some kind of macabre nightmare. "He is... was a cop." She forced herself to take a deep breath before she turned to meet Cole's gaze. "Do you think he was the one who attacked us?"

But before she could finished asking her question, he answered it. "Who else?"

"But why?"

Cole ran a hand over his hair, which was still tousled from sleep and their lovemaking. "I guess we'll never know."

Walking back into the cabin, Anne felt numb as she pulled the hooded sweatshirt over her head and then rejoined Cole and Seth outside. Their conversation stopped when they saw her, but not before she heard the words *sheriff* and *coroner*.

HALF AN HOUR LATER, they'd finished digging out the snowmobile Seth had tried to ride to the cabin only to have it bog down in a drift just off the road. By the time they reached the spot where Seth had parked the ranch truck, Anne's socks and shoes were soaking wet and she couldn't ever remember her feet feeling so cold. Besides the cold and the wet, thirty minutes of glare off a sea of white snow had given her a headache the size of Mount Sneffles.

While she sat in Seth's truck trying to warm herself, Cole and Seth unloaded another snowmobile and stood for a few minutes in conversation at the back of the truck. It wasn't difficult to know what—who—they were discussing.

The image of Dan lying dead in the snow would haunt her for a long time. Even though now she had to believe he'd been involved in Stan's killing, Anne still cringed when she allowed herself to think about him trapped in last night's deadly storm, unable to make those last few precious feet to shelter.

"Are you going to be all right?" Cole asked as he opened the door next to her. With one hand on the roof and the other on the back of the seat behind her, he went on, "It'll be a chilly ride on the snowmobile, but once we get back to the house, you can sit in the hot tub for as long as you like. It's going to take Seth and I a few hours to finish clearing the road. And—" he hesitated "—to deal with the sheriff when he arrives."

"We should call Nyguen," she said.

He nodded. "He'll want to question both of us when we get back to Denver."

*Denver,* she thought. How ironic that just a few short days ago she could think of nothing but going back. Now, however, Denver meant only one thing—the end of her time alone with Cole, the one person in all of this she truly trusted.

As she climbed onto the back of the snowmobile and slid her arms around his waist, she felt a deep sadness welling in her chest, a sense of aching personal loss that went straight through her heart and all the way to her soul.


"I THOUGHT they were my friends," she said as she stepped into the distinctively male bathrobe he held out to her.

She accepted it gratefully and huddled deep in its soft folds. She sat down across from him on one of the wicker chairs arranged on the glass-enclosed redwood deck, which accommodated the hot tub. Sunlight streamed in from all directions, and Anne, feeling finally warmed after the long, leisurely soak in the hot tub, began to feel the physical and emotional jolts of the past twenty-four hours creeping up on her.

Her neck and shoulders ached, and her legs felt leaden. Her senses, however, were humming and fine-tuned again. In light of what had transpired between them in the hazy gray light of morning, she wondered how he could affect such a businesslike attitude. In the clear light of day, he was once again Cole Spencer, bodyguard, investigator. A man in control of himself and his surroundings. Thinking back to his spontaneous display of pure passion warmed her and evoked a stirring inside her—a primal appetite for him that, instead of being sated by their lovemaking, seemed to have been merely whetted.

"Can you be ready to leave soon?"

"Sure. Since I don't have to think much about my wardrobe, packing should be easy."

He smiled, a tired, humorless smile that stopped short of his eyes. "If we get back to Denver early enough, we'll pick up a few more things for you on the way to the hotel." He went on to explain how, for the first night at least, they'd be staying on the west side of town.

She didn't have to ask to know that he'd already mapped out their strategy for getting around Denver, for keeping her hidden until... Until what? Was he still planning to hand her over to another bodyguard? Had what they'd shared this morning weakened or strengthened his resolve to remove himself from her case?

"As you probably know, he retired from the force four years ago," he said, jerking Anne out of her private conjecture. "He'd kept in close touch with a number of friends in the department."

She leaned forward in her chair. "Did Nyguen make any guesses as to who else might have been involved?"

He stood with his back to the tub, leaning against the rail, his arms crossed over his chest. In his softly faded denim shirt and jeans, he could have been the model for an ad touting Colorado life-styles. "I'm sure he has suspects in mind."

She got the distinct feeling he was holding back. "What did he say, Cole?" she asked, pressing him. "What does he plan to do next? Do they have any leads, or has this case hit another blind alley?"

He didn't answer immediately, but looked past her, seemingly intent on studying the white-capped mountains in the distance. After a moment, his gaze shifted to her face. "He wants me to bring you to his office, to smuggle you in so that you can listen and watch without being observed. He especially wants you to listen to the officers he intends to parade past you."

Anne almost couldn't believe her ears. "But that's exactly what I've wanted to do from the beginning."

Cole's expression darkened, like the clouds gathering around the peaks in the distance, his own shadows made him seem distant, cold and untouchable.

"So, what did you tell him? Did you tell him we'd be there? You had to know I'd think this was a great idea."

"It's a lousy idea," he said. "And I have no intention of letting you do it. It's too big a risk. What if Hagan's accomplice recognizes you?"

"He won't. I'm sure we can come up with a disguise that would work."

His dubious expression told her what he thought of her plan.

"All right. So what if he recognizes me?" She stood and moved a step closer to him. "He can't very well come after me in the middle of the police station."

"But what about later? Have you thought about that?" His obsidian eyes shot flinty sparks.

"I haven't thought that far," she shot back. "I didn't think I'd have to."

"Oh, is that right? And just why the hell not?"

Even in his anger, with his eyes locked on hers, she sensed his deep feelings for her. She could see, almost touch them, and suddenly she experienced a euphoric surge of delicious power. "Because I have you, cowboy," she said. "And I'm betting you won't let me down."

A slow, cynical smile curved his wonderful mouth. "Oh, you are, are you?"

"Yes," she said quietly. "I think I am."

The intensity of his flinty stare stole her breath, but she wouldn't look away. Determined to match his stare with one of equal intensity, she clenched her fists at her side so he wouldn't see her hands shaking.

"But what if you're wrong?" His voice was low, almost ominous.

She held her breath. "I don't think I am."

His expression didn't change, but he shifted his gaze to the window and the view beyond. "You wouldn't be the first woman I've let down."

Where the courage came from she didn't know, but before she knew it, she said, "Finish telling me about her, Cole. Tell me about Meredith."

For a long moment he just stood there, staring out at the mountains. The soft gurgling of the hot tub was the only sound, and the wisps of steam were the only movement in the room.

"She was pretty. Charming. Young. And unbelievably rich. She was spoiled in every way the super-wealthy spoil their kids—private schools, lavish vacations and lessons in everything from fencing to elocution."

Quite a contrast between childhoods, Anne thought. Except for Cole, it seemed she and Meredith Hackett had little in common. "Go on, Cole."

"Anyway, I met her when she came to the agency, after her parents were killed in a boating accident while vacationing in Greece."

"She was looking for her half sister."

"Right. She was spoiled, had everything materially that anyone could wish for. The one thing she didn't have, all her money couldn't buy...."

"Family," Anne whispered.

His eyes flicked to hers. "Yes. Family. It seems no matter what her parents did for her, Meredith had never really felt connected to anyone in that way every child yearns to belong. She experienced a deep disappointment when the half sister was finally located and not particularly interested in establishing a relationship with Meredith. She was just so needy, she chased people away. She wanted so much to have what everyone else seemed to have."

She knew all about that feeling, Anne thought, and a surge of compassion for the lovely heiress swelled inside her, almost smothering the twinges of jealousy she felt toward Cole's former lover.

"Anyway, I guess maybe that's why she became so attached to Drew and me. At first she seemed to want to just be around us, feel part of that family situation. Anyway, before long she and I..."

"Became lovers."

He nodded and his gaze drifted away from her again. "Became lovers," he said softly. "For a short time, anyway."

"What happened? Why did it end?"

"It just wasn't working. Not for me, anyway. The physical attraction was intense, I won't lie to you about that. But for me, there just had to be more. And for Meredith, that more meant everything. Enough was never enough for her. No matter how much attention, gifts, time anyone gave her, it was never enough. She was never satisfied, always hungry for more."

She marveled at the lack of bitterness in his voice. If any emotion was reflected, it was sadness. She walked over to stand beside him, gazing out at the peaks that seemed to hold his complete attention. Clearly, he couldn't look at her while he divulged his deepest hurt.

"Tell me about the murder," she coaxed him gently. "Were you there when it happened?"

He shook his head. "I hadn't seen Meredith in over a month. When I ended our... relationship, she went a little crazy, started running with a very fast, very rich crowd. From London to Aspen, they spent money and consumed enough cocaine to build a small mountain range. By the time she touched back down in Denver, she was one sick kid."

He shook his head and walked to an overstuffed love seat and sat down. Without his invitation, she joined him. Wanting more than anything to touch him, she forced herself to keep her hands in her lap.

"I checked her into rehab, and for a while it looked as though she'd made great gains. When she was released, however, she had the mistaken impression that things between us had changed. She'd interpreted my concern for her recovery as something else."

"Love?"

He looked into her eyes. "Yes. But it wasn't. Not ever. I cared about her. Cared what happened to her and wanted to help her. But I know now it was never love."

She could no longer resist touching him, and her hand came up to trace the fine line that winged from the corner of his mouth to his cheek. He captured her hand and kissed

the palm, and she said, "Go on, Cole. I want to know a
of it."

He released her hand reluctantly and took a deep breath
"Anyway, when I didn't respond to her demands, sh
turned up the pressure." He shook his head and almos
smiled, a humorless expression that stopped far short of hi
eyes. "I don't have any sisters, you know, only brothers
and I'd never seen a woman throw a tantrum."

"It isn't a reaction confined to the female gender," sh
reminded him gently.

"Right. Well, anyway, things were going from bad t
worse, and as you might suspect she went back to her fas
friends. The one she shot...they'd been involved, o
course. He'd also been supplying her with the coke. Wh
knows which of them was sicker? No one was there tha
night, and I guess we'll never really know what happened
But after the shooting, like everyone else, I believed he
story. That she'd killed him in self-defense."

A deep skepticism lodged in his eyes. "When the truth
came out, she was desperate for a way out. She begged m
to cover for her, provide an alibi, say I was there...anythin
that would bail her out of the murder charge."

"But, of course, you couldn't do that."

"No," he said quietly. "I couldn't."

For a long moment they sat in silence. Anne waited fo
him to find the right words.

"She'd threatened to hurt herself countless times," h
began. "It was part of her routine. That night was no dif
ferent. When she called, she sounded drunk, and when
refused her demands, she threatened suicide. Again. Bu
this time she went too far. She made good on her threat
The combination of the pills and the booze..." His voic
trailed off.

"Then it wasn't intentional?"

He shrugged. "Who knows? She was miserable, no on
can deny that. Desperate. Depressed."

Anne took a moment to collect her thoughts. "Cole, yo
can't possibly blame yourself for Meredith's death."

He rose slowly and walked over to gaze out the window again. "I should have taken her threats more seriously."

"I'm sure you did. You said you and Drew arranged for her to go into rehab. You did what you could."

He turned, almost challenging her. "Did I?"

"Of course you did. You tried to save her, to protect her. But protecting someone from themselves is almost impossible. From the things you've said, it sounds as if she'd been working on self-destructing for a long time."

"But I should have known. As you said, we work with desperate people, we're the ones they turn to. And when we're not there...then what?"

"You were there. But you couldn't change what she was determined to do." She laid a gentle hand on his arm and peered deeply into his eyes. "Your caring wasn't enough. It never would have been. She needed too much, too many things you didn't—couldn't—give her. Her obsession with you, with life, had to do with devouring, possessing. The woman you described didn't know how to love. To love is to share. To give and take. People like Meredith don't know how to give." It had been the same with Gregg, she thought. She'd never been good enough or given enough love in just the right way to satisfy his insatiable needs— needs that had nothing to do with her and everything to do with his own intense emptiness.

Cole studied her face, and she knew he longed to believe what she'd said. As she looked into his eyes, her thoughts took flight, and every delicious memory of their lovemaking came back to her. The feel of his skin beneath her fingertips, the way his hands had felt on her skin. Something in his eyes, an almost imperceptible softening, told her that his thoughts had transported him to that magical predawn experience when the two of them had left every external sadness behind to share one perfect, golden moment.

"We'll leave in an hour," he said quietly as he rose and walked into the house, leaving her with nothing to do but sit and watch him go.

When she heard his shout from the hallway, she jumped. Responding to the alarm in his voice, a jolt of adrenaline shot through Anne, but despite that intense physical reaction, it seemed her legs wouldn't move fast enough.

"Anne!" he shouted again. "Anne. Please. For God's sake, come here! Quick!"

In the space of a few agonizing seconds, she rounded the corner at a run, only to be stopped, momentarily paralyzed in her tracks by the sight of Bess Spencer's limp and lifeless body on the floor.

AGAINST THE STARK environment of the metal and glass of her intensive care room, Cole's aunt seemed impossibly small and frail. The bandage over the hideous wound to her head covered one of her eyes. But her other eye was open, and even in her grievously injured state, Anne saw the Spencer determination shining through. How she'd managed to free herself from the ropes Dan had used to bind her wrists and ankles, Anne couldn't imagine.

When Cole asked her, Bess muttered something about it taking more than a few slipknots to keep a good woman down. "I think it was the hangers she used to untie the knots that did most of the damage," the nurse said as she applied ointment to the angry welts on Bess's wrists.

"That's all I can remember," Bess said, her voice so weak it had become almost inaudible. The uniformed policeman standing beside the bed jotted a few notes on a pad.

"I saw the man on the phone in Cole's office, and the next thing I knew, I woke up on the floor of my closet, trussed up like a Thanksgiving turkey with . . . with a headache the size of Texas."

The officer smiled, but the expression on Cole's face was one of raw anger.

"That's all right, Mrs. Spencer. When you're feeling better, you might remember more details. I'll be back to see you later."

Her thin, vein-lined lid dipped lazily, and Anne realized that the drugs running through clear plastic tubes were beginning to take effect.

"We'll let you rest now," Cole said, taking his aunt's small, thin hand in his much larger one.

Obviously weakened by her injuries, she merely nodded before lapsing into a semiconscious state.

Drew put his hand at the small of Anne's back and they walked into the hallway. They were met by a gray-haired nurse with a sympathetic smile.

She took Cole's arm and led him to the desk. "Now listen, she's going to be fine. The doctor said that gash on her head isn't nearly as bad as it looked at first. I've been helping patch your family up for more than twenty years—since this one was in short pants," she confided to Anne, "and I know you're all as hardy as those fine quarter horses you raise. She just needs rest now and a little time to recover. No more questions for tonight, though. No more visits from the police."

Cole nodded solemnly.

"Tomorrow or the next day she'll remember a lot more of what happened."

He reached for Anne's hand, and together they left the hospital for the airport.

BY THE TIME the charter flight landed at the small private airport east of town, the sun had dropped behind Denver's scraggy skyline. Cole took her hand, and they walked across the tarmac together to where Drew stood waiting for them just inside the high chain-link gate. The first thing Cole noticed was the absence of a cast on Drew's right leg.

"Miraculous recovery."

"Yes, when we've got more time, remind me to tell you all about it."

"I can't wait."

Drew smiled when he glanced at Cole's hand wrapped around Anne's. But when he asked, "How's Aunt Bess doing?" his smile quickly faded.

"She was roughed up pretty badly," Cole replied solemnly. "But the doctors say she'll recover fully."

The anger on both brothers' faces told Anne that if Dan Hagan weren't already dead, he'd rue the day he'd heard the name Spencer.

"But what happened? How did she come to be in the house? I thought she was on her way to Phoenix," Drew said.

"We all thought so, too," Cole said. "Seth took her to the airport, but when she learned that her connecting flight had been delayed, she insisted he go back to the ranch. Seth offered to wait with her, but she was adamant—you know how she can be when she gets her mind set."

Drew smiled and nodded.

"Anyway, when her flight was eventually canceled, she caught a ride back to the ranch with a friend."

"It's a miracle she survived," Drew said in the car on the way to the hotel where he'd reserved a room for them.

"Has Jenetta been told?" Anne asked.

"Drew and I questioned her briefly this afternoon," Nyguen said, turning around in his seat to face Cole and her in the back seat. "Obviously, she's pretty upset."

"Especially since we couldn't tell her much about how it happened," Drew put in. "Anne, would you be willing to talk to her for us?"

She hesitated. What would she say to her friend—if Jenetta was, or ever had been, her friend? Had Jenetta been involved in Dan's deceptions, or would she be as shocked by his duplicity as Anne had been?

"If you think it would help, I'll try."

"She might possess valuable information about her husband's accomplice. What about your aunt, Cole? Was she able to give you any leads?"

"As I told Drew when I called from the airport, she said she walked in on Hagan after he'd broken into the house. He was on the phone. It shouldn't be too tough to trace that call, if it went through."

"Francine's working on it. We should have the answer soon."

*Answer.* With all the turmoil and shocks of the past few days, she hardly knew where to start with her questions. Had Dan been responsible for Stanley's death? Was he the accomplice or the murderer? And why? Why Dan? Had he fallen into this tangle innocently, as she had? Or had he been pretending all along to be her friend? What about Jenetta? What about Zach? Were Zach's involvement with Webster Renfrow and Stanley Lewellyn's crusade against Brian Renfrow merely coincidence? And where did Marty fit into all this? Could he really have been harboring a murderous rage toward Stan all this time? Had he been Dan's accomplice, or was it the other way around?

And finally, what about her feelings for Cole Spencer? What future, if any, could there be for a man who was afraid to care again, and for the woman who'd fallen head over heels in love with him?

IT WAS AFTER SIX when Drew arrived with Jenetta in tow. One look at her friend's face and all trepidation flowed out of Anne. Without thinking, she put her arms around the woman.

For a full minute, Jenetta's shoulders shook as she sobbed in Anne's arms. Finally, she followed Anne to the couch and slumped down. Her eyes were puffy and red from crying.

"Anne, I'm so glad you're here." She reached for Anne's hand and held it in a desperate grip. Seemingly oblivious to Drew and Cole's presence in the room, Jenetta focused her wide gray eyes only on Anne. "The police have been at our house all day. They brought a warrant and searched every inch."

"Jenetta," Anne began, trying to soothe the hysterical woman by making her voice as calm and low as possible. "I want you to know that no matter what happens, I'm very sorry about what ... has happened."

Jenetta sniffed into the wad of crumpled tissues she clutched in one hand.

"This is Cole Spencer," Anne said softly. "He's a friend of mine. And his brother, Drew." Cole nodded, and Drew took a seat in the chair facing the two women. "They're private investigators, and they want to help you. If you know anything—anything at all about what Dan might have been involved in—"

Jenetta jumped to her feet so fast, she startled them all. "What are you saying, Anne?" she shrieked. "You're just like the rest of them—Marty and the rest. They're acting like Dan was a criminal or something." She shoved her shaking fingers through her hair, making it almost stand on end and giving her the appearance of someone teetering on the edge of sanity.

Anne didn't realize how it happened, but Cole and Drew were suddenly poised on each side of the overwrought woman, ready to grab her if she veered out of control.

"He was no murderer, Anne," she cried. "You must believe me! What he did, he didn't do out of meanness or for personal gain," she continued, her voice shaky. "He wasn't a bad person, Anne. Really he wasn't."

It took every ounce of control not to lash out at Jenetta, to tell her of the awful attack on Bess Spencer and the haunted, pathetic look on Stan's face the night his life had been so cruelly stolen.

"Sit down, Jen," Anne said, her voice surprisingly firm. "No one's accusing you of anything. We just need answers."

Jenetta seemed almost ready to believe what Anne had told her. "But what about the police? What about all those things they took out of our house?" She tugged at the front of her sagging cardigan while her eyes darted from the men at her side to Anne.

"They just want to get to the truth, Mrs. Hagan," Cole said, his voice never smoother or more calm.

"Please sit down, Jen," Anne said again. "Please."

When Jenetta finally relented, Drew took a deep breath and said, "I think everyone could use some coffee, Cole. Why don't we see if we can find our way around that kitchen?"

Cole was obviously reluctant to leave her alone with Jenetta. His eyes searched and found Anne's.

"It's all right," she whispered. "Jen and I are old friends."

When the men finally left them alone, Anne saw Jenetta visibly relax.

"Oh, Anne. I told him not to do it," she said in a desperate whisper. "When he asked for the records on Shannon Browers, I thought he just wanted to try to help the kid out. But then when I found out about the money he'd taken out of the police benevolent fund, all the rest of it came out. I almost left him," she cried. "Believe me, I tried to get him to turn himself in. I told him he'd be caught! I told him he'd have a better chance if he'd just confess and make some arrangement to pay it all back. But no!" Her voice rose unsteadily, angrily. "He wouldn't listen. And now, just look at what's happened!"

*Yes,* Anne thought. *Just look!*

## Chapter Fourteen

When Zach came home from work to see Brian Renfrow sitting beside Karli on the floor, he felt his heart drop. With his long, thin, midnight black ponytail at his nape, tattooed arms and pierced ears, Brian Renfrow represented everything Karli thought cool and everything Zach knew was bad.

From the beginning, the last thing he'd wanted was for his family to come in contact with Webster Renfrow's dangerous brother. He stared at his sister a moment, remembering how she'd looked a few years ago, just a kid, with her soft cap of curls three shades lighter than his own. Too quickly she was turning into a woman, as never evidenced more clearly than tonight, dressed as she was in a pair of tight black jeans and a skimpy cropped sweater.

"Where's Ma?" he asked his sister tersely as he dropped his jacket on the chair beside the door.

"She's down the block." It was their family way of saying Reno's, the grimy bar on the corner where their mother spent too many of her days and nights.

Karli still hadn't looked at her brother. She seemed transfixed with what Brian was doing—and just what he was doing, Zach couldn't tell. Littered with empty soda bottles, tin cans and rags, the living room reeked of gasoline.

Zach watched Brian filling one of the empty soda bottles with gasoline. He wasn't particularly careful, and he seemed oblivious to the gas running down his arm and the sides of the bottle.

"What the hell are you doing?" Zach asked, stalking across the room to open the window behind the tattered floral couch. "You'll asphyxiate us all with that stuff!"

He'd arranged for Brian to stay in the furnace room, on a cot he'd hauled out of someone's long-abandoned storage area behind the broken washers and dryers that hadn't seen a load of wash in years.

Brian looked at Zach for the first time. His eyes were glassy, and his smile was just a snarl in disguise. "I kind of get off on it, buddy. Want a whiff?"

Everything inside Zach screamed for him to jerk Brian up by the collar of his torn black T-shirt and throw him out into the street. Instead he barked, "You ought to be in bed, Karli. It's late. You've got school tomorrow."

"Ah, Zach," she whined. "Can't I just watch—"

"No! You can't," he snapped as he headed into the kitchen to get a drink. "Now go to bed, Karli. Do it now!"

To his amazement, he heard his sister padding out of the room. Later, he would explain to Karli what bad news Brian was, how she shouldn't be hanging around him or anyone like him.

Brian had invaded their home early this morning, before Zach was even out of bed. He didn't know what he'd expected, perhaps a nervous fugitive on the run. Instead, Brian seemed almost arrogant in his escape, amused that the authorities still hadn't caught up to him. Like his brother, Webster, Brian seemed impervious to rules or laws.

Zach hadn't wanted to leave Brian alone in the apartment, so he'd skipped school. He could only hope Anne wouldn't find out before he could get rid of Brian and find some way to explain. Unfortunately, he hadn't been able to bring himself to leave Mr. Jenkins shorthanded at work, so he'd pulled his regular shift. Now, seeing the mess on the living-room floor, and worse, coming home to see Karli alone with Brian, he vowed that until Brian left, his job would just have to wait.

"Close the window," Brian growled. "You're freezing me out of here."

"Get that crap out of the living room," Zach said.

Brian didn't move to comply.

"I said—"

"Shut up, you stupid shit!" Brian warned. "I'm trying to work."

Zach started for him, but before he could make it halfway across the room, Brian pulled out a six-inch switchblade. Trying to stop, Zach almost fell forward into the knife's deadly tip.

Karli's head appeared in the doorway. "What's going on?"

"Go back to bed," Zach shouted. "Now!"

Karli disappeared into the bedroom, but she didn't close the door.

"I've got work to do, so get the hell out of here," Brian ordered.

Zach stood dumbfounded, staring at Brian as he returned his attention to his "work." There was no way he was leaving the apartment, leaving Brian and Karli alone again. He had to tread softly, he told himself, realizing that Brian had been sniffing—or huffing, as they called it on the streets. The gasoline fumes that filled the apartment also filled Brian's brain, making him not only sky-high, but as dangerous as a hand grenade with the pin pulled.

"What are you doing, Brian?" he asked carefully, treading lightly toward a different approach.

"Why should I tell you?"

"Just wondered. Forget it," Zach said over his shoulder as he walked back into the kitchen. "You want something to eat?"

"It's fireworks," Brian said lazily, his tongue thick and his speech slurred. "We're gonna have a show later. You want to watch?"

Despite the fear Brian's erratic behavior ignited in Zach, he affected indifference. "Maybe. Where?"

"Like I'd tell you. But hang around, you'll find out. And I guarantee it'll be a good show." He had the same dead eyes, the same wicked smile that Zach had felt every time he'd seen Webster. It was almost as though Paxton, Webster and Brian were all part of one evil body. A body with more arms and legs than an octopus. Since the day he'd delivered the message to Webster at the jail, Zach had felt those arms and legs wrapped around his throat, slowly squeezing the life out of him.

"What the hell is going on?" he demanded.

"Huh!" Brian snorted. "Like I'd tell you! From what I hear, you've turned into a real good little citizen, cuz."

"Go to hell," Zach mumbled.

"Yeah, Paxton tells me you've got something goin' with that probation woman of yours, that Osborne woman."

*How the hell did he know her name?*

"I hear she's real good lookin'. Is that right, Zach? How is she, man? As good as she looks? Maybe I oughta find out for myself."

Zach tried to shake off his anger, but it had a grip on him, digging its claws into his chest. "Shut up, Brian. You don't know what you're talking about."

"Yeah? Well, I got a little something for your woman, Zach. Something she's gonna get a real charge out of." His laugh was more of a hoarse coughing sound.

"Hey, what's up, Zach? You look a little nervous. Has your woman been holding out on you? I heard you calling her on the phone, man."

When Zach started, Brian smiled. "Yeah, that's right. I heard everything you said. We've got a little party planned for her. I can hardly wait till she shows up. How about you, man?" He smirked. "Hey, you look real nervous, man. What'sa matter, has she found herself another man—another boy? You know, word has it up at Mountainview that she's real good to all her boys... *real* good."

Zach threw everything into the first blow. He caught Brian in the jaw in mid-smirk, sending him sprawling into the bottles, sending gasoline spewing all over the room, sloshing across the TV screen and his mom's broken recliner.

Luckily for Zach, Brian's impaired state slowed his reflexes, and when he reached for his knife, Zach had time to kick it out of Brian's fist, sending the glittering blade spinning crazily across the floor.

Brian lunged at him, but Zach quickly subdued him despite Brian's superior size. With a satisfying twist, he pinned Brian's arm behind his back.

Brian yelped. "Hey, man. Back off. Back off!"

"Just shut up about her, all right?" Zach growled, giving Brian's arm another meaningful jerk before he released his grip.

"Yeah, sure. Whatever," Brian snarled, rubbing his arm and swiping at the long dark hair that fell over his eyes. "Keep your whore."

Zach grabbed a bunch of paper towels from the kitchen and mopped up the gas that hadn't already evaporated. The room reeked. Jerking the window open wider, he took a deep breath and fought the light-headedness that swarmed over him. When he turned around, he saw that the knife was no longer on the floor.

ANNE'S HEART HURT as she watched her friend slip into a pathetic state of numbed resignation, and the phrase "protective custody" took on new meaning for her when she watched Nyguen and two plainclothes female police officers escort Jenetta out of the room.

"What happens now?" she asked Cole.

"She could be indicted, I suppose, especially if it can be proven that she tampered with court records."

From across the room, Drew said, "Cole's right. It's all a matter of degree. But I tend to think the D.A. would be more interested in striking a bargain for Jenetta's testimony than convicting her. Even though she knew about her husband's embezzlement and his association with Webster Renfrow, she's still a minor player. It isn't clear yet whether she was directly involved in the corruption in the department. She claims she stumbled over Dan's activities just a few weeks ago."

"But what about Stan?" Anne asked, slumping onto the couch. "Do you think it's possible she was involved in some way in his murder?"

"If she was involved or knew anything about the murder, she's the best liar I've ever seen," Cole said, sitting down beside her.

"I'm convinced she didn't know," Drew concurred. "And if I'm reading Nyguen's reaction right, I don't think he suspects her, either."

"They found a set of pictures in her purse," Cole told Anne. "Copies of the ones you and Bess took of the ranch."

Anne felt a stress headache creeping up behind her eyes. "The pictures I sent to Zach," she said almost to herself.

When Drew and Cole exchanged a meaningful glance, her head began to pound in earnest. "Zach sold me out, didn't he?" she asked, rising to pace a few feet across the room. "He and Jenetta knew what Dan and Renfrow were up to."

Cole rose and moved over to where she stood beside the glass doors that led to a small enclosed balcony. "We don't know that for sure. Nyguen said Jenetta seemed truly shocked when she learned that Dan had tracked you to the ranch."

"So where does that leave Zach?" Anne asked wearily.

Cole thought a moment before he answered. "Well, Jenetta hasn't said anything so far that would incriminate him. If he is involved, it's beginning to look as though he's just an unwitting courier."

Hearing Cole defend Zach gave her a thread of hope. "That would explain the visit to Renfrow. The visit he insisted he made as a favor to a friend," Anne said.

"That friend might have been Hagan," Drew put in. "But it could have been any one of Renfrow's dealers. I doubt Zach had much choice if he was confronted by one of those characters."

"Intimidation is their mode of operation," Cole said.

"Dan found me because of those pictures, didn't he?" she asked, fighting to keep her voice steady.

Cole nodded. "It looks that way," he said quietly.

She searched his face and the depths of his dark gaze, and found no hint of the blame he had every right to hurl at her. "I'm sorry, Cole," she said softly. "You tried to warn me, but I just wouldn't listen. I couldn't believe Zach would do anything to hurt me, or sell me out. But he did, didn't he?"

Cole put his hands on her shoulders and gazed into her eyes. "Don't jump to conclusions, Anne. Jenetta's version of how Zach inadvertently left those prints behind jived exactly with what he told you. It's a very good possibility that the only thing Zach's guilty of is being in the wrong place at the wrong time."

"With the pictures I sent him just *accidentally* ending up on Jen's desk?" In light of Dan and Jenetta's horrendous betrayal, she was finding any coincidental scenario difficult to believe.

"I heard her explaining the prints to Nyguen, and I believe she was telling the truth," Drew said over his shoulder from the sink where he was preparing another pot of coffee.

"How about you?" Anne asked, turning to face Cole.

He shook his head. "At this point, I really don't know. Jenetta said Zach had been as excited as a kid on Christmas to get those pictures from you."

He'd never know how badly she wanted to believe that.

"She said she had no idea where those pictures were taken."

"It wouldn't have been difficult to identify Mount Sneffles," Drew pointed out, and Anne remembered Cole telling her it was one of the most photographed peaks in Colorado.

"Dan always planned their vacations. He loved the mountains and spent a lot of time hunting and fishing in the high country. He would have recognized the area easily.

From there, it was only a quick process of elimination for him to pinpoint my precise location." Anne felt tears just behind her eyes. "Knowing now how much pressure he was under, I'm surprised he didn't approach me to try to involve me in some way in his scheme."

"My guess is, he knew you too well," Cole said.

Her eyes posed the question.

"In the short time we've been together, I already know what your reaction would be. Your loyalty to the friendship would have ended where his criminal activities began. Dan would have been blind not to know that."

She sat down again and leaned into his arms when he offered them. What Jenetta had told them was almost unbelievable, that Dan had enabled countless criminals to cheat the probation system. With an accomplice whom Jen swore she didn't know, Dan worked the probation department, paid officials to rig parole and probation hearings, to change records and basically corrupt and tilt the system in order to put criminals—most of them juveniles—back on the streets to do Webster Renfrow's bidding.

The reality of what had been happening right under her nose suddenly sent a surge of indignant anger coursing through her. She sat up straight and shouted, "Damn it! I feel like such a fool."

"You're no fool, Anne," Cole said gently, pulling her back into his arms. "And that's why Dan came after you. Because sooner or later you would have figured out his scheme. Even if you hadn't identified his voice, your dedication to the truth would have led to his undoing. You're anything but a fool," he assured her again. "But you are exhausted. Why don't you go into the bedroom and try to get some rest? It could be hours before we get the answer to our phone trace."

He stood and reached for her hand and pulled her to her feet. On the way to the bedroom, she hesitated.

"I promise I'll let you know the minute we have more information."

Reluctantly, she allowed him to lead her into the bedroom. His kiss was reassuring and breathlessly tender.

"Promise you'll wake me?"

"Promise," he said and closed the door. Ten minutes later, hovering at the edge of troubled sleep, Anne was startled awake when the telephone rang. Someone in the other room picked it up on the first ring. A moment later, the door opened and Cole stepped into the room. Anne got to her feet and met him at the door with every nerve in her body humming.

"Nyguen's on his way," he said. "They've got the phone number Hagan called from the ranch."

DREW LEFT moments before they did, but somehow they all managed to converge at the same time on the dark and rain-slicked street in front of the County Annex building. Two plainclothes cops flanked Nyguen where he stood just inside the building waiting for them.

"Have you been up to the fourth floor yet?" Cole asked.

Nyguen shook his head. "We waited for you."

Inside the elevator, Nyguen turned to Anne and handed her a slip of paper with numbers written in black ink. "Do you know this number?"

Anne shook her head, experiencing a surge of relief when she didn't immediately recognize the numbers. One betrayal from someone within her immediate circle was enough. "The prefix indicates our building, but I don't recognize the last four numbers. I'm sure they're the direct numbers for someone's private office."

"Obviously, Hagan wanted to contact his accomplice directly rather than chance going through the building operator," Cole noted.

"And if Jenetta is telling the truth," Drew added, "if she really didn't know the identity of her husband's accomplice, she'd have questioned his call if he'd tried to route it through her line."

After what seemed to Anne like the longest elevator ride of her life, the doors slid open and they all stepped out into the dimly lit fourth-floor hallway.

"We should be able to find a list of each extension somewhere on Jen's desk," she said, leading the way to the receptionist's area.

It only took a few minutes to realize that the phone on Jenetta's desk had been programmed for speed dialing, allowing her to connect each department extension with just one button. Enduring the frustrated glances of the men hovering around her, Anne sat down in Jen's chair and began a methodical search of the desktop.

After a few minutes, her search came to a successful conclusion. Holding the laminated master list in her hand, she scanned the numbers for each member of the probation team.

When she didn't immediately locate the four digits Nyguen had given her, she searched the list again. "This number isn't listed here," she said finally.

"What do you mean?" Nyguen asked gruffly, snatching the list out of her hands.

"I mean it's not there," she repeated. "I should have realized it the moment you showed me those numbers." She reached for the phone.

"Realized what?" Cole asked.

"All the numbers in our department begin with four. For example, my extension is four seven one five. Four for the fourth floor and seven one five for my office. My boss's number is four seven one four. This number—" she picked up the piece of paper with the mysterious numbers written on it "—is three five nine zero. Three for the third floor. Five nine zero for the office—"

Her explanation stopped as the truth revealed itself to her in a blinding flash of recognition. Immediately, a mental picture of the third floor formed in Anne's mind. As did the image of the individual who occupied office number five nine zero.

NYGUEN MOVED with dizzying efficiency, placing all the necessary calls and requesting the proper warrants in short order. "We should have our man in custody before dawn," he said before leaving the building with his grim-faced officers following him.

Drew left a short time later, and finally, with the small digital clock on Jenetta Hagan's desk reading one forty-five, only Cole and Anne were left in the hauntingly quiet reception area.

Anne felt bone tired and heavyhearted. "Well, it's over," she said, slumping against the wall while they waited for the elevator that would take them to the ground floor.

Cole nodded, but seemed strangely distracted.

"I think it will take a few days for everything to sink in, before any of this becomes real to me," she said.

But still Cole didn't respond, didn't seem to hear, even though he was standing within touching distance. Anne couldn't help feeling that, mentally anyway, he was as far from her tonight as her life in Denver was from his world at the Spencer ranch.

"Anne," he began slowly. "I'd like you to do one more thing for me before we go."

"Sure," she said as he took her arm and led her back to Jenetta's office. "What? What are you thinking, Cole?"

"Do you have a voice-mail system here?"

"Of course." At first she'd hated it, but within a few weeks she'd begun to see the merits of the system.

"I'd like you to check your messages before we leave. Hagan may have tried to warn you. He might have left valuable information we can use to help clear some of this mess up. Do you have the key to your office with you?"

She thought a minute. "Unfortunately, I don't. But we keep a master key in here for emergencies."

After retrieving the key from the sturdy metal box in one of Jen's desk drawers, Anne unlocked her office and headed for the phone. Cole followed her inside, and while she glanced through a stack of scribbled memos, he picked up the framed picture that sat on the corner of her desk. "You look pretty happy here," he said.

She smiled. "Go ahead. You can say it. 'And a lot younger, too.' That's Max," she said, coming around beside him. "She'd just helped me register for college. She was so proud that day. I felt pretty proud myself, just to have made it that far."

Without warning, he set the picture down and pulled her into his arms. With his chin resting on the top of her head, he said, "She'd be even prouder now." He hugged her tighter and kissed her hair.

Anne slid her hands up his back and pressed herself against him. Beneath her fingers she felt the solid strength of the man who held her heart in his hands. From that first horrible night, she'd somehow sensed his deep capacity to give the kind of love that, until now, she'd only dreamed of experiencing.

He kissed her again, then whispered, "You'd better check those messages before we both forget what we came in here to do."

She slid out of his arms and keyed in the code to activate her messages. After listening to half a dozen calls from probationers performing their weekly check-in, Zach's voice came on the line.

Cole took a step closer to the phone, as did Anne, to hear the young man's raspy whisper. "Anne . . . Ms. Osborne, please if you get this message, please, I've got to see you!" His words and his desperate tone were just short of sheer panic. "I don't know if you'll get this message, but God, I hope you do! It's important. Please—" When his voice cracked, Anne's eyes flicked to Cole's. "Please call me. I've got to . . . I've got to talk to you. I'm in . . . trouble." An awful feeling of dread caused Anne's stomach to drop, as though she was standing on the edge of a ten-story building staring straight down.

"Please," Zach said again, "I need to see you. As soon as you can. Alone! Please! Please don't bring anybody with you," he blurted, apparently as a desperate afterthought.

According to the digital readout, Zach had left his message at ten-fifteen that morning. God only knew what had happened. His mother might have been picked up again and consigned to detox. Or something could have happened to Karli. In Zach's unstable world, most anything could have happened. Anne felt dizzy with the grim possibilities that spun through her mind.

Grabbing the phone out of its cradle, she didn't wait for the taped message to finish before she started dialing.

"You've got to come alone!" Zach's recorded voice was saying as the phone on the other end of the line started to ring.

"Yeah?" The male voice sounded familiar, but before Anne could place it, the sound of voices in the background distracted her.

"Zach?"

"Hang on," came a curt response.

After a few seconds of muffled conversation, Anne heard the phone being transferred to other hands. "Hullo."

"Zach!" she said, the urgency she felt churning inside her making the word come out as a shout. "Zach, it's Anne Osborne. I got your message. What's happened? Are you all right?"

"She ain't here," Zach replied, although his voice seemed so strained, so tight she barely recognized it as his.

"Zach, I know it's you. What's wrong? What's going on?"

"I don't know anything about that. She ain't here and she won't be back till, uh, after two. When the bar closes."

"Zach, I know you're trying to tell me something. Just answer yes or no."

"Okay," came the sullen response.

"You're in trouble."

"Yeah, you could say that."

"Can I see you?"

"I . . . sure hope so."

"When?"

An uncertain silence followed before he blurted, "Like I said, she won't be back till after two. Call back then."

The sudden silence came so unexpectedly that Anne was left blinking, still expecting Zach to somehow be there when she called his name again. "Zach! Are you still there? Zach?"

She didn't realize she'd been holding her breath until the line went dead.

IT TOOK SOME DOING, but Anne convinced Cole to let her meet Zach. It took a lot more persuading, however, to get him to agree to her going into the run-down building alone. Only when they pulled up in front of the apartment did she discover that *alone* had a very different meaning to a bodyguard.

"I'll be just out of sight," he said, kissing her quick and hard. "I'll be waiting. If you aren't out of that building in fifteen minutes, I'm coming in. I don't care what the kid said."

"I don't know how much time I'll need—" she began, only to have him cut her off.

"Fifteen minutes," he said again.

"Cole—"

"Look, it's two o'clock in the morning, and we're in one of the worst neighborhoods in the city. You're walking into a building that probably has a crack addict behind every other door. The kid you're meeting has done time and he could be implicated in a murder. Give me a break, Anne. I'm bending as far as I can. But if I had really good sense, I'd have you in a flak jacket."

"The only flak I'm getting now is from you," she said.

"Very funny. But seriously, Anne, if you need me, remember, all you have to do is yell. And I mean yell. Scream as loud and long as you can. I'll be there. I promise."

"I've never been much of a screamer."

"Well, it's time you learned. Don't worry. I won't be that far away. You just get in there, find out what the kid wants, and get out."

"I'll be fine," she told him again, as much for her own assurance as his. "I just can't believe Zach would hurt me. I know it looks bad right now. But I just have to believe. Can you understand that, Cole?"

His gaze caressed her face. "I can. And I want to believe in him as much as you do. But the fact is, we don't know under what circumstances he made that call."

"It's true we don't know what was going on during that second call," she agreed. "But you heard the message he left. And when I called, he sounded scared silly. He's trusting me to help. And I have to try."

Cole slid his hand gently along the line of her jaw to caress the back of her neck. "I know. I understand why you have to do this. I just hope you understand that I can't let anything happen to you." He looked into her eyes with such intensity, such warmth, that he left her breathless. "I never dreamed someone like you would come into my life. But now that you have, I don't intend to let you go, not without one hell of a fight."

His words thrilled her, filling her with incredible joy. "Now listen to me, cowboy. I only have enough courage to walk into that building because I know you're behind me, and I know when I come back out, you'll be waiting."

"I'll be here," he promised and sealed his vow with another unforgettable kiss.

Hugging Cole's denim jacket around her tighter, she pulled open the sagging front door and walked into the dingy hallway. She'd only been inside Zach's home one other time, during the obligatory home assessment. The smell of rotting garbage had permeated the air that day, seeping into the Turner apartment, despite the fact that someone had opened a window and lighted scented candles before she'd arrived.

She remembered the apartment as being small and sparsely furnished, but surprisingly clean. Zach's mother had seemed nervous and years older than Anne knew her to be. Before her destructive life-style had taken its toll, Zach's mom had probably been a natural beauty, judging by the startling resemblance she bore to Zach's sister, whose flawless skin, small, even features and large, doleful brown eyes gave her a strikingly pretty face.

Climbing the narrow stairway to the second floor, she felt invisible eyes boring into her back. But when she turned around, no one was there. The eerie feeling persisted all the way to Zach's door. "I hope that's you, cowboy," she muttered as she braced for the trouble that awaited her on the other side of the door.

She knocked once and then again, harder. The scuffling sound inside the apartment caused fresh concern to well up inside her. Her fist was poised to knock again when the door creaked open a scant couple of inches.

Zach's face appeared, looking incredibly pale, but a flood of color swept his cheeks when he saw her. "Anne," he gasped, but before he could say more, he was jerked backward and the door opened wide to reveal the tall, husky kid who'd tossed Zach aside.

Before she could react or make a sound, the kid brought the butt of a gun crashing down on Zach's head.

Anne opened her mouth to scream and lunged at the gunman, only to find herself shoved back with the gun in her ribs. "Don't even breathe," he growled. "Now, get going," the kid ordered, emphasizing his demand with a jab of the gun. With a last look at Zach lying unconscious on the floor, Anne turned toward the stairs.

The cryptic tattoos she'd noticed on the gunman's knuckles told Anne she was dealing with a kid who was associated with a gang. His young face belied the viciousness he'd shown himself capable of doling out.

"Down there," he ordered, pressing the gun roughly into her ribs. The smell of gasoline and smoke sent her thoughts racing back to the explosion that had destroyed her apartment, and fear engulfed her.

With the gun in her side, Cole's instructions to scream taunted her. Fighting hysteria, her mind scrambled for a way out as her captor shoved her along the first-floor hallway to stairs that led to the basement.

Her heart sank when she stared down the narrow, concrete stairway.

"Keep going," the kid commanded when she glanced over her shoulder into the empty hallway behind her. *Cole! For God's sake, where are you?*

The gunman shoved her so hard she would have fallen face first down the stairs had he not grabbed her by the hair to jerk her to her feet. She yelped at the cruelty, which brought hot tears to her eyes.

Each step took her deeper into the trash-strewn, vile-smelling cellar. At the bottom of the stairs, he ordered, "That way," and shoved her around a corner into a laundry room, or what was left of it. By the light of a single bare bulb suspended from the ceiling by a frayed wire, she saw a couple of battered washers. One had no lid and the other had been knocked over on its side. Both were covered with unintelligible and multicolored graffiti. The lone dryer's controls had been ripped from the front panel, and the empty sockets stared blindly at a battered couch on the other side of the room.

"In there," the kid with the gun directed, grabbing her arm roughly to steer her through a small doorway, which opened into a cobweb-encased furnace room. A metal cot had been placed in the corner, and a hot plate sat on a cardboard box next to the narrow bed. Fast-food wrappers littered the floor, along with half a dozen empty beer cans and crushed cigarette butts.

In the midst of all the hovel, in stark contrast, stood one tall, well-dressed, impeccably groomed man. "Hello, Anne. Come in. My friend Brian and I have been waiting for you."

Gilbert Pembrooke's cool blue eyes had never looked more cold.

"You bastard!" She spat the words out.

Now she realized it had been his voice she'd recognized on the phone when she'd spoken to Zach earlier. More importantly, his voice had been the voice she'd heard giving the orders inside Stan's office the night of the murder.

"You killed him!" she cried. "You killed Stan in cold blood."

Unruffled, Pembrooke said, "Sit down, Anne. Close the door, Brian. And keep the gun on her."

"You won't get away with this," Anne cried.

"Oh, really? And who's going to stop me? Your boy-friend the bodyguard?" He shook his head. "Sorry. But we had a little run-in outside, and I'm afraid he won't be rushing to your rescue this time."

Anne felt her heart break in a thousand pieces. If Cole was...no! She refused to think the worst. Her life had taken on new meaning with Cole and she wouldn't accept losing him.

"They'll get you!" she screamed at him. "It's only a matter of time. They've traced Dan's last call, and even now there's a warrant being issued for your arrest."

Gilbert smiled and shoved her down on the bed.

"Oh, Anne," he said, standing over her. "You are so naive. By the time Nyguen finds a judge and cuts through all the legal red tape, I'll be sitting on a beach in Mexico sipping margaritas. Now, let's get down to business. My friend here wants to prove his abilities as an explosives expert."

Despite her best resolve to remain brave, she felt her last reserve of courage slipping. With Zach hurt and Cole out of the picture, she was trapped here, helpless in this god-forsaken rat hole with a cold-blooded killer and a de-ranged kid.

Grasping for any thread that might buy her crucial moments, Anne stammered, "Why? Why did you kill him, Gilbert? What did Stan do, refuse your dirty money?"

"Oh, come on. We both know how he was. Straight arrow all the way. He and that idiot Marty. You know, in a way it was Marty who helped me get to Stan, though he never realized it. When they went to battle over my young friend, here, I caught on to the scam Webster was running." He glanced at Brian, who stood blocking the door, the gun still aimed at her heart. "Unfortunately, it was

Brian's case that alerted Stan, as well. At first, I thought maybe Webster had gotten to Marty, but as it turns out, Marty really did think the kid should be tried as a juvenile." He shook his head. "What a sap! Anyway, during the dogfight between departments I learned that Stan was onto something, that he suspected the money flowing through the system that kept Webster's—what shall we call them?—errand boys out on the streets."

"And what about Dan? Was he *your* errand boy?"

Pembrooke scoffed. "Hagan's a fool."

"Was," she corrected. "Dan's dead." If the news came as a surprise or touched Pembrooke in any way, it didn't show. "You sent him to kill me, but your plan backfired."

"Not that it makes any difference, but I didn't send him. He had some misguided notion about offering you a cut of the take. Did you know he was waiting for you at your office the day of Zach's hearing?"

"The day you discovered I was being protected by Cole Spencer . . ."

"Yes. But by the time I found that out, Nyguen surprised me with a change of venue. I couldn't get to Hagan in time and the next thing I knew he struck out on his own to find you. Ironic, isn't it? I guess he was a better investigator than I thought." He shook his head and almost smiled. "The damn fool tracked you to Telluride on his own."

"You're despicable," Anne hissed. "I hope they lock you up for the rest of your life."

"Much as I'd love to sit and discuss the merits of jurisprudence with you, Ms. Osborne, I've got a red-eye flight to Cancún waiting. But Brian has a fireworks show he's prepared to rid the neighborhood of you and this blight on the landscape." He glanced around the room with disdain. "Do you have everything ready, kid?"

Brian nodded, his scraggly ponytail bobbing behind him. "This place will go up like a matchbox." Handing the gun to Pembrooke, he withdrew several bottles from a cardboard box beside the door. From his pocket he took a small red lighter.

"Looks good. I see you're prepared."

"I learned a lot from blowing her place," Brian said, an almost demonic gleam in his eye. "If I'd just used more gas and less gunpowder—"

Brian's words were lost to the fast-breaking chain of events that erupted before Anne's disbelieving eyes. At the same time she sprang up from the bed to grab Brian, the door was kicked open with such force that it flew off its hinges and sent Gilbert Pembrooke flying across the room and into the wall. The gun discharged, its deafening retort echoing off concrete with an ear-splitting scream.

Cole grabbed Anne's arm and shoved her toward the doorway. "Get out of here!"

"Look out!" she screamed, when out of the corner of her eye she saw Gilbert lunging.

Out of nowhere, Zach appeared and stepped between the two men before Cole could stop him. The gun was in Pembrooke's hand, and it exploded again. Its retort echoed, along with Anne's screams, to rip through the air.

Zach crumpled, a burst of red exploding in the middle of his white-and-blue Burger Shack uniform.

Pembrooke's face turned ashen. "Don't move," he warned, backing to the door, the gun unsteady in his hand. "Get out of here, kid," he yelled at Brian. "Find Paxton and get the hell out of town. Both of you."

Brian seemed unable to move. He just stood staring down at Zach bleeding on the floor. The smell of gunpowder, blood and gasoline permeated the air.

Cole's anger radiated off him in waves, and Anne's heart ached. In a few precious moments, all hope for the dreams they could have shared would be crushed. Their chance for happiness destroyed by the cold, calculated precision of Gilbert Pembrooke's gun.

Suddenly, a movement in the doorway behind Pembrooke caught Anne's eye. He must have seen it at exactly the same time, because he spun around to see the young girl standing behind him. Her mouth was open, but the scream seemed frozen on her trembling lips. "Zach," she gasped.

Pembrooke moved toward her, but the knife in her hand stopped him. It was all the distraction Cole needed. Gilbert collapsed with one blow.

# Epilogue

Zach pretended embarrassment, his thick lashes dipping over his dark eyes shyly when Anne leaned over the bed and kissed him on the forehead. Karli leaned against the windowsill, her arms crossed over her chest, like a sentinel standing watch over her brother, where he lay with tubes connecting him to machines in the corner.

"He's going to be all right," Karli told them. "The doctor says he's got nine lives."

Zach's sister had aged ten years in three days, Anne thought. On the mean streets of the neighborhoods like the ones she and the Turner kids had learned to survive, childhood didn't seem to last very long.

"Hey, Zach, remember those pictures Anne sent you?" Cole asked.

Zach nodded weakly.

"Well, I found one she forgot to send, and I think it might interest you more than those pictures of the mountains."

Cole handed Zach the picture with his left hand. His right arm was immobilized by a sling, due to the damage Pembrooke's gun had rendered to his shoulder when the two men had collided in the alley.

With an effort that made Anne cringe, Zach reached out to accept the snapshot Cole held out to him. "B-but that's...your pickup, isn't it?"

Cole nodded, and Anne slipped around behind him to take a closer look. Zach was right. In the center of the snapshot was Cole's pickup, although she might not have recognized it since she'd never seen it so clean and shiny before. But there was something else about the picture that intrigued her. "What's that big red bow doing tied around your truck, cowboy?" she asked.

He frowned. "Oh, that. Well, how else would you expect me to wrap a birthday present?" he asked her, feigning impatience.

Understanding dawned gradually, and when she realized what he'd done, her heart overflowed with love for him.

Karli moved up beside them and took the picture out of Zach's hand. "Hey, you mean—"

"That's right," Cole interrupted. "Happy birthday, Zach."

"But that's your truck," Zach stammered. "You mean you're giving me..."

"I sure am," Cole said. "It's all yours now. Happy birthday, buddy."

Zach's smile flooded the room like sunshine, warming all of them. The tears that pooled in his eyes caused a band of emotion to tighten around Anne's heart.

"I expect you to drive your mom and sister up to the ranch to see Anne and me just as soon as you're out of here," Cole said, his voice suddenly hoarse with restrained emotion.

"The ranch?" Anne asked, pulling him aside while Karli listened to Zach extol the virtues of what was destined to become his prize possession.

"But what...what would *I* be doing at the ranch, Cole?" she asked him. "You remember, don't you, about my life in Denver? My job, my commit—"

"I know, I know," he said impatiently, brushing her hair behind her shoulder and bending to kiss her quickly on the cheek. "You've got a job, a life, friends in Denver. Well, so do I. And I want them back. But first we've got a colt to name, remember? And oh, yes, there's the wedding to plan."

Before she could respond, he took her hand and led her into the hall. "Drew will be my best man, of course. And if Zach agrees, I'd like him to stand up with me, as well. Hey, maybe Karli could be a bridesmaid, or a flower girl? They still have those, don't they? Flower girls?"

"Yes. But—"

"And we can't forget Bess. She'd never forgive us if we tried to plan the reception without her, so we'd better talk to her before we get too carried away with—"

"Flower girl? Reception?"

"And then there's our house. But that can wait. Besides, I think we can finish most of the remodeling after we move in."

"Our house?" With what little bit of breath he hadn't stolen, she managed to ask, "We have a house?"

"Remember that change of venue?"

"Sure... Wait a minute! That was *your* house?"

"You like Victorian, antiques, that sort of thing?"

"I love them. Why?"

"Well, I'm going to need your help furnishing it. What the heck does a cowboy like me know about what a woman wants in her new house?"

She returned his sly smile and slid her arms around his neck and drew his face within inches of hers. "Flower girls. Receptions. Furniture. You wouldn't be trying to take control of my life again, would you, cowboy?"

"No ma'am," he drawled innocently. "When the bullets started flying you showed me just how well you can handle yourself. A woman in complete control."

"But that doesn't mean I won't always need you there to cover my back." She stared into his eyes and the love shining back at her almost took her breath away. "You will be there for me, won't you Cole?"

"You can count on it. I'll even trade my hat in on a white one, if it makes you happy."

"Keep your hat." She smiled. "Now, what were you saying about a house . . . ?"

"I want it to be your dream house, ma'am." He brushed her lips playfully with his. "Your home."

She kissed him and then lowered her voice to a sexy drawl. "All I want in my dream house . . . all I need is you, cowboy."

For today. For tomorrow. For a lifetime of new dreams, all she wanted, all she ever needed was his love.

# MILLION DOLLAR SWEEPSTAKES
## AND
## EXTRA BONUS PRIZE DRAWING

No purchase necessary. To enter the sweepstakes, follow the directions published and complete and mail your Official Entry Form. If your Official Entry Form is missing, or you wish to obtain an additional one (limit: one Official Entry Form per request, one request per outer mailing envelope) send a separate, stamped, self-addressed #10 envelope (4 1/8" X 9 1/2") via first class mail to: Million Dollar Sweepstakes and Extra Bonus Prize Drawing Entry Form, P.O. Box 1867, Buffalo, NY 14269-1867. Request must be received no later than January 15, 1998. For eligibility into the sweepstakes, entries must be received no later than March 31,1998. No liability is assumed for printing errors, lost, late, non-delivered or misdirected entries. Odds of winning are determined by the number of eligible entries distributed and received.

Sweepstakes open to residents of the U.S. (except Puerto Rico), Canada and Europe who are 18 years of age or older. All applicable laws and regulations apply. Sweepstakes offer void wherever prohibited by law. Values of all prizes are in U.S. currency. This sweepstakes is presented by Torstar Corp., its subsidiaries and affiliates, in conjunction with book, merchandise and/or product offerings. For a copy of the Official Rules governing this sweepstakes, send a self-addressed, stamped envelope (WA residents need not affix return postage) to: MILLION DOLLAR SWEEP-STAKES AND EXTRA BONUS PRIZE DRAWING Rules, P.O. Box 4470, Blair, NE 68009-4470, USA.

## FAST CASH 4032 DRAW RULES
## NO PURCHASE OR OBLIGATION NECESSARY

Fifty prizes of $50 each will be awarded in random drawings to be conducted no later than 11/28/96 from amongst all eligible responses to this prize offer received as of 10/15/96. To enter, follow directions, affix 1st-class postage and mail OR write Fast Cash 4032 on a 3" x 5" card along with your name and address and mail that card to: Harlequin's Fast Cash 4032 Draw, P.O. Box 1395, Buffalo, NY 14240-1395 OR P.O. Box 618, Fort Erie, Ontario L2A 5X3. (Limit: one entry per outer envelope; all entries must be sent via 1st-class mail.) Limit: one prize per household. Odds of winning are determined by the number of eligible responses received. Offer is open only to resi-dents of the U.S. (except Puerto Rico) and Canada and is void wherever prohibited by law. All applicable laws and regulations apply. Any litigation within the province of Quebec respecting the conduct and awarding of a prize in this sweepstakes may be submitted to the Régie des alcools, des courses et des jeux. In order for a Canadian resident to win a prize, that person will be required to correctly answer a time-limited arithmetical skill-testing question to be administered by mail. Names of winners available after 12/28/96 by sending a self-addressed, stamped envelope to: Fast Cash 4032 Draw Winners, P.O. Box 4200, Blair, NE 68009-4200.

# REBECCA
## 43 LIGHT STREET
# YORK
# FACE TO FACE

*Bestselling author Rebecca York returns to "43 Light Street" for an original story of past secrets, deadly deceptions—and the most intimate betrayal.*

She woke in a hospital—with amnesia...and with child. According to her rescuer, whose striking face is the last image she remembers, she's Justine Hollingsworth. But nothing about her life seems to fit, except for the baby inside her and Mike Lancer's arms around her. Consumed by forbidden passion and racked by nameless fear, she must discover if she is Justine...or the victim of some mind game. Her life—and her unborn child's—depends on it....

Don't miss *Face To Face*—Available in October, wherever Harlequin books are sold.

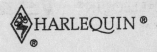

# HARLEQUIN ®

®

43FTF

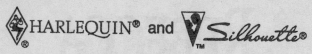

**HARLEQUIN® and Silhouette®**

are proud to present...

# HERE COME THE GROOMS™

Four marriage-minded stories written by top
Harlequin and Silhouette authors!

Next month, you'll find:

| | |
|---|---|
| *Married?!* | by Annette Broadrick |
| *Designs on Love* | by Gina Wilkins |
| *It Happened One Night* | by Marie Ferrarella |
| *Lazarus Rising* | by Anne Stuart |

**ADDED BONUS!** In every edition of
*Here Come the Grooms* you'll find $5.00 worth
of coupons good for Harlequin and Silhouette
products.

On sale at your favorite Harlequin and Silhouette
retail outlet.

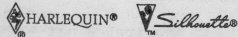

HCTG996

# Free Gift Offer

With a Free Gift proof-of-purchase
from any Harlequin® book, you can receive
a beautiful cubic zirconia pendant.

This stunning marquise-shaped stone is a genuine cubic
zirconia—accented by an 18" gold tone necklace.
(Approximate retail value $19.95)

## Send for yours today...
## compliments of ◆HARLEQUIN®

To receive your free gift, a cubic zirconia pendant, send us one original proof-of-purchase, photocopies not accepted, from the back of any Harlequin Romance®, Harlequin Presents®, Harlequin Temptation®, Harlequin Superromance®, Harlequin Intrigue®, Harlequin American Romance®, or Harlequin Historicals® title available in August, September or October at your favorite retail outlet, together with the Free Gift Certificate, plus a check or money order for $1.65 U.S./$2.15 CAN. (do not send cash) to cover postage and handling, payable to Harlequin Free Gift Offer. We will send you the specified gift. Allow 6 to 8 weeks for delivery. Offer good until October 31, 1996 or while quantities last. Offer valid in the U.S. and Canada only.

# Free Gift Certificate

Name: _____

Address: _____

City: _____ State/Province: _____ Zip/Postal Code: _____

Mail this certificate, one proof-of-purchase and a check or money order for postage and handling to: HARLEQUIN FREE GIFT OFFER 1996. In the U.S.: 3010 Walden Avenue, P.O. Box 9071, Buffalo NY 14269-9057. In Canada: P.O. Box 604, Fort Erie, Ontario L2Z 5X3.

---

## FREE GIFT OFFER                                    084-KMF

ONE PROOF-OF-PURCHASE

To collect your fabulous FREE GIFT, a cubic zirconia pendant, you must include this
original proof-of-purchase for each gift with the properly completed Free Gift Certificate.

---

*You are cordially invited to a*
# HOMETOWN REUNION

*September 1996—August 1997*

Where can you find romance and adventure,
bad boys, cowboys, feuding families, and babies,
arson, mistaken identity, a mom on the run...?
Tyler, Wisconsin, that's where!

So join us in this not-so-sleepy little town and
experience the love, the laughter and the
tears of those who call it home.

## WELCOME TO A
# HOMETOWN REUNION

Twelve unforgettable stories, written for you by
some of Harlequin's finest authors. This fall,
begin a yearlong affair with America's favorite
hometown as **Marisa Carroll** brings you
*Unexpected Son.*

Available in September at your
favorite retail store.

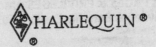

Look us up on-line at: http://www.romance.net

HTR1

# You're About to Become a *Privileged Woman*

Reap the rewards of fabulous free gifts and benefits with proofs-of-purchase from Harlequin and Silhouette books

# Pages & Privileges™

It's our way of thanking you for buying our books at your favorite retail stores.

**Harlequin and Silhouette—
the most privileged readers in the world!**

For more information about Harlequin and Silhouette's PAGES & PRIVILEGES program call the Pages & Privileges Benefits Desk: 1-503-794-2499

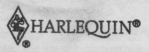

HARLEQUIN®